2

Witches of Bourbon Street

Books by Deanna Chase

Haunted on Bourbon Street
Witches of Bourbon Street

Witches of Bourbon Street

A Jade Calhoun Novel

Deanna Chase

Bayou Moon Publishing

Copyright © 2012 by Deanna Chase

First Edition 2012

10 9 8 7 6 5 4 3 2 1

Library of Congress Control Number: 2012901712

ISBN: 978-0-9837978-2-1   Trade Paperback
         978-0-9837978-3-8   ePub Version

Cover and Interior Design: The Printed Page, Phoenix, AZ
Cover image: © Detelina Petkova — Fotolia.com
Cover image manipulation: Kyle Crichton
Back cover image: © Natalia Bratslavsky — Fotolia.com

Bayou Moon Publishing
dkchase12@gmail.com
www.deannachase.com

Printed in the United States of America

Acknowledgments

A huge thank you to Lisa Liddy, Jennifer Spiller, Angie Ramey, Susan Sheehan, and Rhonda Helms. Your help and tireless work on this project means the world to me. Thank you to my family. Your love and support has never gone unnoticed. And to Greg, my heart is with you always.

Chapter 1

I sat cross-legged in Bea's cheery, yellow living room, trying not to scowl. White witch, my ass. After two hours of trying to manipulate my so-called power, I was ready to tell Bea and her nephew, Ian, exactly what they could do with their magic lessons.

Only, I couldn't.

While battling with an evil spirit three months ago, Bea's energy had been compromised, and she'd never recovered. For some ungodly reason she was convinced I was a witch and the answer for a cure.

I took in the dark circles rimming her eyes and her pale, waxy skin. The vibrant southern lady I'd come to admire had been replaced by a tired shell of an elderly woman destined for a retirement village.

All my irritation vanished. I had to do something. Anything.

Determined to get it right this time, I held one hand out to Bea and the other to Ian. Sweat trickled the length of my nose. It clung to the tip before landing silently on the patchwork area rug. For the hundredth time that day, I opened my senses, trying to harness Ian's energy and hold it in my awareness long enough to transfer it to Bea. Ian's anxious anticipation pressed against my skin, making me flinch.

"Focus, Jade," Bea said. "Remember what I said about compartmentalizing."

Stop focusing on what Ian is feeling, and focus on his essence.

When I'd given her a blank look, she'd gone on to explain: *The essence of an individual is made up of both their soul and spirit. Spirit is basically life energy, while the soul is what gives a person the ability to feel compassion, love, and all the things that make one human.*

Okay. Essence. I could do that. I'd done it before, only I'd thought of it as emotional energy. Somewhere in the corner of my mind, I closed the door on my empath ability. The three of us sat there holding sweaty hands as I tried to mentally connect with Ian. As usual, nothing happened. All right. Time for a new tactic. Instead of trying to get into his head, I concentrated on his heart. Slowly, the threads of Ian's inner light started to tickle my senses. I imagined a siphon attached to a glass beaker and focused on capturing the essence Bea needed to be strong again. A swirly mist started to fill my beaker.

Success! After weeks of instruction, I'd finally grasped the technique Bea insisted I had the skill to master. Elation caused me to redouble my efforts.

With a full container of mist, I turned my attention to Bea, intent on sending her nephew's strong energy into her being. Instantly, my imaginary beaker exploded. Ian's hard-won healing essence evaporated into nothing.

"Damn it," I growled.

"Negativity won't help anything, dear." Bea slumped back against her sunflower print loveseat.

Argh! I yelled in my head and looked at Ian helplessly.

He wiped his face with a cloth handkerchief and stood. "I'm getting some more tea. Anyone else?"

"Please." I pulled my shirt away from my body and leaned toward the oscillating fan to my left.

Ian studied his aunt. "Bea? Tea or water?"

"No, thank you. I'm fine." She rose gracefully to her feet then settled into the loveseat under a ray of sunshine. She tilted her face, warming it in the light. With each passing day, her ability to stay warm diminished, and despite the stifling heat, she wore black slacks and a long-sleeved shirt, topped with a cardigan sweater.

Just looking at her raised my internal temperature ten degrees. I stood. "I'll be outside. I need a break."

"I'll meet you out there," Ian said from the kitchen.

With effort, I managed to not slam the French door behind me as I escaped to the screened-in patio. The overhead fans rotated full force, showering me with a steady stream of much-needed air. I sat directly beneath one and stared out onto the perfectly manicured lawn, edged with a vibrant bed of hibiscus plants. What else would one expect from a carriage home in the Garden District of New Orleans?

While it was still beautiful, I missed the variety of colorful annuals that had long since given up in the summer heat. I'd offered to help Bea with the fall garden, but she'd waved me off, saying I had better things to do with my time.

Like figure out how to energy meld. After banishing Roy—an evil spirit who used to haunt the club in my building—Bea had never fully recovered, leaving her cold and weak. When her doctor didn't find anything wrong, he'd prescribed a vitamin regimen. It wasn't helping, though Bea had said all along she knew it wouldn't. Her essence had been zapped, and there were only two ways to restore it: time or the help of another witch. But not just any witch. Apparently it took a white witch. Something both Bea and Lailah—her shop assistant—insisted I was. I didn't agree. I'm an empath, someone who can read others' emotions, not a witch. Or at least not a powerful one, judging by my lack of ability to transfer Ian's energy to Bea.

The door squeaked and Ian's frustration reached me before he did. "It's not working." He handed me a tall glass of sweet tea and sat down opposite me, stretching out his long, gangly legs.

"I told you not to get your hopes up." I took a long sip and didn't make eye contact.

"If you had a better attitude, it would help."

My head snapped up. I opened my mouth, ready to let him know exactly what I thought of his opinion, but closed it. The fatigue etched around his pale blue eyes gave him a hollowed-out, almost ghostly appearance. If he hadn't been so worried about his aunt, it would have been funny, considering his obsession with ghost hunting.

I breathed deeply, trying to release some of my bottled-up frustration. "I'm trying."

"Shit. Sorry. I didn't mean it the way it sounded. I only meant positive energy flows more freely and all that crap." He brushed back his sweat-dampened, sandy blond hair.

I laughed. "All that crap?"

He shrugged, giving me the first real smile I'd seen on him in days. I searched for a resemblance of the man I'd met three months earlier, after a ghost scare in my apartment. That day he'd been all smiles, easygoing, and dressed in all black, looking very much like a pro skateboarder. Today he wore khaki shorts and a pinstriped, button-down, short-sleeved cotton shirt. Only the Converse shoes remained from his previous persona.

"What's with the makeover? I thought T-shirts and jeans were all you owned," I teased.

He glanced down at his shirt, looking pained. "I'm a little behind on laundry. Plus, with the heat in there, this is a little cooler."

Sobering, I leaned in. "She's getting worse, isn't she?" It seemed each time I saw her, Bea got a little paler and a little thinner. If I couldn't master the energy meld soon and transfer some healthy energy to her...I didn't want to finish the thought.

Ian nodded. "I've been noticing her decline for the last few weeks. But I don't understand it. Enough time has gone by that she should be getting better."

I bit my lip. "Maybe it's her age. Older folks don't bounce back as easily."

"She's not that old. In her sixties, I think. She makes sure none of us know what year she was really born in."

I smiled at that. Bea owned a new age shop in the French Quarter. From the outside it often embodied everything you'd expect a tourist shop to be. But one foot inside from someone with knowledge of the craft, and you knew she was one powerful witch. With that kind of skill, Bea could be eighty and no one would be the wiser. In fact, I'd guessed she was in her fifties. "Either way, with how strong she was, this doesn't make sense."

Ian rubbed his temples. When he dropped his hands, he looked me dead in the eye. "Ready to try again?"

No. My shirt was practically soaked through. I had plans with my boyfriend, Kane, in a few hours, and I'd promised to call my aunt Gwen before I went out. I pushed my chair back and grabbed my empty glass. "Let's do it."

Ian held the door for me. I set my shoulders and walked willingly back into the sauna that used to be Bea's living room. After a stop in the guest bathroom to splash my face with cool water, I took my place on the area rug.

Bea slid to the edge of her seat and, with shaking arms, carefully lowered herself to the floor. The small effort left her winded.

I took her hand and peered into her eyes. "Tell me again why I can't just transfer some of my own energy?" In the past, I'd been successful in replenishing both my own strength and the strength of others by tapping what I used to think of as emotional energy. I'd thought it was just part of my gift. But when Bea had explained the energy meld she was trying to teach me, she'd said I wasn't transferring emotions at all. I was taking and receiving pieces of the inner essence we all possessed.

"Remember how weak you were the last time you loaned your strength to someone? Didn't you tell me you'd drained yourself to the point you'd become bedridden?"

"But I can give you just a little, to at least help you feel a bit better?"

"No." Her voice was full of conviction. "You don't have control yet, and that's why you exhaust yourself. Use Ian. You'll learn something and you'll both recover fast." She held her hand out to her nephew and gave him a pointed look.

Joining our circle, he shot me a look that implied I'd better get to work.

With their hands in mine, I once again concentrated on Ian. His familiar essence flowed easier this time, and before I could devise a new way to capture it, the weight of it settled into my bones. I sat straight up as my nerve endings tingled, overflowing with the urge to move. It was too much. The energy meld had worked, only I'd accidentally absorbed it instead of transferring it to Bea.

"Release it now!" Bea commanded.

My head snapped in her direction. Rigid and ready to jump out of my own skin, I stared her down. She met my gaze, and suddenly my back arched as Ian's essence was pulled from me.

Ian's hand went slack in my death grip, but I couldn't move my fingers to release him. I sat frozen, locked in Bea's gaze until every last tingle faded to numbness. My body slumped forward. I sat there half-lying on the floor until Ian's strong arms lifted me back into a sitting position.

"You okay?" he asked.

I lifted my weak head, giving him a small nod.

He cradled my head on his shoulder and whispered, "Look."

Bea stood over us, her cardigan sweater shed, fanning herself with a book. "When did it get so warm in here?"

I smiled. "It's about time you noticed."

A low chuckle vibrated in Ian's throat.

"Can you turn the temperature down now? Some of us don't prefer a slow roast," I teased. Though, for once, I wasn't sweating. My hands and feet were still numb, and the rest of my body had started to tremble.

Ian's arm tightened around me. "Don't worry. Bea has a special vitamin that will pick you right back up."

"Huh?"

"It kick-starts your inner strength."

Right. I'd never heard of this so-called miracle pill. "Is it altered?"

He laughed. "It's spelled, if that's what you mean. Bea keeps them around for emergencies."

I pushed myself away from his embrace. "No, thanks. I'll recover on my own."

Ian sat back and crossed his arms. "This again? You just did a spell. You've been trying to master it for how many days—no, weeks, now? And yet you won't take a pill that will have you feeling right in no time because a witch enhanced it? I hate to tell you this, Jade, but you're a witch, too. A white one. A very powerful one and, to be honest, you can't afford to be drained."

"Wha—"

"Don't sass the girl. She just cured your aunt." Bea handed me a tall glass of sweet tea and pointed the fan at Ian.

"Thank you." I gulped down three-quarters of the liquid before coming up for air.

Bea's smile turned to a grin. "No point trying to force a pill down her throat when tea will work just as well."

I tilted my head in confusion then frowned as my nerve endings started to come back to life, reviving my extremities. My body started to hum, much in the way it did after a good workout at the gym. "Bea! Tell me you did not just drug me without my knowledge."

"Heavens, no. I wouldn't do that. I did crush up an enhanced vitamin, though. You needed it after that impressive display of energy work."

Her satisfied smile made me want to scream. But as I took in her rosy cheeks and the glint that had been missing from her eyes, I softened and shook my head. "You know I don't like to be manipulated."

"Who does?" Bea called as she headed toward the back door. "I had to do something after you botched the essence transfer."

"Botched? What do you mean? Looks like it worked to me. You're upright, looking better than you have since the exorcism."

"Yes, botched." She opened the back door. "I'm not saying it didn't work. In fact, I'd say it worked better than anyone expected it to. But I also told you not to transfer any of your essence. Too bad you don't take direction well. Don't worry— we can work on that." The French door shut with a soft click.

I glanced at Ian. "I didn't mean to. It just happened."

He patted my hand as if I were a five-year-old then got up and headed for the kitchen.

"I didn't do it on purpose," I called.

Ian poked his head back into the living room. "I know. This is why you need to study."

I clamped my mouth shut and glared.

"That's what I thought you'd say." He disappeared again, leaving me alone with my jaw clenched and arms folded tightly against my chest.

"A thank-you would have been nice," I said to no one.

Chapter 2

Frustrated, I grabbed my purse and left. From the yard, I gave Bea a terse wave before stalking off to the trolley stop on Saint Charles. Ian would've given me a ride home if I'd asked, but that would've involved talking to him.

My gut reaction to reject all magic had taken over my common sense. Again. I couldn't help it. The memory of the coven leader standing on my doorstep that late summer night twelve years ago still brought tears to my eyes.

Her bloodless face, lined with despair, had frightened me more than the gut-wrenching fear and sorrow she hadn't been able to hide from me. She'd tried. Her defenses had been in place, but she'd been too weak to hold any of it in. From what I'd learned, the leader had wielded so much magic that night she'd come within an inch of burning out.

I hadn't cared. My mother had disappeared. Nothing else mattered.

My demands for her to return to the circle and cast until she found my mother had fallen on deaf ears. The leader stared at me with wide, empty eyes, allowing me to rage at her until my voice went hoarse. When I'd finally collapsed in a heap on my front step, she touched my forehead and whispered a spell. Through my sobs, I'd missed the incantation, catching only the familiar phrase I'd heard my mother say a million times before: "Blessed be, child."

I'd fallen into a deep sleep and woke up two days later in the psychiatric hospital. The doctor said I'd suffered a mental break from traumatic grief. But it was a lie. I'd been spelled to save me from my immediate pain.

A week later, I moved into a foster home and never spoke to any of my mother's coven members again. Despite a number of attempts from a few of them, I'd always refused. They were the reason my mother went missing. The group and the magic they loved so much. Neither had been welcome in my life after that. They still weren't. But for Bea, I'd do what I had to.

I knew the herbal remedy she'd spiked my drink with was mostly harmless, and it had helped. I just had zero tolerance for all magic forms, especially when they were used on me without my knowledge. But Bea didn't know that. No one did. My mom's disappearance wasn't something I talked about. It was too painful.

By the time I'd taken a shower and gotten ready for my date, my irritation had vanished. Bea had only been doing what she thought was best. It wasn't her fault I had baggage. Still, after a day like mine, a girl deserved a little chocolate and wine. On my way to Kane's, I stopped at a neighborhood market and picked up supplies.

Twenty minutes later, I used my key and called out as I let myself in Kane's house.

"In here," he answered from the kitchen.

I found him at the table with a stack of papers, a ten-key calculator, and his laptop.

"How's my gorgeous witch this evening?" He reached for my hand after I dumped my haul on the island counter.

Rolling my eyes, I let him pull me into his lap and ignored the nickname. "Better now that I'm here."

"Any progress?" A five-o'clock shadow lined his chiseled jaw and his dark, wavy hair stuck out in unruly clumps. I couldn't resist smoothing it down.

A genuine smile tugged at my lips. "It finally worked. When I left, Bea was outside sprucing up her flower garden."

"She's better then?"

"Yes. And I'm free from witch training, spells, and all things supernatural."

"Good." He leaned in close, brushing his lips across my cheek until he found my mouth and sank into a deep, sensual kiss. His expert tongue darted sinfully over mine, exploring and stroking until I lost my breath. When he finally pulled back, he gave my lower lip a nip that initiated a small moan from the back of my throat. His words came out low and husky as his mocha colored eyes bored into mine. "Dinner's ready."

"If that's dinner, I'm going to need seconds."

He laughed and lifted me up as he stood. "No, that's dessert. Dinner first." He planted a light kiss on my forehead and strode over to the stove.

"Evil. Pure evil." I put away the strawberries and chocolate and opened the wine. While setting out the plates, Kane retrieved dinner from the oven. Instantly, the mild spicy aroma of the kitchen turned into a meaty, roasted garlic mecca of goodness. "Oh, my. What did you make?"

"Short ribs over Cajun pasta with garlic mashed potatoes and roasted tomatoes for an appetizer." He placed the meals on the counter next to a plate of baguette slices and then poured the wine. He eyed the Cabernet label. "Perfect."

I smiled, helping myself to a generous amount of goat cheese for the bread. "Where did you learn to cook? Pioneer Woman?"

He paused before taking his first bite. "Who?"

"Never mind." I chuckled then popped a tomato in my mouth and sighed in pleasure over the sharp tang of herbs and rich cheese.

"I used to help my grandmother on Sundays when I was a kid. It was our tradition. I kept it up through my teenage years out of obligation, but when I moved back after college, I realized I actually enjoyed it. So up until we lost her a few years ago, every Sunday afternoon was spent with Mamaw right here in her kitchen."

A soft glow of joyous affection illuminated his skin, warming my hand where I touched him. My heart swelled, and I had to blink back the tears from the emotions welling in my chest. I'd known his grandmother had been important to him, but I hadn't known just how much. "I wish I could have met her."

He turned and cupped his hand over my cheek. "She would've adored you."

"I doubt it. Considering the amount of time you spend at my place on Sundays, it sounds like she'd have resented the heck out of me." Since Kane spent most Saturday nights at his club, Wicked, I'd gotten in the habit of using that time to focus on my glass bead business. Sometimes I worked at my apartment, but usually I could be found in my studio. It was often right before sunrise when Kane picked me up. It meant we slept late and stayed in bed even later, frequently not getting up until around dinner time.

His mocha eyes crinkled as his lips turned up in a rueful smile. "No doubt our current schedule would've been a conflict. We'd have figured something out." He leaned in and kissed me, tasting of wine and garlic.

"Dinner is delicious," I said.

"Compliments to Mamaw."

"To Mamaw," I echoed, turning my attention to the pile of papers on the table. "Looks like you've got a lot to do. Is that for the club?"

He shook his head. "No. I've got a new financial client. His assets and portfolio are a mess. I told him I'd have a proposal for him in the morning." His expression clouded as his regret washed over me.

"That's too bad. I'd planned melted chocolate and strawberries for dessert."

He groaned and his intense eyes caught mine. A flash of his desire shot through my middle, making me catch my breath. His elevated pulse confirmed my reaction hadn't gone unnoticed. Without speaking, he tugged me off the stool toward his bedroom.

"Hey, I wasn't finished."

"There's more in the fridge."

His lips closed over mine, cutting off my protests. Despite his implication of needing to work, we took our time undressing each other one piece of clothing at a time, using our lips to explore every inch of newly exposed skin. The passion we each harbored grew hot and fierce as we tumbled into his bed, forgetting everything but each other.

It was a long time before we lay wrapped together in a tangle of limbs, spent and languid. Kane ran his fingers through my hair and kissed the top of my head. "I love you, pretty witch."

I was too content to scold him for using the unwanted nickname. Instead, I traced the back of his fingers with my own and smiled into his chest. "I love you too, my pioneer man."

He pulled me close, wrapped his arm over my middle. His good humor tickled my senses just before he fell asleep. I lay awake, listening to his steady breathing.

After some time, I finally faded into a restless dream state. A faint trace of humor grabbed my attention, and my fuzzy mind tried to focus on the familiar energy. Slowly, an image began to appear, shapeless at first, then transformed into a woman's silhouette. I squinted, trying to make out her identity, and grinned when my mother appeared in our old kitchen back in Idaho.

She scooped a bunch of strawberries into a bowl and glanced at me. "Whipped cream or chocolate, Shortcake?"

"Mom," my fourteen-year-old self moaned. "You have got to stop calling me that. I'm two inches taller than you."

Her eyes twinkled as she lightly grabbed a handful of my strawberry-blond hair. "With a gorgeous color like this, you'll always be my Shortcake."

I pulled away, laughing and embarrassed at the attention.

She moved to our old-fashioned, robin-blue refrigerator that matched the porcelain sink. "So, which one?" She held up a bag of dark chocolate chips and a container of heavy whipping cream.

"Both." I pulled out the double boiler to start melting the chocolate.

"That's my girl."

The dream faded, taking the warm, happy glow of the cherished memory with it. I woke feeling empty and alone, the way I always did after I dreamed of my mother.

A light shone under the bedroom door. I got up and followed it to the kitchen. Kane, with a serious case of bed-head, sat in front of his laptop, gripping a giant mug of steaming coffee.

The rich aroma made my stomach growl. "What time is it?"

"About two." He yawned. "Did I wake you?"

"No. Just a dream." I shuffled to the refrigerator and pulled out the strawberries. I scanned the shelves looking for cream, frowning when I came up empty. "How long have you been up?"

"A few hours. The proposal wasn't going to write itself." He tapped a few keys then paused as I pulled out a slow cooker from his cabinet. "What are you up to?"

"Dessert." I sent him a small smile and dumped the chocolate into the pot. "Someone interrupted my dinner and I'm in need of a two a.m. snack."

"Need help?"

"No, thanks."

With the chocolate set to low, I washed the strawberries and took my time slicing them. How many times had I shared the activity with my mother? I couldn't possibly say. It had been our favorite dessert. She'd always said, "It can't be that bad. Look at all the fruit on the plate."

Then I'd read her the fat grams from the heavy cream container. In response, she'd stuff a giant spoonful of freshly whipped cream in her mouth. The image always made me giggle.

"What's so funny?" Kane came up behind me.

"Just something my mom used to do when I was a kid." I grabbed a strawberry and dipped it in the melted chocolate. "Here."

He took a bite, looking thoughtful. After a moment he opened the refrigerator, rummaged around a minute, and came up with a spray can of whipped cream. "Didn't you once tell me this was your favorite dessert as a kid?"

I grinned. It wasn't freshly whipped, but it would do.

The only bad thing about working at The Grind was the ungodly hours. Five a.m. should be outlawed. By nine-thirty I was ready for a serious nap. Stifling a yawn, I absently cleaned the espresso machine as the last of the morning rush filed out of the café.

The minute the door closed, Pyper swept her electric-blue-streaked dark hair into a bun and said, "I need a favor."

"Sure." I started wiping the counter down, but when she didn't elaborate I paused and looked up. She stood at the counter, pretending to straighten a display of chocolate-covered espresso beans. The ones I'd just finished restocking.

She stilled when she realized I was watching. "Sorry. I was thinking."

"I can see that." I eyed her. Was she nervous? I'd never seen Pyper anything but all brass with confidence to spare.

"Are you guys busy tomorrow night? You and Kane, I mean?"

I shrugged. "I don't think so. Unless he's working at Wicked." Technically, Kane's professional job was a financial consultant. But he also owned the strip club next door. He had a manager to run it, but he wasn't exactly a hands-off guy. At least when it came to the money end of things.

She waved a hand. "Charlie's working. He doesn't need to be there."

I laughed. "Charlie does such a wonderful job running the place that he never needs to be there. But that doesn't stop him. Or you, for that matter." Pyper had been the manager prior to Charlie taking over, and even though Pyper didn't need to spend half her life there, she still did. "You both need Workaholics Anonymous."

"Yeah, yeah. Whatever. Anyway, tomorrow." Her lips quirked into a shy smile and she blushed. Actually blushed. "Are you busy for dinner? I have someone I want you to meet."

"Why, Pyper, have you met a man you want to introduce to the family? Or a woman?" I teased, remembering she didn't discriminate when it came to love.

Her blush vanished and a glint lit her eyes. "Something like that. Seven okay?"

"Sounds good." My phone buzzed and I pulled it from my pocket.

A text from my best friend, Kat, read: *News alert, I've got a date!*

I typed back: *Awesome. Who with?*

Almost instantly, she replied. *Someone I've had my eye on for a while. I'll call you later.*

Smiling, I glanced at Pyper. "You're not the only one with a new love interest—wait, is that who I think it is?" I pointed past her toward a tall, dark-haired man and a very familiar bohemian-chic woman standing in front of the café.

Pyper peered over the counter as the woman pulled the man into her arms and gave him a kiss on his cheek. "Looks like Lailah's found a boyfriend. It's about time. I thought she'd never get over Kane. It's been forever since they dated."

I choked on an intake of breath. After a gulp of water, I spat out, "What the hell is she doing with Dan?"

Pyper's eyes went wide. "Your ex?"

Transfixed on the scene outside, I barely heard her.

"Jade?"

"Huh?"

"You okay?"

"I…" The initial shock started to fade, but I couldn't help but be annoyed. What the hell? Did everyone I know have to date him? We'd been together all through college and had almost gotten engaged before we'd destroyed our relationship. Not long after that he'd started dating Kat…until he assaulted me in the club a few months back and she dumped him. I turned on Pyper. "If you ever so much as even think about going out with Dan, I'm going to have to resign as your friend."

She scoffed. "Date him? You're kidding, right? Why would I ever go out with a homophobic asshole?"

Her matter-of-fact, flippant tone released the tightness in my chest as Lailah entered the café.

"Where's the douche canoe?" Pyper asked her.

I opened my mouth, but laughter bubbled out in the form of a chuckle.

"Um, what?" Lailah asked.

"The douche canoe. Jade's ex. The guy you were slobbering all over." Pyper stood with her hands on her hips, staring Lailah down.

Lailah set her purse on the counter. Her normal light, intuitive energy turned thick as a tiny amount of irritation escaped her essence. "You mean Dan?"

I sobered and mirrored Pyper in her confrontational stance. "Yes, Dan."

She gritted her teeth. "I'm not dating him. It's…" She looked around, no doubt checking to see if we had any patrons. "I'm working with him."

"Didn't look like work to me," Pyper mumbled.

"On what?" I asked.

"It's confidential."

Pyper and I stared at her.

"I'd tell you if I could, but—" she raised a finger and pointed skyward, "—it's angel business."

"Oh. Right," Pyper said with a snort.

"Look, I just came in to say hello and order a chai, but if I'm not welcome—"

"No, no. It's fine." I went to work on her drink, trying very hard to not say anything. She'd told us once she was a low-level angel, but none of us knew what the heck that meant. And she hadn't explained other than to say she could wield spells, but didn't really need incantations and potions. What any of that had to do with Dan, I didn't know, but I was dying to find out.

While I steamed the milk, I studied the angel. "How does it work? Do you have assignments?"

"I'm sorry, Jade. I can imagine you're curious, but I really can't talk about it."

I shrugged, feigning disinterest. Then I remembered, while she wasn't an empath, she had enough intuitive energy that she could see right through me. I sighed and finished her drink. Just as I placed it on the counter, the door swung open and in walked Dan.

He strode right up to the counter, ignored Lailah, and stared pointedly at me. "Jade."

"Dan." I backed up, even though the coffee bar and another three feet separated us. "Pyper will take your order."

"I don't want anything, thank you. I'm here to see you."

Pyper stepped forward. Her protectiveness came through loud and clear. I placed a hand on her arm to stop her before she said anything.

The last few times I'd run into Dan, he'd been a real prick. Today there was something different about him. I studied him, trying to figure it out. After a moment it hit me. His emotions were under tight control.

A twinge of guilt settled in my gut, but I sent my energy out anyway. It was an invasion of privacy, and the reason Dan and I had broken up, but if I was going to talk to him, I needed to know his state of mind.

With his emotions locked down, it was hard to get a read. On the surface, he was doing a very good job of projecting a layer of calm. There was something else there, though, and it tugged at my senses. What was it? Arrogance? Determination? Maybe a little of both. I pushed deeper. Fear. Deep-seated fear.

Why in the world would Dan fear me? That's when it hit me. My gift. He feared I'd know exactly what he was feeling. Crap. He was right. Instantly, I erected the imaginary glass barriers I used when I wanted to shield myself from unwanted emotions. It probably wasn't necessary since he was keeping his in check, but it made me feel better.

"What do you want, Dan?" I asked in a measured tone.

He took a deep breath. "To apologize."

His words hit me in a wave of confusion. I stared at him in disbelief.

"I know I did and said some terrible things after we broke up. I have no excuse. I won't even try. I just wanted you to know I'm sorry, and it won't happen again."

His words and tone were so much like the Dan I'd been friends with, and then dated all those years, that when he held his hand out, I automatically took it without thinking.

He gripped my hand, shaking it, and continued to apologize. I didn't comprehend a word. My hand started to smolder in a slow burn in all the places his skin touched mine.

"Let go!" I yanked my hand back, cradled it against my chest.

"What the hell?" Pyper stepped in front of me, shielding me from Dan's view. She turned on Lailah. "Get him out of here."

"But," Dan said, "it's part of my anger management classes."

"What? Crushing her hand?" Pyper asked.

"I didn't…Jade, are you okay?" The softness in Dan's voice went against everything I'd felt coming from him. The burn had been a reflection of his inner self. The mark of a man marinating in toxic energy.

"I'm fine." I craned my neck to see around Pyper. The concern in his eyes made me look away. "You should go."

A moment later the bell on the door chimed, signaling they had left.

"What the hell just happened?" Pyper demanded.

I shook my head. "I have no idea."

Chapter 3

The grooves in the metal ladder pinched the arch of my bare foot, making me wince as I reached forward and secured the portrait to the wall. "If I'd known you'd have me doing manual labor, I would have worn more suitable shoes," I called down to Kane.

"Sorry." He gave me a rueful smile. "I forgot I'd promised Charlie I'd help with the promo stuff for the Halloween party."

"Hey, Charlie." I glanced over my shoulder at the club manager. She'd recently clipped her shocking red hair, and it stood up in random gelled spikes. Her slim build and heart-shaped face made her perfect for a career as a high-fashion model. Instead, she spent all her time managing the club and working her way through business school. "I hear it's your fault I'm on this death trap in my little black dress."

Her appreciation tickled my skin the way it always does when she's feeling flirty. "Girl, if that skirt was a few inches shorter, we could turn you and that ladder into a new act."

Kane chuckled and tilted his head for a better view of my backside.

I turned back to the portrait, ignoring both of them. Every few days one of them made a crack about recruiting me to work at Wicked. On occasion I helped out tending bar, but stripping was never going to happen and they both knew it.

"I think we're out of luck," Kane said to Charlie.

"You never know," she mused. "I could spike her drink next week at the party. Then maybe we'll see some of that peachy flesh."

"For God's sake." I choked through my laughter. "That's enough embarrassment for one night." My already warm face burned hotter as Kane's desire caressed my psyche. Last night's dreamwalk flashed in my mind, making all my sensitive places ache. My eyes met Kane's and I knew he was remembering our encounter. It had been one of the rare occasions when we hadn't spent the night together. But since Kane is a dreamwalker, and can consciously will himself into my dreams, it hadn't slowed down our sex life. On the contrary, the things he'd done to me... Mmm.

Charlie rapped her knuckles on the bar. "Are you two horn dogs done mentally undressing each other? 'Cause we've got about twenty minutes to finish this before the doors open."

"You started it," Kane said, still gazing at me.

Stop, I mouthed to him and climbed down the ladder. Stepping back, I cocked my head to one side. "How does it look?"

The grotesque, mixed media 3-D portrait of papier-mâché and acrylic epoxy featured a wrinkled hag staring down at us, one eye wide open and the other squinted. Her long, narrow nose sat slightly off center directly over an oversized, chipped tooth. The only two redeeming qualities were her thick, auburn-brown hair and the deep emerald green of her eyes.

"Ah, Priscilla, you're looking especially fierce," Charlie said.

"Priscilla?" I asked.

"Yep. Her name's etched in the frame. That's Meri—" she pointed across the room to a skeletal-faced hag, "—and this is Felicia." Charlie held up a third portrait. The woman would have been beautiful, with her Caribbean blue eyes and silky blond hair, had it not been for half of her face peeling off.

"Jeez. Poor Felicia. It must have been quite a blow to her ego to be given such a deformity." I grimaced, following Kane as he moved the ladder.

Charlie's lips twitched. "She's my favorite."

I shook my head. "Do you ever stop?"

"Nope. Now get your skinny ass back up on that ladder so we can get this done."

After I tied my hair back, I climbed up one more time and held my hand out. Kane handed me Felicia, and I secured her frame to the wall. As I was straightening the unusual piece of art, a foreign stream of sadness filtered through my being. I stiffened. Emotional energy has a distinct imprint specific to each person. The sadness didn't belong to Kane or Charlie, which meant either a stranger was in the club, or we had another ghost.

I turned and studied the empty room. "Did someone just pop in for a moment? One of the dancers, maybe?"

"No. Why? Did you hear something?" Kane scanned the room.

"No, I thought I sensed someone new. I could've been mistaken." But I had sensed *someone*. I took a deep breath, let it out slowly, and opened my awareness. Stale, gritty lust crawled over my skin. Great, now I needed a shower.

There was a reason I usually avoided the club. Even when it was empty, it retained a sexual imprint of its past patrons. I did my best to push the lust aside and focused on Charlie. Her normal playfulness now housed a thread of worry as she studied me. I forced a smile and shut the door on her energy.

Kane's wouldn't be so easy. Ever since we'd gotten together, I could tap into his emotions as if they were my own, making it virtually impossible to fully block him out. I could push it aside, but when he was near me, I always knew how he was feeling, whether I wanted to or not. It was one of the reasons I'd refused to move in with him, even though he'd asked. Sometimes I just needed my own head space.

The longer I remained silent, the more his trepidation grew. "It's all right," I said. "Nothing's here."

"You're sure?" he asked.

It was a reasonable question. Three months ago, I'd been in a coma while, Roy, the evil ghost and former owner of Wicked, kept me locked in another dimension. Roy had first captured Pyper after a failed spell by Lailah. I'd managed to free her by tapping her emotional energy, but had, unfortunately, taken her place in the process. The only reason I'd escaped was because Kane had pulled most of our friends into a dreamwalk, and combined with Bea's powers, we'd been able to banish him to Hell. Once you've gone through something like that, anything seems possible.

"I'm sure." I smiled reassuringly at the pair of them and turned back to the portrait. "Let's finish this. Is she straight?"

"A little to the left," Charlie said.

The peeling paint was rough on my fingertips as I nudged the frame.

"A little more."

I pushed harder. The frame swung wildly, and I grasped it with both hands to keep it from falling. "Oops." I straightened it. The earlier foreign emotional energy returned, this time full of glee. I yanked my hands back. The glee vanished. "Oh, shit."

"What?" the pair below said in unison.

I climbed down off the ladder, keeping my eyes on the blue-eyed, disfigured beauty. "There's someone in that portrait."

"What?" they said again.

"The foreign energy is coming from her. That weird art project has something…or someone trapped in it." Could this be happening again? We'd just gotten rid of two spirits. I sure as heck didn't want to deal with another one. I turned to Kane. "Can you move the ladder? I want to probe the other two."

His expression and energy betrayed his skepticism, but he did as I asked. When I was in position, I deliberately placed both hands on Priscilla's frame. A stirring of curiosity trickled up my arms. I gripped tighter, but didn't tap into anything else. As soon as I let go, the curiosity disappeared. Interesting.

I repeated my experiment with Meri, but no amount of probing produced anything. I climbed off the ladder and sat in one of the blue, crushed velvet chairs. "That's weird. The first two give off energy, but Meri doesn't."

"Are you sure it was coming from the portraits?" Charlie sat beside me and downed a shot of amber liquid. The sweet aroma of rum filled the air.

I rubbed my forehead. "I think a couple of ghosts are trapped in those frames."

"Huh," Charlie said. "I guess there is something to that rumor."

"Which one?" I asked.

"The one about the three ugly ghosts."

A vague memory of Kane explaining the club's tagline surfaced. The marquee out front read: *Hundreds of beautiful women and three ugly ones*. When I asked what it meant, Kane had said they were ghosts. Later, he had assured me it was an urban legend made up for the annual Halloween party.

"But I only felt two." I frowned.

She shrugged. "Maybe Meri followed someone home."

"She was joking," Kane said over his menu. "She found those portraits at a secondhand store last week and bought them for the Three Ugly Women costume party the club is having on Halloween."

"Costume party?" I peered at him over my wine glass.

"Each year we have an Ugly Woman contest. The ladies dress up in their scariest, ugliest costumes, and at midnight they strip, unveiling their natural beauty. The crowd votes on the best costumes and the dancing. The winner gets a weekend stay at one of the hotels in the French Quarter. Plus she gets crowned Halloween Queen and all the free drinks and lap dances she wants."

"Sounds fun," I said dryly.

He laughed. "It is."

"So what do the portraits have to do with it?"

He shrugged. "Nothing. Charlie saw them and thought they'd be good decorations for the event."

They would have been great for the party, but after my revelation, Kane had taken them down and stored them in the supply room. He wasn't taking any chances on freaky paranormal activity. Frankly, I'd been relieved. "I'm sure she'll find something else."

Kane nodded. "I thought you said we were meeting Pyper and her date?"

"We are." I glanced at the time on my phone. "I'm sure they'll be here any minute."

"Never mind." He jerked his head toward the front door.

I spotted Pyper standing at the entrance of Muriel's, the restaurant she'd picked for the night's double date. She smoothed the skirt of her black and white print dress, smiling as the front door opened and her date joined her.

Wine lodged in my throat, forcing a coughing fit.

"Everything all right?" our waitress asked.

"Fine," I wheezed.

Kane stared at me. "Ian's her date?"

I didn't have time to answer.

"Sorry we're late," Pyper said from behind me. "Ian took me on a ghost hunt."

"What?" I turned around so fast I almost tipped over. She caught the back of my chair, sparing me from landing flat on my back with my legs in the air. "A ghost hunt? You?"

She took a seat next to me, but not before she snagged a sip from my wine glass. "Thanks." She handed back the wine. "And yes. I figured the only way to get over my anxiety is to learn more about ghosts. So, I asked Ian to take me."

That made perfect sense. The terrifying, claustrophobic sensation of being nailed down and trapped in a glass box came roaring back, making me fidget uneasily. After I'd freed Pyper from Roy's hold and taken her place, I'd been able to stave off the ghost's punishments. She hadn't been as lucky; she'd been tortured for three days. I nodded my understanding and tried to ignore Kane's stifling irritation. "Long time, no see," I said to

Ian, noting his signature all black ensemble. Black jeans, black T-shirt, and black short-sleeved button-down shirt.

"Better today?" He flashed a knowing smile.

He knew damn well I was better. Had been right after Bea tricked me into drinking that tea. I smirked and tried to block out the memory of the last time I'd been at Muriel's with Ian. That time we'd been on a date, and he'd spent the whole night scanning the place for ghosts. I prayed we wouldn't be witness to a repeat performance.

"When did Ian turn into your date?" I whispered to Pyper.

"About two hours ago when I asked him. Are we ready to order?"

A waitress appeared from nowhere and jotted down our requests.

When she left, Pyper filled her wine glass and turned to me. "When are you going to tell me about the haunted portraits?"

Ian's interest piqued and pressed on my skin. I bit my lip. Damn. Now we'd have to have the discussion in front of Ian, who no doubt would want to investigate. It was what he did. "How did you know about that already?"

"I talked to Charlie."

"Go ahead. They're going to find out sooner or later," Kane said.

I leaned over and kissed his cheek. After a bite of buttered bread, I set it down and explained what happened. As predicted, Ian wanted to get some readings. When he asked if he could get a reading with me, I shook my head before Kane could say anything. "No. I'd rather not. Go ahead and take readings if you want or have Bea or Lailah check it out, but I'm happy staying out of this one."

Ian looked disappointed, but perked up when Pyper said, "I'll help."

I sat straight up, ready to diffuse the coming argument. No way was Kane going to let that go. Pyper and I were the two most important people in his life. He didn't want either of us involved.

Pyper seemed to be channeling my thoughts because she sent Kane a pointed stare, daring him to say something.

He sucked in a breath. I barely noticed him bite the side of his cheek before he raised one shoulder in a slight shrug. I could tell it was killing him to stay silent by the way his irritation poked at my psyche. I sent him some of my own calm, mostly because I didn't want anyone causing a scene.

Pyper and Ian filled us in on their uneventful ghost hunt all the way through dinner. To my surprise, Ian didn't crane his neck once to look for the famed ghost that supposedly haunted the French Quarter restaurant. By the time dessert came, I was actually relaxed and enjoying myself.

Kane and I shared a crème brûlée, and Pyper and Ian had a molten chocolate cake.

"I've been craving this all day." Pyper closed her eyes and moaned her appreciation.

Ian watched her with a pleased smile, ignoring his half of the cake.

"What?" She loaded her fork.

"Just enjoying my dessert." His eyes never left hers.

"Oh." A blush crept up her neck and a nervous laugh escaped her lips before she stifled it.

Nervous? Pyper? Where was the confident, sassy spitfire I'd come to know and love? I turned to Kane and found his expression mirroring my own confusion. There was only one conclusion. Pyper had a thing for Ian.

As we left, Pyper and I walked together behind our dates. I leaned in and whispered, "Ian, huh?"

Her lips turned up in a sly smile. "Why not? He's cute."

"What about the guy you wanted us to meet?"

Her expression turned blank. "What guy?"

"Yesterday at the café, remember? You said you wanted to double date." Hadn't she said she'd just asked Ian two hours ago?

"Yeah. I meant with Ian. I meant to ask him right after work, but we were playing phone tag. All I wanted was something casual just in case, but since it's going so well, I think we'll call it a night." She grinned and called out. "Hey, Ian. Ready to walk me home?"

"Sure," he replied.

"I think we might need more dessert." Pyper winked.

Ian's gaze ran the length of her tiny body. "If you insist."

"You have no idea." Her voice came out low and sultry.

"Night, Jade, Kane," Ian said, not looking back at us. He wrapped an arm around her shoulders and the pair walked off toward Jackson Square.

"I don't like that guy," Kane said.

I laughed. "It's a good thing you're not going home with him then."

Chapter 4

The next day, after working a six-hour shift at The Grind, I dragged myself up the third flight of stairs to my one-room apartment, ready to collapse on my lumpy couch. When I got to the door, I froze. It stood slightly ajar and soft voices echoed within.

Slowly, I backed up then spun. I'd made it halfway down the stairs when I heard the door swing open. Footsteps echoed in the hall.

Shit! My body jerked forward, propelling me around the corner to the second floor.

"Jade!"

Grabbing the railing, I came to an abrupt stop then poked my head into the adjacent stairwell. "Pyper? What were you doing in my apartment?"

"Waiting for you. Sorry to barge in, but I had to use the restroom."

"It's okay." I shook my head and climbed back up to my apartment. "The door was open and, well, I thought I had an intruder."

"Oh, gosh." Pyper made a face. "I hadn't thought about that."

Her silver high heels clacked on my wood floors as I followed her. "You're dressed up today. Where are you headed?"

She spun, showing off her red, vintage, nineteen-fifty's-style pinup dress, and smiled. "I have a lunch date."

My eyebrows shot up. "With Ian?"

She gave me a coy look and walked behind my couch. "We need your help with something."

"We?"

Right then the bathroom door opened. Lailah came strolling out with Duke on her heels. Once she stopped, the ghost dog sat and stared up at her in pure adoration.

"Lailah," I said.

"Jade, you're looking...satisfied." Her lips curved in a teasing smile.

My faced burned. Since Lailah was supposedly some sort of angel, she could sense and see things others couldn't. In particular, she could read auras, and mine probably had a healthy glow of red surrounding the normal purple haze. Red was the color for passion. Something Kane and I weren't lacking in these days. If anything, it was growing. We couldn't keep our hands off each other, and when we couldn't be physically together, Kane always visited me in my dreams. Sometimes even right after...well, anyway. Having a boyfriend who dreamwalks has its perks.

I cleared my throat. "What brings you by this morning?"

Lailah turned her attention to Pyper. "She didn't know we were coming?"

Pyper ignored the question and turned to me. "Lailah could use your help."

"What's going on?"

Pyper reached behind the couch and came up with a portrait in each hand.

"I can see their auras, but I can't get a read on their emotions or intentions," Lailah said, holding the third portrait.

My attention focused on the mutilated beauty in Pyper's left hand. The desperation flowing from the portrait distracted me from Pyper's attempt to make a case as to why I should help.

Felicia's blue eyes seemed to lock hold of my gaze. Everything in the room disappeared. Suddenly I was trapped in her energy.

Strong-willed and stubborn, Felicia held her emotions close. They were thick and weighted down. Not what I'd expect from a supernatural being. Unless they were inherently evil, their emotional signatures—like mine—were light and easy to navigate. Hers pushed, prodded, and wrapped around my limbs like heavy tentacles. Desperation began to seep into my pores.

"Jade?" Pyper called.

I blinked, and the tainted energy dissipated. "Yeah?"

"Are you listening?" Pyper waved a hand in front of my face. "I know you said you didn't want to get involved, but we're just asking for a reading to understand what's going on."

I studied Felicia again. What had happened to the soul trapped in that portrait? Despite my reservations of dealing with another spirit, I nodded. "Okay."

"You don't have to do anything else. Ian's already got readings with Lailah. He just asked if we could jot down what you sense from them."

I barely heard Pyper's reply. Felicia's energy force had found me again, and I'd started moving toward the portrait. It was like a personalized, mystical gravitation pull. Like I wouldn't be able to break away even if I wanted to.

When I reached Pyper's side, I held my hands out. She set one of the portraits down and passed Felicia to me. As soon as my hands clasped the frame, my world turned black.

No, not black. A crescent moon peeked out from behind the clouds. A few stars twinkled in the midnight sky. I spun, taking in the wide clearing among familiar pine trees.

My heart dropped to my stomach. I took a deep breath and choked on the overwhelming pine scent. I knew this place. I hadn't been there for over ten years. Not since before my mother had disappeared.

"Why here?" I asked.

Felicia floated over the dirt-packed earth and stopped in front of me. Her perfect, non-deformed face radiated light and beauty. She studied me then began to move in a circle. On her third pass, she paused. "To remind you of what you lost."

The panic I'd been fighting vanished. My voice turned cold and flat. "I don't need a reminder."

Felicia floated higher and loomed over me. "Then why do you do nothing?" she asked in an icy tone.

"Nothing?" I cried. "What am I supposed to do? A whole coven of witches couldn't bring her back! The very ones who lost her to the other side. If they can't do anything, what makes you think I can?"

"You ignore your power. Every day you deny your gift is one more day Hope is a slave to the otherworld."

My throat closed. "Hell?" I choked out. "You're saying my mother is trapped in Hell?"

She nodded.

I crossed my arms and glared up at her. "No. That's not possible."

Felicia floated back down to my level and moved in close. Her eyes never left mine, but her suffocating energy wrapped around me. "Isn't it?"

I struggled to break her hold, but with each movement, her tentacles only wrapped tighter. I stilled, searching for calm. Some energy feeds off of fear. I wouldn't give her the satisfaction. "My mother disappeared during an earth spell. Agents of Hell cannot tolerate that kind of magic. She'd sooner be trapped in a tree than living in the underworld."

Trapped in a tree. My insides recoiled at the thought. She could certainly be trapped in one of the very trees right here outside the circle. *No. The coven would have found her.*

I consciously relaxed each muscle one at a time. Slowly her hold started to ease. She redoubled her efforts, but the more relaxed I became, the harder she struggled. Eventually her perfect face started to deteriorate as the left side peeled off in chunks.

Gross. She must have been using her energy to form an illusion.

I cocked my head to one side. "You should release me now, or you'll lose what's left of your appearance. You'll eventually run out of steam anyway."

Felicia spun, hiding her face. After a moment, she turned back with narrowed eyes. "I know what happened to your mother. Get me out of that frame and I'll lead you to her."

An arrow of pain jabbed at my heart. I kept my voice cool and steady. "Tell me where she is and I'll consider it."

Her lips turned up in a gruesome smile. "I already did. She suffers in Hell."

"Liar!" I screamed.

"See for yourself." Felicia waved one shriveled arm and the scene suddenly changed.

I still stood in the middle of the circle, but now thirteen white-robed witches surrounded me. Each held a black candle in both hands while they chanted a protection spell.

Nobody noticed my presence, and I had the distinct impression I could see them, but they couldn't see me. My suspicion was confirmed when two silver-robed witches stepped into the middle of the circle. One came dangerously close to walking right through me. I moved—no, floated—off to the side and waited.

The chanting grew louder. Energy seemed to vibrate through the air. Strong, powerful energy that could fill one with limitless possibilities. The witch at the northern point of the circle raised her arms and commanded, "Angel Avendale, heed our call. Our circle is true. Break the ties that bind you. Come forth to us, your sisters, your fate."

The coven repeated her words while the pair in the middle burned a picture. I couldn't make out the image.

As the last piece of ash fell from the photo, the witch leading the spell threw her head back and cried, "By the power of the coven, we command you, appear now within the safety of our circle. Join the souls of your sisters."

The power built and pressed in on me. Had I been in solid form, I was sure I'd have fainted or cried out in pain. The strength of it overwhelmed me, weighing me down. This wasn't an ordinary earth spell. Something much more dangerous and powerful was happening.

Blood magic. I smelled the copper tang first, and then turned to find both of the witches in the circle holding knives, each of them red with the owner's blood. They raised their hands toward the sky and prayed while it trickled slowly over their wrists, down their bare arms.

"By the Goddess of heaven and earth, we sacrifice ourselves for our sister, the Angel Avendale."

A heavy wind picked up, blowing out each of the black candles. The roar deafened the low chanting of the coven. Then suddenly, everything stopped and silence followed.

The leader's head came up, and for the first time I got a good look at her face. My heart stopped. "Mom," I whispered.

Of course she didn't hear me. When she spoke again, I realized why I didn't recognize her voice. It was the magic running through her. It transformed her soft-spoken speech into a powerhouse of a spell conjurer.

As if in slow motion, I watched her take out her own knife and run it across the palm of her hand. She held it straight out over the circle. Time seemed to stop as one small bead of blood clung to her palm. It dangled indefinitely, unwilling to complete the blood spell. Finally at last, it splattered on the ground.

All hell broke loose. Literally.

A misty, coal-shaded fog filled the area, blinding me momentarily. When it faded, a tall woman with wild gray eyes stood between the silver-cloaked witches. She reached out and grabbed both of their wrists. "How dare you summon me?" she seethed.

One of them gasped and fell to her knees. The other held herself steady and in a loud, but trembling voice said, "It's too late. She's already turned demon. Close the spell. Now!"

My mother gasped and started chanting again.

"No chanting," the standing silver-cloaked witch commanded. "Not enough time."

A cackling laugh came from the demon. "You're mine now. All of you."

The gray mist rose, swirling in a vortex around the two witches in her grasp. They stood trapped and terrified in their prisons. The mist spread out toward the rest of the witches, but before it reached them, my mother stepped forward.

"No!" Mom's arms came up and power exploded from her. A brilliant white force spread out, protecting each of the coven members from the demon's toxic magic. But inside, the two other witches and my mom were powerless against it. The demon's eyes blazed black and back to gray. Then in one swift movement of her hand, all four of them vanished.

The panicked coven members and their cries of dismay faded away, and I was left once again in the empty coven circle.

Felicia appeared once more. "That's what happened to your mother."

The terror in my heart threatened to seize my entire body. I willed myself to calm down. It couldn't be real. My mother wasn't the coven leader. She didn't perform blood magic. Someone would have told me.

"You expect me to believe that?" I crossed my arms defiantly.

Felicia's eyes narrowed. "You think I made that up? You think I'd show you my demon sister and how she ended the three innocent lives of those who were only trying to save her?" Pure rage strummed through her. "Think carefully, Jade Calhoun. For one of your own is on the verge of the same fate. Help me, and I'll help you before it's too late."

The world turned white for an instant, and once again I was in my tiny apartment on Bourbon Street.

"Jesus Christ, Jade," Pyper said, now holding the portrait. "Where did you go?"

"Put it down," I yelled from the floor at her feet.

Startled, Pyper dropped the portrait onto the couch and stepped back with her hands raised. "Sorry."

I concentrated on air filling my lungs. In, out. In, out. "No. I'm sorry." I shook my head. "I was back in Idaho. I saw…"

The words clogged in my throat. I swallowed. "There are spirits trapped in those frames, and I think it's best if we put them away."

"You can't be serious. I thought they just held an imprint of emotions," Pyper said.

I studied my friend, the twinges of fear seeping from her. I didn't want to think about what had happened, much less talk about it. I needed time to process, but since they'd both seen me check out, I had little choice. "Felicia's in there. She sucked my consciousness into another dimension. Different than what we experienced with Roy, though."

"How?" Lailah asked.

"I don't know exactly. Partly because I was in a place I knew, here in this world. But the other part was it felt different. With Roy, I was trapped. With Felicia, I wouldn't say that was the case. Just pulled there, but not imprisoned."

"What did she want?"

"To be freed," I said softly.

Lailah's energy reached out, engulfing me.

I jumped to my feet and stepped back with narrowed eyes. "Stop it. I don't want to be read."

She cocked her head. Her voice turned airy and dream-like. "Something happened while you were gone. Your aura changed. Deep sadness has settled over you. Whatever it was, Felicia touched a nerve."

"It's none of your business," I snapped, not caring if I hurt her feelings. It was rude to read someone when they didn't want you to. Even worse to comment on it. Lailah and I just weren't that good of friends. Not even friends. More like acquaintances. At least when I read people's emotions, I kept the information to myself.

Pyper kept her gaze on the portrait as she moved to my side. She took my hand and squeezed it. "Sorry," she whispered. "I'll tell Ian he's on his own."

The contrition in her voice had me sending her a small smile of acknowledgement.

"No, he isn't." Lailah moved forward and grabbed all three of the portraits. "I can't leave them in there."

"But—"

She cut me off. "No. I have to figure out a way to free them. It's an angel's duty to help the lost souls." Lailah sailed through my front door before either Pyper or I could say a word.

"Damn it!" I followed her, suddenly worried Felicia's warning was about Lailah, but by the time I made it to the stairs, she was long gone. I trudged back into my apartment and flopped on my bed.

Pyper eased down next to me. "What happened?"

I took one look at her concerned face and all my defenses crumbled. I started with the day my mom disappeared, how the coven had told me a routine earth spell had backfired and Mom had just vanished, and then moved onto Felicia and the vision she'd shown me. By the time I was finished, a tight ball had formed in my gut.

A few moments of silence ticked by after I'd finished talking. Then Pyper's deep blue eyes met mine. "Do you think it's possible Felicia was telling the truth?"

"Yes." I leaned against the ornate floral, wood-carved headboard. "I think it is possible, but if it is, I don't know what to do about it."

"It sounds like Lailah might be the one to ask."

"Sure, if I didn't think she was crazy."

"But we have to if what Felicia said is true about your mom and…one of your own is on the verge of the same fate. Do you think she meant on the verge of turning evil?"

"I have no idea." I rubbed my temples, trying to block out the tension headache seizing my brain.

Pyper shook her head then got up and moved toward the door. "I think you're right about Lailah. She is crazy, but what choice do we have?"

I sighed. "Again, no idea."

Pyper's face softened. "I really am sorry. I thought facing my paranormal fears would help me feel more in control after what happened this summer, but seeing you mentally disappear like that…" She focused on my wide-planked pinewood floors. When she spoke again, her voice was barely audible. "It's like it happened all over again."

The strong woman I'd come to call my friend vanished with those words, leaving her weak and vulnerable.

A small tremor ran the length of my spine. I could almost feel the barbed wire that had been wrapped around my body while I'd been imprisoned by Roy. I shook it off, rose from the bed, and stepped in Pyper's path. "It's over. Felicia wasn't anything like Roy. I wasn't trapped so much as transported. Trust me—it wasn't the same at all."

When she looked up, her eyes seemed to have regained a fiery spark. "Good. I want to say it's best we let it alone, but if there's any chance of you finding your mom, you know I'm here for whatever you need." She gave me a quick hug and left.

I crossed the room to my kitchen, and with shaky hands, poured an extra large glass of merlot. All I could focus on was Felicia's words. *Hope is a slave to the otherworld.* Was that at all possible? If she was, there wasn't anything I could do about it. Or could I? Bea and Lailah kept insisting I was a witch, but that wouldn't solve anything. All I knew how to do was transfer a little energy.

Pyper was right; I'd have to seek Lailah's help. A small tremor of apprehension rippled through me. What was she doing with those portraits? I picked up my phone and called her. It went straight to voicemail. After a quick message, I called my aunt Gwen. She knew about these things, though we rarely talked about them. As a teenager, after Mom disappeared, I didn't want to have anything to do with the coven. Gwen, however, did. I knew she didn't attend their rituals, but she did socialize with a few of them.

Again, the phone went straight to voicemail. I frowned and left a message for her to call me, but left out the details. Gwen always knew when I was upset. In fact, I was surprised she hadn't already called herself. She has intuitive tendencies, especially when I'm involved.

I tossed the phone on a small end table. Duke, my ghost dog, appeared and settled next to me. I looked at him. "You couldn't have warned me about Felicia? You spent two weeks barking at Roy. What gives?"

The golden retriever turned toward the window, rested his head on his paws, and heaved a heavy sigh.

"My thoughts exactly."

Chapter 5

I blame shock. It's the only reason I remained on my couch, drowning my fears in a bottle of wine. If I'd been convinced what I'd seen in the vision was real, I probably would have hunted Lailah down or gone straight to Bea's or even Ian's house. But I couldn't reconcile the events with the mother I'd known: The sweet, kind witch who drew her pure healing magic from the earth. Not a witch who messed with blood magic. The kind of magic that often resulted in horrific consequences.

Just like it had in the vision. The blood spell had failed, producing a demon instead of the angel they'd called. Or had it? One of the witches had said it was too late, she'd already turned demon. Then maybe the spell had worked.

A tiny thread of doubt sprouted in my mind. Had my mom agreed to perform blood magic because it was the only way to help the silver-robed witches?

My heart pounded. That I could believe. If I wasn't mistaken, the silver-robed witches were trying to save an angel from turning demon. Would I do the same for Lailah? The answer came instantly, without thought. Yes. I didn't know much about angels, but there was no way I'd let one succumb to such a fate. Even it if meant using blood magic.

Lailah needed to know what I'd seen. She was in danger. The warning had to be about her. She was the only angel I knew. I jumped up, ready to run over to her house, but the room tilted and my floor rolled. I sat and once again the world righted itself.

Maybe when the wine wore off. I stumbled over to my bed, climbed in, curled up in a tight defensive ball, and promptly went to sleep.

Passing out before your boyfriend shows up is the perfect way to avoid answering questions. That is, until he appears in your dreams demanding answers. Damn, a girl can't even enjoy a good drunken stupor.

I knew it was a dream. Kane's slight silvery outline gave him away. Anticipation curled in my belly. When he visited, things always got heated. I smiled up at him and ran a fingertip down his thigh. "What are you doing way over there?"

He sat on the edge of the bed, staring down at me. Usually he alerted me to his presence in a much more intimate fashion. He frowned. "What happened today when Lailah came over?"

I turned over on my side and propped my head up with an elbow. "Did Pyper tell you they ambushed me?" I asked, evading his question. I wanted to tell him when I was awake and sure I was thinking clearly. I didn't always remember all the details when Kane pulled me into a dreamwalk. It wasn't the best time for a serious conversation.

Irritation and impatience slammed into my consciousness, making me flinch.

"Sorry." Kane made an effort to rein in his emotions. "My chat with Pyper did not go well."

"Imagine that." I flipped onto my back and stretched.

"What the hell was she thinking? You'd already told her you didn't want to be involved." Kane got up from the bed and started pacing the floor. "Christ." He ran a hand through his thick, dark hair. "Why is she so stuck on exploring this?"

I rolled off the bed and crossed the room to stop in front of him. Wrapping my arms around him, I pulled him close. "Is it so hard to understand? Roy took something from her. It's her way of getting it back."

He closed his eyes, struggling to control the anger that always surfaced at the mention of Roy. I could relate. Roy had been an asshole when he was alive, and he'd turned evil in death. "He can't hurt her now."

I shrugged. "We hope not, but it really isn't about him. It's about how she sees herself. She needs to get her confidence back. Confronting the paranormal is how she's chosen to go about it."

He gazed down at me. "And what about you? Do you feel the same way?"

"No."

Kane leaned down and kissed my nose. "Care to elaborate?"

"If you haven't noticed, I'm not much of a fan of the paranormal world. It hasn't exactly brought good things to my life." I tried to pull away, but Kane's arms tightened around me.

His lips twitched. "You can't think of one positive thing?" One hand traced the length of my neck before he bent and nibbled my jawline. "Would you really trade all those dream hours away?"

I shook my head and leaned into him. "You might have a point."

He trailed kisses along my neck, igniting the familiar hum I always felt when his lips brushed over my skin.

"Hmm," I sighed.

He let me go then lifted me effortlessly into his arms. The gentleness of his gaze made my heart swell.

The next moment we were lying on the bed. My clothes had changed to a silky, jade-green night slip. I had to smile at Kane's choice. He always loved to dress me in colors that matched my eyes.

He gathered me close with one arm, cradling me next to him. "I won't let anything happen to you," he whispered.

"I'm counting on it."

His love fluttered over my skin before wrapping me in a protective layer. I glanced up with a warm smile and froze when my gaze landed on someone standing right next to the bed.

"What?" Kane sat up. "Lailah?"

Her black, cotton negligee rode up her thigh as she lifted her arm and crooked a finger at him.

He rose from the bed, clad only in his boxer briefs. A moment later he vanished. And took Lailah with him.

I woke with a start. Beside me, Kane slept soundly with a tiny smile on his lips. I placed my hand on his shoulder and nudged. When he didn't respond, I lowered my lips to his ear. "Kane, wake up."

"Hmm," he mumbled.

"Wake up," I tried again, my voice pitched a little louder.

He rolled over and I heard a low rumble of another woman's name. "Lailah."

A slow burn started in the middle of my chest. The thought of Kane spending any time at all with his ex-girlfriend, even in a dream, produced a variety of violent impulses. I pushed them back, grabbed my pillow, and headed for my lumpy couch.

The next day I gritted my teeth when Pyper asked about Kane.

"He must have said something to you," she prodded. "I know he isn't happy I'm working with Ian or that I brought Lailah to your apartment yesterday. But he'll get over it, right? I don't want to spend the next week fighting with him."

"I don't know. Just talk to him." I threw the metal milk pitchers into the stainless steel sink, satisfied when the noise drowned out Pyper's response.

She stopped restocking the coffee cups and turned to me. "Are you okay?"

My shoulders slumped. "Sorry. No. Besides the weird thing with the portrait, something else happened last night that has me in a funk."

She leaned against the counter. "Want to talk about it?"

I shook my head. "Not when customers can hear." I gestured toward a couple stumbling in through the door of The Grind.

She pursed her lips and nodded before turning her customer-service smile on the pair holding each other up. The moment they dragged each other out with their blended, double-chocolate, mocha lattes, she flew to the door and flipped the closed sign.

I glanced at the clock and raised my eyebrows.

She shrugged. "It's only fifteen minutes early. The tourists are too drunk to notice what time it is anyway."

She had a point. The Saints had played and won that day. It had turned into a full-on street party on Bourbon Street. We hadn't seen a sober person in hours.

Pyper pulled out a chair to one of the tables. "Sit."

"Wait a minute. This requires reinforcement." I grabbed a cup of ice, filled it part-way with chai concentrate and the rest of the way with soy. After a quick stir, I joined her at the table.

"You call that reinforcement? You're pathetic." She jumped up, making a lock of electric blue hair fall from her otherwise black ponytail. She leaned over the counter, searching for something under the register. She came up with a small, hotel liquor bottle.

"What's that?"

"Chocolate liqueur."

I rolled my eyes. "Yes, I can see that. But why do you have such a small bottle of it?" The club next door was full of regular-sized bottles. Usually she swiped whatever she wanted from the stock room. Kane never said a word about it. Not that it would stop her if he did. They were best friends, but they acted more like brother and sister.

"I got it a few days ago from a hotel on Royal when I was out with Ian."

"You did?" Surprise rang in my voice. She'd told me the night he'd walked her home they'd only kissed good night. That had been less than a week ago.

She poured a generous amount of chocolate liqueur into my drink and nodded. When she looked up, she laughed. "Yes, but it's not what you think." Her lips curved into a sly smile. "At least, not yet."

I took a sip of my drink and waited. I knew she was waiting for me to react. I just wasn't in the mood.

After a few moments, she relented. "Oh, all right. I was on a ghost hunt. One of the hotels asked Ian to check out some paranormal activity and ward it off if he could. Seems someone was freaking out one too many guests in the middle of the night."

A smile broke out on my face for the first time that day. "That's wonderful. I know Ian's been dying to check out some of the businesses around here. And he got paid for it too."

Pyper nodded. "Not much, though. They paid a consulta- tion fee, and if the haunting stops, they'll pay him a bonus."

My smile vanished. "Who decides if it was successful?"

"That's the rub. No one really knows for sure, do they?" Pyper picked up the tiny liqueur bottle and poured some into her coffee. "The hotel is keeping a log of customer complaints. After three months, Ian can go take more readings, and if there aren't any more incidents, he gets paid."

"That doesn't seem fair. Ian should get paid a flat fee for services."

"I agree, but he said he was willing to compromise for the opportunity to gather data."

"That sounds exactly like something he'd say." I drained my spiked chai tea. "And what did you think of the hunt? Anything unusual happen?"

She laughed. "Not unless you count Ian not paying one speck of attention to me."

"Was he supposed to?"

The expression on her face told me everything I needed to know.

Laughing, I raised both hands palms up. "Sorry, I forgot. All men, especially cute school-boy types, should be fawning over your every word."

She snorted. "Maybe not every word, but they should acknowledge I'm there, even if they are caught up in their life's work." She leaned back and fixed me with a stare. "Now, what happened last night that's got you in a funk? I know Kane spent the night. I saw him take off up the stairs to your place.

Usually you're disgustingly chipper after the two of you bump uglies all night." A mock look of alarm transformed her face. "Don't tell me he's having equipment issues."

My neck grew warm and I spread my palms on the table, trying to relax. Pyper used to manage Wicked. Talking about sex never embarrassed her. Unlike me, who up until three months ago only ever had one friend to talk to about such things. I took a deep breath and prayed my face wasn't turning the color of a tomato. "No. Actually, I passed out in a red wine haze before he got there."

"Hangover?" Before I could respond, she shook her head. "No, you would've just said so. The customers around here are intimately familiar with that particular issue."

"Well, I did wake up with a craptastic headache, but one of Bea's herbal packs took care of it." That morning, with my pounding head and queasy stomach, I'd broken down and taken a smidge of one of her all-purpose healers. The instant relief told me they were, in fact, enchanted. At once I'd felt both comforted and heartsick. I'd grown up with all sorts of similar herbal cures, but after Mom had disappeared, I'd sworn off all magic, including enhanced herbs. Funny how fast the righteous fall when suffering from too much wine.

"Jade?" Pyper asked.

"Hmm?" My glazed eyes focused on her concerned face.

"Where did you go?"

"Just thinking—crap. Kane's coming and he's not happy."

"So?" Pyper leaned back and stretched out her legs as if she didn't have a care in the world.

Kane's irritation intensified the closer he got. I straightened, planted my feet, and crossed my arms over my chest. My eyes stayed transfixed in a glare on the back door I knew he'd be stalking through any moment. Whatever he was upset about, it would have to wait.

For normal people, dreaming of another woman could be forgiven. But Kane was a dreamwalker. He controlled what went on in his dreams. I didn't know if he brought Lailah into our dream or if he'd only taken her out, but to continue to dream of her—or possibly with her—afterwards…well, he had some explaining to do.

"Pyper," Kane yelled as he plowed through the swinging door from her office. "What the hell do you think you're doing now?"

She took a swig from the hotel liquor bottle and placed it carefully back on the table before glancing at him.

He'd come to a full stop, looming over her. Electric shots of fury crackled around him, making me flinch. He wasn't just annoyed, he was ready to explode.

Pyper's lips turned up in a pitying smile. "Discussing your impotence issues. Maybe you need a little blue pill."

A surprised bubble of laughter escaped before I clamped a hand over my mouth and avoided Kane's sideways glare. Pyper never put up with Kane's moods and today was no exception, but he wasn't in his usual annoyed state. Whatever was going on with him was different. I'd never seen him this angry.

To his credit, he completely ignored her jab. "Why the hell couldn't you leave it alone like I asked?"

Her eyes got wide. "Why, Kane, I haven't come anywhere near your failing male parts." She turned her innocent expression on me. "Jade, trust me when I say I don't have any interest in your boyfriend's wanker."

"Pyper," I warned and got up to move beside Kane. I touched his arm, almost flinching at the current of unease running through him. "What's going on?"

"You mean she hasn't dragged you into this yet?" His tone had softened slightly as he spoke to me.

"Into what?"

Now Pyper was on her feet, indignation taking over her playful mood. "Stop accusing me of shit I didn't do. And if you're talking about yesterday, I already told you I'm sorry for what happened with Lailah."

The mention of Kane's ex had me scowling and backing away. He sent me a questioning glance, but I lowered my gaze and retreated behind the counter. I leaned against the wall and waited.

"You haven't been to the club today?" he asked Pyper. "At all?" The shocks of fury he'd been throwing off vanished, replaced by a swirling cloud of wariness.

"No. I've been here all morning, with Jade. If you don't believe me, ask her. I'm sure—"

Kane held up his hand, stopping whatever else she was going to say. "I believe you. But you'd both better come over to the club. There's something you need to see."

Chapter 6

Kane led us out the back and down the hallway toward Wicked. I followed Pyper on the short walk, but as we got closer to the door, I fell behind. My chest started to constrict. A cold sweat broke out on my skin. I dug my fingernails into my palms, stopped, and pressed one shoulder into the wall.

"Jade?" Kane turned around suddenly. "What is it?"

I met his worried, dark eyes. "I don't know." Everything in me wanted to close the ten feet between us, wrap myself in his arms, and bury my head into his chest. But fear paralyzed me. I couldn't move forward. I just stood there, sagging against the wall.

Pyper got to me first. Her small hands clutched my forearm. Worry rippled off her, rushing into my being at an alarming rate.

My stomach turned. "Let go," I cried, yanking my arm from her grip. The relief wasn't enough. My knees gave and I started to crumple.

Just before I slammed onto the tiled floor, Kane caught me. Instantly, the sickening foreign energy disappeared. It took a moment to feel normal again, if not a little weak. "Get me out of this hallway," I said, my words muffled against his shoulder.

Despite my garbled speech, he picked me up and carried me the short distance to the club. Kane headed straight to a small sofa and sat, positioning me on his lap. I tried to shift to sit next to him, but he held me firm, his protective instinct unwilling to let me go.

"It's okay," I said. "I'm better now."

Sometimes if I'm weak, a weird thing happens when Kane touches me. It's almost like the energy meld I'd been working on with Bea, only not quite. I can take and send emotions to and from most people, but it takes conscious effort. With Kane, it just happens. His emotional energy seems to complement mine, making it easy for him to calm me.

He kissed my temple. "I'm glad to hear it, but I won't be letting go just yet."

My insides warmed as I relaxed against him.

"I hate to break up this Hallmark moment," Pyper said lightly then sobered. "But maybe you can tell us what the hell just happened?"

Turning his head in her direction, Kane's irritation returned in full force.

I tensed.

"Sorry." He made a decent attempt to relax as he brushed a strand of hair back from my face. "What did happen out there?"

"I…" A terrifying realization came over me. I'd experienced those awful, sickening emotions on a hot July afternoon twelve years ago. I'd been trapped in a shabby, wood-sided house with my best friend Kat as we were forced to witness the beating of a boy intent on keeping us safe. Fear lodged in my throat. "Has Dan been here?" I finally choked out.

"That slimy ex of yours?" Pyper asked.

"Why?" Kane's body stiffened.

His hand tightened on mine, and I stared down at it, not sure what to say. I'd only ever spoken of that day once before after we'd been rescued. Kane and Pyper had no idea what the three of us had endured.

"You felt an emotional imprint of him, didn't you?" Kane accused. "He was here, wasn't he?"

"Maybe. I don't know." The pair of them stared at me, waiting for answers. "I felt him, I guess. But not the Dan I know today. The one I knew as a teenager."

"What does that mean?" Pyper stood with her hands on her hips. "And how does a teenage boy who was a friend of yours make you look like you're going to throw up? You liked him then, didn't you?"

I steeled myself and told them how Dan had protected me and Kat from a sexual predator when we were fifteen years old. "He risked his life for us, took a beating that put him in the hospital for weeks. He came very close to dying that day. If he hadn't been so determined, I don't know what would have happened to us." A hollow emptiness filled my chest. I'd long ago stopped crying when I thought of that day. The only thing left was cold hatred for the man who'd called himself my foster father.

"You not only watched, but you experienced his terror along with him, didn't you?" Kane said gently.

I gave him a short nod.

"And that's what you felt out there?" Pyper's horrified expression made me curl tighter against Kane.

He took in a short breath as he realized the truth of her words. "Jesus, Jade. No wonder your essence was torn from me." He'd told me once he could feel my energy. He wasn't an empath, but apparently his dreamwalking was enough of a supernatural ability that he could sense me when others couldn't. He couldn't feel anyone else, though. It was odd, but I'm used to odd, so I never spent time dwelling on it.

I took a moment to process what he said. Torn from him would suggest he couldn't sense me anymore. Had I recoiled into myself? Probably. I slid off Kane's lap, relieved he didn't try to stop me. Telling them about that day had helped, made me stronger, like I was in control. I stood and faced Kane. "I'm okay. I think you should check the doors and security cameras. I don't know why Dan was here or why he appeared to be reliving that day, but I'm certain it was him. What we went through that day and how he felt isn't something I'd forget or confuse."

Kane stood. "I have a good idea what he was doing here. What I don't know is why."

Pyper and I stared at him, waiting.

He opened the office door. "Come with me." Clasping my hand in his once more, he led us into the middle of the club near the stage.

"Where did those come from?" Pyper asked.

"What?" I whirled. But she didn't need to answer. Lined up against the wall were three life-sized voodoo dolls, only instead of being generic, they each had very distinct faces. They were cute, even. I was about to say so when one caught my attention. Without thinking, I found myself standing in front of her with my hand stretched out.

"What are you doing?" Kane pulled my arm back.

Startled, I stepped back and blinked. "I don't know." Had there been some sort of magnetic pull, or had it been my imagination?

"Why would Dan put giant voodoo dolls in here?" Pyper asked.

I frowned.

Kane and Pyper were arguing about how Dan may have gotten in when I interrupted them. "Hey." I pointed to the doll in front of me. "Take a look at her. What do you see?"

Pyper gasped. "Oh my God. It's Felicia, only without half her face burned off."

"And I'm pretty sure the others are Meri and Priscilla."

Kane nodded. "Right. Now you know why I was so worked up."

I squinted and moved closer. Then I stopped breathing. "Guys," I whispered. "Meri's the demon from yesterday's vision."

"You're kidding," Pyper said, shock replacing her curiosity.

"What?" Kane asked, confused.

I sank into a chair, staring at the black-haired doll. The characterization was spot-on with her long, straight hair and gray eyes, but it was the sewn-on expression that made it clear the doll was her. High arched-eyebrows, defined cheek bones, and slightly puckered lips. I'd know her anywhere.

"You sure?" Pyper asked.

I nodded.

"Can someone fill me in please?" Kane demanded.

Oh. Right. I hadn't actually given Kane the details, since I'd passed out before he'd arrived the night before. Then this morning, I'd left for work before he'd woken up. And let's face it. I hadn't wanted to talk to him anyway after the Lailah dreamwalk incident. The irritation from the night before came roaring back. I pushed it aside. This was much more important than some dream right now.

Kane stayed silent through my entire explanation. When I finished, he just stared at me.

"What?"

He cocked his head and eyed the Meri voodoo doll. "You're saying this doll represents a demon? And that your mother helped two witches summoned her, causing your mother's disappearance?"

"Yes. I mean, no. They were *trying* to summon an angel, except she'd already fallen and had become a demon."

"Didn't Felicia say the three of them were sisters? Doesn't that mean these other two are angels also?" Pyper asked, confusion pinching her face.

I shrugged. "I guess they could be."

Kane shook his head. "Not likely. Angels are born into witch families and are very rare. It's unheard of to have two in the same generation."

I narrowed my eyes. "How do you know that?"

He shrugged. "I dated Lailah."

Jealousy coiled in my belly. Was it wrong to hate an angel?

"Why do you think Dan brought these here? I mean, what's the purpose?" Pyper moved in front of me, getting closer to inspect Felicia.

"That's the question of the hour," I said. Felicia's warning came roaring back. Had she meant Lailah? And would her involvement with Dan be the cause of her downfall?

I was about to voice my concern when Pyper traced her finger over the stitched X on the left side of the Felicia looka-like. As she did, a soft white glow encompassed her and the doll. It appeared suddenly, and when Pyper pulled her hand away, it vanished. Considering her and Kane's non-reaction, I had to believe I was the only one who had the ability to see it.

When Pyper stepped back, I couldn't help myself. After what happened with the portrait, touching the doll was a stupid thing to do, but I had to know. Before I even made contact, the light, airy, familiar essence merged with my own, a comfortably warm sensation. My fingertips grazed the X and everything intensified.

Memories flashed through my mind: A child's stuffed puppy, ragged and loved in the bed; mixing up a batch of cookies while Mom chanted spells over a bowl of herbs; a first kiss with a boy named William. I jerked back as if I'd been burned.

Kane's hands grabbed my shoulders, and he steadied me. "Why do you insist on doing that?"

"I didn't…I mean, it wasn't planned." My voice seemed far away as I processed what had happened. I turned to Pyper, who was leaning against the stage. "Did you feel anything?"

She shook her head. "Nothing but the cotton they used to stuff her with."

"I thought so." I walked behind the bar and poured myself a tall glass of water. What I really wanted was a Guinness, but now was so not the time. After draining the glass, I looked up, not surprised to see Kane and Pyper staring at me. I sighed. "That voodoo doll has witch energy trapped in it."

Pyper frowned. "I didn't know witches messed with voodoo dolls."

"They don't," I said. "Or at least, I've never known one to. But the Felicia clone not only has traces of witch energy, she also carries memories."

"What?" Kane strode to the hanging dolls. "That's it. These need to go."

He grabbed the rope Felicia dangled on and almost had it over her head when I cried, "Stop."

He let go of her immediately, and the blinding light that had encased him vanished. He spun, staring at me expectantly.

"They aren't evil. We have to help them." I pushed him out of the way and started carefully untying the Felicia doll.

"Jade." Kane put a hand on my arm, but I barely noticed. Felicia's young life was flashing through my mind: Her sitting in a wood-sided house on a hot day, eating oranges with another young girl; playing in a cool river, laughing off a warning to be careful of water snakes; dancing close with a young man in a large barn as a teenager while a band played country music for the growing crowd.

"Jade!" Kane shook me.

I dropped Felicia into a nearby chair and looked at him, tears filling my eyes.

He wrapped his arms around me. "It's okay, baby. You're fine now."

Trying to pull back, a small chuckle escaped my throat when he tightened his embrace, not willing to let me go. I brushed a soft kiss across his lips and said, "I'm okay." After the portrait incident, I couldn't blame him for being protective. But this time was different. "Sorry." I gently separated myself from Kane and flashed them both a smile. "It's not what you think. That doll is infused with Felicia's happy memories. Everything coming from her is joy. There isn't anything evil about it."

"Except that her happiness is trapped in a voodoo doll," Pyper said, voice laced with disgust.

Pyper's words sank in. Turning to the other two dolls, I sent out my energy. Faint traces of their contentment pressed against my psyche, confirming my suspicions. Suddenly, I found myself sitting in one of the velvet chairs, holding my head in my hands.

What the hell was going on? Had all their positive emotions been stripped from the portraits and embedded into the dolls?

If so, then by who and, more importantly, why? And how was Dan involved? He hadn't even a trace of supernatural ability. I would know after living with him for two years.

I glanced up to see Pyper and Kane staring at me. "What?"

"You know, none of this stuff started happening until you showed up." Pyper's lips twisted into a curious smirk.

"Pyper," Kane warned in a hushed tone. "It's not her fault her ex is a psycho."

It could be my fault. He'd been tortured as a fifteen-year-old because of me. Then I'd lied to him for years about my empath ability, basically spying on his deepest emotions without his knowledge. When I'd finally come clean, I'd witnessed firsthand the sense of betrayal and personal invasion he'd experienced. After that, he'd changed into someone I didn't even recognize. I suppose he saw me the same way. But I wasn't intentionally messing with voodoo dolls. At least, not yet.

I stood. "We have to put them somewhere safe."

Kane's eyebrows rose as he contemplated me. "Why?"

"Why are boys so stupid?" Pyper reached out and picked Felicia up out of the chair. "Because if someone with a fetish for stick pins gets a hold of these, we could end up with another Roy on our hands."

She was right. I moved to help her, but she shooed me away. "I got this. We don't need you getting whisked away into more memories. Your face goes slack and you start to resemble a post-op lobotomy patient."

"Lovely." I moved back toward the bar to deter myself from touching any of the dolls again. I wasn't scared. Everything about them was pleasant, inviting even. My heart swelled with warmth as I remembered the little girl laughing in the river. But that's what made it so dangerous. Anything could go wrong. When messing with the mystical plane, even the best of practitioners made mistakes. Being an empath—and quite possibly a white witch, if Lailah and Bea were to be believed—meant that dealing with any unknown curses left me particularly vulnerable. And make no mistake; joy sucked out of trapped spirits was a curse. A dark one.

Pyper and Kane started carting the dolls toward the back door.

"Where are you taking them?" I asked.

"My place," she called over her shoulder. "It's the only logical choice."

I nodded. I couldn't take them. Kane wouldn't risk having them at his house since I spent so much time there. Leaving them in the club was out of the question. Too many people coming and going. Still, I hated the thought of her spending time with the cursed dolls. Just because she didn't have any natural intuitive or magical abilities didn't mean she wasn't susceptible to wayward curses. "Lock them in the spare room and don't touch them any more than you have to," I called back.

A moment before the back door clicked closed, I heard Pyper's faint reply. "Yes, Mom."

I pulled out my phone and called Kat. Crap! Voicemail. I disconnected and sent her a short text: *Where are you? Call ASAP.*

When Pyper and Kane returned, I said, "Come on. We need to talk to Bea about this."

Chapter 7

The tires of Pyper's VW Bug squealed when Kane rounded the corner onto Bea's street in the Garden District. The car bounced over a pothole, and a teeth-grinding scrape of metal against asphalt made me wince.

"Sorry," he said.

Pyper scowled. It was a testament to her restraint that she hadn't clubbed him after he cut off a dozen cars and possibly lost her muffler in one of the road craters.

There was no way to avoid the gaping holes in the narrow streets. You'd think being the Garden District, the city would do something about the failing roads. No such luck. He should have slowed down, but my desire to see Bea had me secretly pleased Kane was impersonating a Formula One race car driver.

We pulled up to Bea's gate a mere seven minutes after we'd left Wicked. The French Quarter wasn't far, but not that close, considering the street lights on Saint Charles.

"If there's any damage, one scratch, you're paying for it and a rental car while it gets fixed," Pyper seethed from the back seat while we waited for the gate to inch open.

Kane ignored her and sped through the barely open gate, past the main residence, and screeched to a stop in front of Bea's tiny carriage house.

Thank you, I mouthed to him and jumped out before either had even undone their seatbelts. "Bea?" I called through the screen door.

"In here, dear," her voice floated from inside.

The screen door shut with a soft click behind me.

Bea sat at her kitchen table, grinding dried herbs. "What a nice surprise. Let me get you something to drink." She rose, but I waved her down.

"I'll get it." The act of finding glasses and filling them with ice gave me a moment to collect my thoughts. So much had happened in the last few days, I hardly knew where to start.

By the time I had the iced tea ready, Kane and Pyper had joined Bea at the table.

Pyper, God bless her, jumped right into the thick of things. "Bea, is it possible to trap a spirit in an object?"

Bea put down her pestle. "You mean magically bind a spirit to something?"

Pyper nodded.

"Sure. If the witch is powerful enough."

"Why would someone do that?" I asked, handing Bea a glass.

"Any number of reasons, but usually it's done to control a spirit. Keep her from expelling any of her own energy." Bea peered at us. "It's a highly dangerous curse and not one condoned by the coven."

"Don't worry," I assured her. "No one here is interested in working that kind of spell. We just need information."

"Right," Pyper said. "Now, is it possible to put part of a spirit in one object and another part in something else—say, a voodoo doll?"

Bea frowned. "Witches don't use voodoo dolls."

"We just want to know if it's possible." I fingered the rim of my glass.

She shook her head. "But one could trap the soul and the spirit separately. Such a curse would be very dark. Very dangerous."

No one said anything.

"I think it's time you filled me in." Bea pushed her mortar away and clasped her hands together.

I closed my eyes then let it all out. I started with the night my mother had disappeared, and moved on to the portraits, my vision, Lailah running off with them, Felicia's warning, Dan's energy, and the voodoo dolls. When I finished, Bea got up and retrieved a notepad from a small desk.

"What does it all mean?" I finally asked in a hushed tone.

Bea looked up from her notes. "It means someone has trapped the souls of those three sisters in the dolls and their spirits in the portraits."

The memory of what I'd felt from the dolls came rushing back. Love was the underlying factor. Bea had told me the soul was what gave humans their ability to love. Oh, man. No wonder I hadn't detected anything warm and fuzzy from the portraits.

"Demons have souls?" Pyper asked.

"In the early stages of demonhood, yes," Bea said. "When an angel falls, his or her soul gets corrupted. After enough time goes by, it will eventually die."

I bit my lip. "Does that mean there's hope to save Meri from demonism? If her soul is safe in one of the dolls?"

Bea frowned. "Unfortunately, no. Once angels fall, their souls are damned." She made another note. "Someone has gone to an awful lot of trouble to get a few witches and a demon out of the way. Meri is beyond our help, but the other three we have to save." Bea jotted down some notes then made a phone call. When she hung up, she smiled. "Lailah will be here shortly."

"Three?" I asked, barely able to breathe. The two witches in the circle, the demon they'd summoned, and… "Does this mean you think we can find my mother?"

"If Meri isn't too powerful, it's a possibility." Bea continued to scribble notes.

For the first time in twelve years, a small tremor of hope started to blossom in my chest. Tears blurred my vision. "How? When?" I whispered in a shaky voice.

"We'll have to summon the three sisters from Hell, extract their souls from the voodoo dolls and their spirits from the portraits, and then reconnect both with their physical bodies. Meri will be an issue, but if her soul isn't too far gone, the rejoining will weaken her, and we should be able to banish her back to Hell, where demons belong. Hopefully, Felicia will lead us to your mother." Bea glanced at her calendar. "It's best if we do it during the full moon. That gives us two days." She eyed me. "You have work to do. I'll need every bit of your strength to make this happen."

I barely registered Kane's apprehension or the hand he clasped around my arm. "Anything. Where do we start?"

"With Lailah." Bea rose and crossed back to her desk. She pulled out a thick leather-bound volume. Only a lone pentagram graced the cover. "We'll need her strength to deal with the demon. It's her specialty. Plus, she might be of some use in finding out what your friend Dan has to do with this."

"Excuse me, but can you explain something?" Pyper asked Bea. "Why would anyone split someone's spirit and soul from their body? Especially if the person is in Hell?"

Bea pursed her lips. "Without knowing the details, I can't say. But they could have been trying to save Felicia and Priscilla. Being trapped in Hell would make it hard to not turn to black magic. That's just as bad as an angel falling."

I froze. "What about my mom? Can she have survived this long?"

"We can't know until we find her," Bea said gently.

Silence filled the room, until finally Bea flipped to the back of her book and ran her finger down a list in the appendix.

Pyper cleared her throat. "How are angels different from witches?"

I sent her a silent thanks for thinking of all the questions I was too preoccupied to ask.

Bea cocked her head and eyed my friend. "They're here to help people. God gives them special powers to aid them in their journey, but if they abuse them, they fall." Her eyes turned sad and wary. "It's a heavy burden to bear."

Fall. If Lailah slipped up, she'd turn demon and be banished to Hell. I shuddered, wondering how bad she'd have to screw up to suffer that fate.

Light steps sounded on the porch. I looked up just in time to see Lailah stroll in, wearing a long peasant skirt and blouse cinched at her waist with a knitted belt. With her long, blond hair, she looked like she'd just stepped out of a nineteen-seventy's fashion magazine.

Her smile vanished the instant she spotted us at the table. Something vaguely resembling unease crossed over her features. She waved, pulled a small tin out of her felted purse, and then handed it to Bea. "I have the supplements you asked for."

"Thank you." Bea popped the tin open and shook out two green pills, downing them with the last of her tea. She smiled at my worried expression. "Just a precaution. I'm fine." She took two steps and stumbled before grabbing the back of one of her wing chairs. Her face turned pasty white right before she crumbled to the floor.

"Bea!" I cried, springing from my chair.

Her eyes fluttered open and her breath came in short, labored huffs. "Poison."

"Oh my God." I fumbled in my back pocket for my phone. It slipped from my grip and slid under the chair. "Damn it. Someone call nine-one-one."

"No," Bea said with enough force I almost believed it had been a false alarm. But when I touched her arm, her skin burned. "It's a curse. Only a witch can fix it."

Hatred seeped from my pores as I glared at Lailah. Was this the start of her impending demise? At that moment, I didn't give a shit about what happened to her. I focused once again on Bea. "Where can I find the coven's numbers?"

Lailah appeared next to me, her face pinched with fear and panic. "They can't help. She needs a white witch. You need to help her."

I pushed her back. "Get away from her."

Pyper grabbed the angel by the shoulders and wrestled her against the wall. "What the hell did you do?"

"I didn't do anything." Tears streamed unchecked down Lailah's stricken face. "I enhanced the vitamins like I always do. I didn't mean to poison her!"

Pyper whipped out her phone and hit a button. "Stay," she said to Lailah. After a short conversation, Pyper turned to me. "Ian's on his way. He said to get her to her room. Something about positive energy."

Kane carefully lifted Bea in his arms and headed toward the stairs. The only thing that kept me from decking Lailah right there was Bea's wavering voice. "Not quite the way I imagined enticing a handsome man into my bedroom."

I started to follow but stopped mid-step. I couldn't leave Lailah in the living room with only Pyper to guard her. If Lailah wanted to, she could turn Pyper into a toad. At least, I think she could.

Pyper solved the problem by producing a roll a duct tape from Bea's desk.

"Perfect," I said, and sent Lailah one more death glare as I gestured to a chair. "Sit."

She held her hands out, trying to back up, but the wall stopped her. "No, I didn't mean to do it. I already told you it was an accident. I can help."

"No." I stalked toward the chair. "I don't trust you, and Pyper can't contain you by herself. Now sit, or Pyper and I will force you."

Pyper stood poised on her tip toes, ready to pounce. The fierce determination streaming from her made me glad I'd never pissed her off.

Shaking, Lailah eased her way toward me. Shame and sorrow oozed off her. Without looking at either of us, she sat and didn't move once as we bound her wrists and ankles together. Worried she could still wield a spell, I tore a piece of tape to cover her mouth. But the way she sat there meekly staring at the floor, I decided against it. What if it had been an accident?

I handed the tape to Pyper. "If she so much as speaks a syllable without being prompted, cover her mouth."

"Will do."

Pyper pulled out another chair, and sat with her arms crossed, keeping guard over the angel. I took off up the stairs.

It wasn't even five minutes before Ian arrived, red-faced and winded. "What happened?" He tucked Bea's hand in his and gave her his full attention.

"Accident," she whispered. "Poison…need energy transfer."

Ian scanned the room and his gaze landed on me. "Jade. Ready?"

Kane kissed my temple. "I'll be downstairs if you need me."

"Thank you," I said into his ear. Because I sensed Kane's every emotion when he was near, it made it hard to concentrate.

When he was gone, I took a seat next to Ian. Bea's sunken cheeks and paper-frail skin scared me. In minutes she'd gone from vibrant and capable to an invalid. Tentatively I touched her cheek, gasping at the heat radiating from her. "Shouldn't we call an ambulance?"

"No," Bea rasped. "The supplement Lailah gave me was laced with an herbal curse and only a witch can reverse it."

"Lailah." I stood and paced. "Why is it that every time something goes wrong, she's involved? I thought angels were supposed to help people."

Ian's pale blue eyes pierced me. Every muscle strained with tension. When he spoke, his voice held barely an edge of control. "Jade. My aunt is moments from succumbing to whatever poison is eating away at her body. Can we just focus on the energy transfer for now?"

Normally easygoing and cheerful, Ian had transformed into someone I didn't recognize. All the anger clutching my heart drained away, replaced by dread. What if I made her condition worse? I wasn't sure I was a witch. Even if I was, I wasn't a practicing one.

I looked up into Ian's intense gaze and swallowed. "Of course. That will fix this?"

"To start." Ian gently nudged me to sit next to him on the bed. "Then, once Bea gets enough to wake, she can walk you through the counter spell."

Crap! They wanted me to do a counter spell? Besides a few energy transfers, I'd never done more than a simple smudging. Swallowing hard, I held out my hand to Ian. "Ready?"

"Ready."

Someone had turned the air conditioning up to tundra level, making gooseflesh ripple over my arms. I tried to ignore the chill as I closed my eyes to center myself. This part was no big deal. I'd been doing energy transfers for years without knowing it. Of course, I'd have to be sure I used Ian—otherwise I might be too drained to work whatever spell was coming next.

At first I grasped Bea's icy hand then decided to place my hand directly over her chest. With any luck, the energy transfer would go straight to her heart, where it could instantly pump life back into her waning body.

Bea's essence held a mere whisper of energy. I sent my senses deeper, searching for something tangible to connect with. Holy Jesus. She was minutes from leaving us permanently. Panic seized my brain. There wasn't any room for error. Wasn't there anyone else in the magical city of New Orleans with skills better than mine? Surely there was a Voodoo priestess or some other witch...or angel who could pull this off better than I could.

Snap out of it, Jade. I mentally shook myself. There was no time to call anyone else. And Lailah apparently caused this mess. So much for angels.

Ian's hand squeezed mine, propelling me into action. I forced my anxiousness down and sent my awareness deep into Ian. Worry clouded every inch of his being. "Ian," I said with as much calm as I could muster. "I need you to block out all your fears for Bea and think only positive thoughts. Right now, what's coursing through you could make her worse."

"Sorry." He loosened his grip on my hand and shifted into a more relaxed position. Still, his energy remained tainted.

"Talk about her. A happy memory. Something that makes you smile when you think of her."

He let out a ragged breath and ran his other hand through his hair. "A happy memory," he muttered. Seconds ticked by, and I wanted to shout at him to hurry. There wasn't anything I could do to keep Bea's faint energy from slipping further from my grasp.

Finally, after what seemed like an hour, although it was probably only a minute, he cleared his throat. "A week after I turned seventeen, a new family moved into the house across from me. The two oldest kids were fraternal twins, a boy and a girl. The girl, Jessie, was shy, the unassuming type, and the most beautiful person I'd ever met." He raised his eyes to mine.

I smiled and nodded for him to continue.

"I wasn't exactly Mr. Outgoing myself at that age, but we had a lot of the same classes, and it wasn't long before we became friends. Of course, she had no idea I'd fallen in love with her at first sight. But her brother had. Jay was good-looking, the type all the girls had eyes for. Like Kane. And just as protective."

The slight edge in his voice when he mentioned Kane made my face burn. Ian and I had never talked about the one and only date we'd had just before I'd gotten together with Kane. It had been obvious Ian had a thing for me. But he had to be over it by now, especially since he was dating Pyper. With nothing else to do, I ignored the barb and waited for him to continue.

"I'm not sure what it was he didn't like about me, or if it was because I was interested in Jessie, but he made it his life's mission to humiliate me as much as possible when she was around. He'd offer to set me up with his castoffs, pretend he thought I was gay when I declined, and tell jokes at my expense. He'd do things like trip me or dismantle the spark plugs in my car when he knew Jessie and I were getting together. Nothing too serious, but enough to erode my fragile seventeen-year-old ego."

Crap. Hadn't I asked for a happy memory?

As if he'd heard my thought, Ian laughed. "Then one day, Bea came by while I was scrubbing the shaving cream 'I heart Ally' from my car."

"Ally?"

He shook his head. "A poor freshman who'd taken to following me around school. Anyway, I was cursing Jay, not only for messing up my car, but because I was late for school too. No way could I let Ally see that."

"Obviously."

"And Bea told me not to worry about it. She'd take care of everything. I didn't know what that meant. Actually, I sort of forgot about it until Jay told Ally I wanted to take her out on a date. Or at least, he *tried* to tell her that. He actually ended up asking her out himself. Imagine this cocky guy strutting up to this poor girl to tell her some other guy was asking her out, but when the words flew from his mouth, he ended up professing his undying love to her." Ian's laughter burst out in full force as he doubled over at the memory. He gasped in a breath. "He couldn't control what he was doing, and the harder he tried to correct himself, the more insistent he became about wanting to date her."

A flash of pity ran through my gut for the poor girl.

"From that moment on, anything Jay tried to do to me came back on him two-fold. Aunt Bea had hit him with one powerful curse."

The love for Bea radiating from him filled the room. Strong and pure, it was the exact thing she needed. I imagined a conduit running from Ian's hand to Bea's heart and tugged. Ian's energy met a wall of resistance, refusing to budge. It shouldn't be that hard. I could take energy into myself pretty easily. I pulled harder, straining with the effort. Nothing moved. Ian's energy held steady at his hand.

He started talking again about how Jay's declaration had ended up turning Ally into one of the most popular girls in school, but I ignored him.

I had to get that energy into Bea. Her own had become all but nonexistent while Ian had told his story. Damn. Abandoning my conduit imagery, I let Ian's emotions flow into me, through my core, and redirected them toward my hand on Bea's heart.

The effect was instantaneous. Bea's eyes fluttered open as she sighed with relief. Her energy pulsed with the radiant white light it usually held. I collapsed in relief at her side.

"Well done, Jade," she croaked.

"Welcome back." Ian took her hand and smiled a wide grin.

"Ian," she whispered, "I told you to never tell another soul I cursed your friend."

"You heard that, did you? I thought you might. I can't help it if I think it's funny. Jay was being an ass. It's not like it hurt him to learn some manners."

She patted his hand. "He was messing with my favorite nephew. I had to do something. Still, I'm not proud of it." She grinned, negating her claim.

"What happened with Jessie? Did you get the girl?" I asked.

"Sure. We dated for a few years." His smile dimmed. "Until she went off to college."

"It happens. And Ally? What happened to her?"

Ian laughed. "She ended up prom queen and had her pick of any guy at school."

"Except you," I said.

He shrugged. "She forgot all about me."

I doubted it. Ian was too nice of a guy for anyone to just forget.

Bea stirred, trying to sit up. Ian automatically reached an arm out to help her while I positioned the pillows against her headboard.

"Can I get you anything?" I asked.

"Seltzer water mixed with crushed vanilla and a teaspoon of lime." Bea picked up a silver hairbrush and started putting her normally immaculate hair back in order.

What were we doing, making some sort of weird cocktails? I was almost through the doorway when she said, "Bring Lailah with you when you come back up."

Her tone sent a shiver that had nothing to do with the frigid air up my spine. "Will do."

"Ian," I heard her say in her normal cheerful voice. "Can you do something about the thermostat?"

Downstairs, Pyper stood with her arms crossed in front of the door.

"What's going on?" I asked as I headed into the adjoining kitchen.

"The angel—" she stressed the word *angel*, indicating she thought Lailah was anything but, "—tried to spell her way out of her binds. I tried to cover her mouth, but she erected some sort of shield and I can't get close enough."

Lailah cowered into herself at Pyper's words. She didn't at all resemble the gorgeous, confident woman I'd come to know. Her face turned pale and she turned to hide from my penetrating gaze.

Without thinking about it, I sent my awareness toward her. My unwelcome probe bounced back. Yep. The barrier held. "Bea wants to see you. Let down your guards and we'll cut away the duct tape."

The air around Lailah shimmered. I knew without checking she'd dropped her shield.

Pyper cut the tape at her feet first. When she got to her wrists, she said, "If you even think of trying anything, remember I've got scissors in my hands."

Lailah only shook her head.

I waited by the stairs with the concoction Bea had requested. As soon as Pyper had her free, Lailah moved toward me. Her panic thrust into my awareness and crawled up my skin. I stepped back, trying my best to separate myself from her. "Calm down. She's fine."

Lailah shook her head, tears shining in her eyes. "I almost killed her."

"Almost," I said without sympathy. Maybe it was cruel, but I couldn't help remembering it was her spell that made it possible for Roy to take Pyper into another dimension. "But she's better now and wants to see you."

The coldness of my tone seemed to ignite some fight in her. She straightened her spine and, without another word, took off up the stairs.

"Was it something I said?" I asked Pyper.

She rolled her eyes and fell in step behind me.

Back in Bea's room, the window had been opened, letting in the warm fall breeze. Bea was dressed in an elaborate deep plum witch's robe, embroidered with delicate gold thread vines.

Lailah dropped to her knees in front of Bea and bowed her head. "I didn't know. I mean, I don't know what happened."

Bea reached out and tilted Lailah's head up. "The supplements were tainted. You were the one who altered them."

"Yes," Lailah whispered. "But…"

Two green pills appeared in Bea's palm. "They contain traces of your spelling signature. No one else's."

Lailah fingered the giant horse pills then snatched her hand back. The tears she'd been holding back spilled silently down her cheeks. "I don't know what happened. I don't remember spelling them."

Bea dropped the pills into a small pillbox. "Stand, Lailah."

Trembling, Lailah did as she was told.

"You are hereby banned from accessing your magic until further notice. A formal inquiry will be conducted. You'll be informed of the hearing once the council reconvenes." Bea held her hand out. "Jade, can I have the seltzer water please?"

Startled, I stumbled to Bea's side and handed her the bottle.

The carbonation sputtered as she twisted the top. When the bubbles settled, Bea poured a small amount in the palm of her hand. She recited a phrase in what I think was Latin, flicked the liquid at Lailah then raised her hands over her head. In a strong, commanding voice, she spoke. "Angel of the earth, heed my command. No magic shall be woven. No spell shall be spun.

No curse shall be uttered. Your threads of power are now tied. By the power of your coven mistress, your Wiccan status has been denied." The air around them shimmered momentarily.

"Shit," Pyper whispered.

My thoughts exactly. I'd known Bea was powerful. She'd demonstrated that when she'd banned a ghost to hell a few months ago. But I hadn't known she had the power to revoke someone's privileges. Not that Lailah didn't deserve it. I'd ban her too if she'd almost killed me. In fact, I was ready to ban her just for invading Kane's dream the night before.

I didn't realize I was scowling until Bea spoke. "It's standard procedure, Jade."

"Huh? Sorry, I was thinking about something else."

Lailah got up and silently left the room. My gaze stayed locked on her until she turned the corner to head down the stairs.

"Want me to keep an eye on her?" Pyper asked.

"Oh no, dear. Lailah's leaving." Bea caught my eye. "Jade, I need your help ridding my body of the rest of the poison."

"Poison? Ah, right." It dawned on me Ian had said she'd need my help, but after the power I'd just seen her possess, I'd forgotten all about it. I scanned her small bedroom. "Where should I...?"

"Let's go out on the porch." Bea swept past me, looking no more like she'd been inches from death just minutes before than any of the rest of us.

Pyper followed her and Ian had to nudge me out the door before I moved. "What just happened?"

"Bea rendered Lailah powerless."

"She can do that?"

Ian chuckled. "Sure looked like she could to me."

I stopped and turned to face him. "You're telling me Bea has spells to bind an angel?" If so, at least I wouldn't have to worry about Felicia's warning. Without magic, it would be hard for Lailah to fall.

"Yep. She doesn't like to flaunt it, but she possesses more individual power than most covens do combined."

I gawked. When covens combined their power, it could reach dangerous levels. Life-threatening levels. Bea could do that all on her own. A shiver ran through me. What was *I* doing here?

"Jade," Bea called from the bottom of the stairs. "I don't want to rush you, but the sooner we can work the spell, the easier it will be."

A wave of sickness rolled in my stomach. I was actually going to cast a spell, something I'd sworn I'd never do, with quite possibly the most powerful witch I'd ever meet. My eyes landed on the woman I'd come to call my friend. The image of her lying helpless in her bed flashed in my mind. Would she end up right back there if I refused?

"Go on," Ian urged in a hushed whisper. "The poison spreads fast."

Indeed, Bea was already starting to pale. Damn. At least if I was going to turn witch, I'd learn from the best.

Chapter 8

The sun hung low in the sky, illuminating the backyard with a soft orange glow. Bea headed down the stairs of the wooden porch and out into the middle of the neatly manicured lawn. "This way," she said.

Ian and I followed her. Pyper and Kane stayed on the deck. I envied them. Heck, I'd have stayed in the house. Or left.

"Jade," Bea said. "Take off your shoes."

"Um..." I stalled. No shoes? Was she crazy? There could be red ants, fleas, chiggers, or any number of painful, vicious bugs in the grass.

"You need the connection to the earth to harness your power." Bea threw off her thick robe and sat cross-legged on the ground.

"But what about the bugs?"

Ian laughed.

"What?" I demanded in a hushed whisper.

"There have never been any bugs in Aunt Bea's yard except ladybugs, butterflies, dragonflies. Things like that. Don't worry about your toes being bitten. They're safe here."

Slowly, I kicked off my shoes. "Does that mean they've been magically removed?"

"Something like that," Bea said. "Please take a seat." She indicated the area directly opposite her.

I crossed the soft, lush blanket of grass and lowered myself until I sat cross-legged in front of her. "You aren't worried about messing up the ecosystem by banishing God's smallest creatures?"

Bea gave me a patient smile. "They aren't banished. Just relocated while we're out here. Once we leave, they'll come back."

"Oh." I fell silent, wondering what else she had altered around her house for convenience's sake. Did the dishes clean themselves? What about the shower? Or refrigerator? Maybe I wouldn't mind being a witch if it cut down on my chores list.

Bea's voice snapped me back to reality. "To work a spell, you'll need to find your inner spark. Every natural-born witch has one. It's where you draw your power from."

"My power." I spread my fingers wide on my thighs, as if I could somehow reach out and grab it. "Where would I start looking?"

She pressed her hand over the left side of her breast. "Here. Look, and you will find it."

Crap. Nothing like a cryptic guru teaching a reluctant supposed witch. *Just look inside. You'll find it, Jade.* Yeah, sure. I was about to protest when I noticed Bea's trembling hands nestled in her lap.

The poison really was taking its toll.

I met her eyes, and whatever she saw in mine made her send me an encouraging smile. "You can do this. I've seen the light you possess many times. It's only a matter of you tapping into it."

Nodding, I took a deep breath. "Once I find it, what do you want me to do?"

"Pinpoint it and focus on it. Then I will guide you." Her voice seemed to falter on the slight breeze. She cleared her throat and in a commanding tone added, "Be confident. Strength will follow."

My desire to help her pushed all the reluctance from my mind. I sat, my face tilted up at the emerging moon, and closed my eyes. Somewhere in my inner recesses, I needed to find my magic source. Effortlessly, my awareness took over. Ian's and

Kane's anxiety, Pyper's intense interest, and Bea's mild disapproval washed through me.

"You're not searching," Bea said. "Your empath ability is a crutch. Cut it off."

Pursing my lips, I imagined my glass silo, the one I erected when I wanted to wall myself off from outside energy.

"How's that going to help?" Bea asked in a gentle tone. "Blocking us out will only lock yourself in."

Frustrated, I opened my eyes and stared pointedly at her. Bea knew things. She felt my energy shift, but she wasn't an empath. There was no way she could know how much it interfered with even the most mundane of tasks. Finding my inner spark with the three of them tainting my energy with theirs would never work. "If I don't block you four out, I won't be able to concentrate."

Bea held still, her expression unchanging. "Don't block us out. Read us, compartmentalize our emotions, and forget us. If you can do that, your day-to-day life will be easier as well."

I huffed. Easy for her to say. Too much intruding energy made me weak and unable to control anything. Still, she was right. If I built my glass silo, how would I send out any magic? All right then. Time to try something new.

With my eyes closed once again, I focused on Pyper and let her interest and unease settle over me. We were close and spent a great deal of time together, so her energy seemed natural, almost an extension of mine. Instead of pushing it away, I let it merge with my own similar feelings. I did the same thing with Kane's concern. I was so used to having him near, it was effortless.

I usually made a point of not invading Ian's emotions. Since he'd once been interested in me, spying on him just wasn't right. I was so used to blocking all but his most superficial emotions, it took a concerted effort to let him in. Intense fear gripped my soul. A soft cry escaped my lips before I could hold it back.

"Let it go," Bea whispered. "Just let it go now."

Releasing Ian's energy eased the tension curled in my stomach, but left me nauseated. I panted, trying to regain a thread of control.

"You're past the worst of it," Bea continued in her gentle tone. "Relax, and we'll be able to continue."

After a soul-gripping read like that, there usually was no hope of relaxing, but Bea seemed to be putting something behind her words because soon the tension eased from my chest and my breathing returned to normal. A faint trace of Ian's fear remained, but not enough to be a bother.

Bea's emotions were guarded and for that I was grateful. I got a trace of her emotional signature, letting me know she was there, but nothing else. I'd take it.

When I relaxed and focused on what was inside me, suddenly it was just me. Well, mostly me. I could still identify traces of Kane, Ian, and Pyper, but for the most part I was on my own. Relief washed over me.

Until I realized I still needed to find my magical spark. Determination pushed away all my doubts and fears. I could do this. Immediately, I concentrated on my heart. Surely that was a logical place to start. The muscle moved in a steady rhythm. *Thump, thump. Thump, thump.* Calm and efficient, there didn't seem to be anything extra or out of the ordinary. Just a heart pumping my life's blood. Next I explored that place deep in the center of my core. The place all my courage and instinct blossomed from. Focusing, I imagined a beacon of light pulsing under my ribcage. Something fluttered inside, leaving me breathless.

"You've found the edges of your soul," Bea whispered. "Your spark won't be there, though it bodes well you're able to find such a place inside yourself. Most people can't."

My eyes flew open. I'd touched my soul? "Why wouldn't it be there?"

Bea's lips turned down into a grim frown. "Only witches have a magical spark, while everyone has a soul. If you combined the two, it would mean giving up part of your soul each time you worked a spell. Do that enough times, and you'd suffer the same fate as a demon."

Gooseflesh popped out over my skin at the eerie foreboding in her voice. "Oh." I closed my eyes once more and this time, followed my blood lines, willing it to lead me to the spark. Blood is extremely magical. It had to get its properties somewhere. If I held on long enough, eventually I'd find my power source. Right?

Wrong.

I sat there searching for what seemed like forever, only to come up empty-handed. Opening my eyes, I heaved a heavy frustrated sigh. "I think you may have made a mistake. There isn't any spark to be found inside me."

"Of course there is." Bea's soft voice barely reached my ears. "I see it…" her words faded away and she slumped forward.

"Bea," I cried and reached to steady her. Her skin burned just as hot as it had earlier when the poison had taken over. "Ian, help!"

He was already by her side, but before he could touch her, Bea held up a feeble hand. "No, Ian. I'm fine." She righted herself and turned a few shades paler in the early moonlight. "The poison is taking over. Jade, listen carefully. When you find your spark, hold it in your mind. You'll need to coax it to do your will. Gently nudge it in the direction you want your magic to go."

A sheen of sweat glistened over her sagging body.

"Okay, but what spell do I use?"

"There—" she gasped for breath, "—isn't one." She looked straight into my eyes. Her upper body tensed and went rigid. With her face frozen in shock, she tilted to the right and fell in slow motion until she landed with a thud on her shoulder.

"Bea!" I scooted forward and rolled her onto her back.

"Do what she said," Ian said harshly as he knelt beside her. I didn't move. I didn't even breathe.

Ian reached out and shook me. "Find your magic!"

"I can't!" I cried, but placed both hands over Bea's chest. Her faint heartbeat skipped a beat. There wasn't time for me to figure out the spell or to transfer Ian's energy, but I could send my own. Determined to save my mentor, I gathered my own energy and forced it into her.

It instantly rebounded back into me. "What the…?" I didn't have time for this. Trying another tactic, I eased my energy once again toward Bea, this time focusing on wrapping her in it like a blanket. Once I had her tucked in, I took her hand and waited.

All of my energy dissipated into the night. "Damn it!"

"Jade?" Pyper said.

"This has to work." In my panic, I stood and reached deep. So deep my toes started to tingle. The sensation intensified, moving quickly through my legs, core, and down my arms. Everything seemed to vibrate. A wild sensation took over, sparking little bursts of energy in my chest.

The energy bursts excited me, setting every sensation I had on fire. The light, warm breeze lovingly caressed my bare arms. The lush grass tickled my feet. The micro-bursts grew, vibrating through my core. Everything inside me warmed with pleasure.

I raised my arms toward the sky and soaked in the glorious night. It was mine for the taking. Anything I wanted. My heart seemed to swell, and suddenly all the new sensations were fading. The night turned warm and muggy. Clouds shifted, covering the moon. The sparks of energy in my chest started to disappear.

The sparks. *My* spark. That was it. Focusing my attention on the last bits of energy, I willed it to clear Bea of the poison.

Nothing happened, except the bursts became almost undetectable. "More power," I whispered. With the words, an unknown force took over my body. My head tilted back and my back arched, as if I were being pulled by something from the sky. Ripples of energy coursed through my limbs. I ached all over. If only I could transfer some of what I was experiencing.

Transfer…to Bea. I barely noticed when I dropped to my knees to hover over her. I was beyond pain, too drunk on the power eating away at me. The moment my hands touched her skin, we both went rigid, powerless to move. My hands clutched hers, but I couldn't drop them. I couldn't do anything, except will the magic to clear Bea's blood of the toxins.

Her eyes slowly fluttered open as my limbs became heavy with fatigue. The world started to spin, and I wondered how long I could keep a hold on the spell.

"Stop it, Jade!" Bea sat straight up and yanked her hands from mine.

"What?" I asked weakly. "You seem to be better. I did good, right?"

"No." She stood and paced before me. "I mean, yes. I'm here. You found your inner spark. Only instead of harnessing your power, you used the source. I told you to coax it into what you wanted it to do. Not just transfer it to me."

My world spun as I jumped to my feet. It was a good thing Ian was around, or else I'd have taken a tumble on the now-dead grass. "What happened? It was green a moment ago."

Kane replaced Ian by my side and wrapped a strong, steady arm around my waist.

"You sucked the life out of it," Pyper said, coming to stand next to me. "While you were standing there, glowing, the grass suddenly turned yellow and started to die."

"Let's go inside." Bea swept past us toward the back door.

"I did it," I said to no one in particular.

"You did something," Pyper agreed.

I raised an eyebrow in her direction.

She shrugged. "Looked pretty creepy to me."

We followed Ian onto the deck. Right before we walked through the back door, I asked, "I was glowing?"

"Afraid so," Pyper said. "It looked cool, though. Wish I'd remembered to snap a photo."

"Oh, God."

"It's too late to be evoking him now," Bea said from inside. "Get in here so we can reverse the damage."

Crap. What had I done now?

Turns out, I hadn't cast a spell with my magic to clear Bea of the poison. I'd sent her part of my magical spark and she'd done it herself. Now she had to send back my power. "Why send it back?" I asked. "I don't plan on using it again." A tiny shiver crawled up my neck. I ignored it. "You're a great witch. Just keep it."

"No, dear. A magic transfer is highly dangerous, for both the recipient and the donor. For temporary use, it worked wonderfully, but if I keep your magic inside me, it would cause all sorts of mayhem in my own power source. It's better for both of us if I transfer it back."

And that's what she did, leaving me vibrating with charged energy.

Chapter 9

Kane walked me to the bottom of my stairs and kissed my temple. "I'll be up in a minute. I have a few things to take care of at the club."

"Hurry." I leaned in and brushed my lips over his.

"Count on it." He strode off, and I worked my way up the never-ending flights of stairs.

By the time I made it to the second floor, the walls seemed to be closing in on me. I quickened my pace and rounded the corner to the third set of stairs. One more flight and I'd be in my apartment, away from the horrid narrowing of the walls. Focusing on my feet, I forced them to move, taking each step two at a time. I had to get out of there.

Finally, the oak door of my apartment loomed before me. With a trembling hand, I fumbled with the key, nearly dropping it before I jammed it into the lock and twisted. The door sprung open, and I stumbled inside.

Duke jumped off the couch and growled.

"Stop it," I demanded and ran to the bathroom to splash cold water over my face. I stood with my hands braced on the pedestal sink taking deep breaths, willing my pounding heart to slow. It only took a moment for my breathing and pulse to return to a manageable rate.

When the heck had I become claustrophobic? I glanced up into the mirror and blinked. The wall behind me started to pulse. I whirled. The tiny room held me hostage as the walls creeped closer. My vision blurred, making me see double. Stumbling, I pushed my way back into my living area.

Duke snarled.

"Shut up, you stupid dog! It's just me." My vision cleared, and I focused on him. He stood across the room with his hackles up. I glanced over my shoulder and back at him. "Did I bring a ghost home with me?" The only other time I'd seen him behave that way was when Pyper had an evil ghost haunting her.

The golden retriever backed down and retreated to the corner.

"I guess not," I said, more than a little relieved. That was the last thing I needed.

The door swung open, making me jump, but I sighed in relief at the sight of Kane.

"You okay?" he asked with concern clouding his face.

"I am now." I buried my head in his shoulder as he pulled me to him. The night's events were too much for me to handle. Ever since I'd ignited my magical source, my body had gone haywire. The spark I'd used to cure Bea hadn't faded. I couldn't sit still or be in confined places. It's a miracle I hadn't jumped out of Pyper's car on the ride home. And Kane's touch was sending shockwaves through my charged body. I was intensely aware of his firm fingers splayed across my back. As I focused on them, a tingling radiated from his touch, spreading through my spine and downward. My body shuddered as the sensation only intensified.

Carefully, I extracted myself from his embrace and stepped back.

He matched my step, filling the void between us. Heat smoldered from his chocolate brown eyes. "You're not going anywhere." He reached out and pulled me back in his arms, this time burying both hands in my hair as he tilted my head up. His lips met mine with a fierce passion that hadn't been there moments before.

Sparks erupted with each caress of his velvet tongue. The night's events vanished as I poured all my pent-up energy into the kiss. Locked in a tight embrace, we each fought for control, nipping and biting, devouring each other. With each contact, each taste, Kane's exploration intensified until I no longer knew where my lips stopped and his started.

The power I'd conjured earlier in the night raged through me, growing with each of Kane's kisses. My body pulsed, vibrating with it. It had to get out; somehow I had to release it.

With a groan, I wrenched myself from Kane's embrace and backpedaled to the door. "I can't," I said in a hoarse voice. "It's too much."

He stalked toward me, pinning me with his gaze. "What is?" His hand cupped my cheek gently.

But the lightning bolt of energy that dove straight to my center made me moan in answer. Before he could say another word, I reached for him, yanking his shirt out of his jeans and over his head in one motion. Shadows from the soft lighting cascaded over his chest. The sight riveted me. I traced my fingers over the curve of his toned muscles, holding back as ripples of energy spiked through my hand.

"I don't know what you're doing," he whispered gruffly. "But if this is an energy transfer, you are forbidden from ever doing it again."

I froze and met his hooded eyes.

"Unless it's with me." Before I knew it, he had me undressed and in his arms. He took three long strides and laid us both on the bed, with me pinned beneath him. Everything pulsed. Every inch that touched him spasmed with power. His lips found my neck, tracing it with soft feather kisses. The pulse in my throat quickened to an alarming rate.

Clutching his shoulders, I held on as he bit down hard at the nape of my neck. I tensed and suddenly convulsed against him.

"How—" he gasped, "—are you doing that?"

"Hmm?" Unable to be pinned any longer, I locked my leg around his and flipped us both, so I was on top. "I'm not doing anything. It's you."

He groaned as I wrapped my lips around his nipple and bit down, flicking my tongue back and forth until it stood erect. As I inched lower, alternatively nipping and kissing his hot flesh, he forced out, "No, love, you've bewitched me."

I grinned and lowered the zipper on his jeans. "You haven't seen anything yet." After stripping him of the rest of his clothing, I ran my hands firmly down the length of his solid thighs. With my eyes locked on his, I bent my head and paused a moment, watching him watch me as I wrapped my lips around him.

Tiny fireworks exploded with every stroke of my tongue. Somewhere in the back of my mind, I heard Kane's strangled moans. I took him deeper, running my lips against his hard length, feeding off the power we were generating, waiting for him to lose control.

His breathing became ragged. I waited for his intense passion to overtake me, like it always did when he couldn't wait even one more second. I was more than ready, slick with need, pulsing with it. But his emotions didn't come. Instead, he yanked me by the shoulders and flipped me on my back. I heard the faint rustle of a condom wrapper just before he buried himself deep inside me.

My insides exploded. The power that had been coursing through my veins concentrated at our joining with each thrust. It built, drawing from our raw hunger, intensified, and sent currents of delicious pleasure through my core.

My mind blurred in the wave of pure sensation until the power crested, sending shock after shock through my limbs. I held on, clinging to him as he quickened his pace, pounding deeper and harder, filling me with all of him, possessing every last inch of me.

Finally, with a guttural cry, he spasmed. All the power we'd built up exploded, leaving me empty and limp in his arms.

We lay unmoving for a long time, until Kane shifted to his side. He gathered me close, ran a hand over the curve of my breast, and whispered, "I think you spelled me, little witch."

Snuggling deeper into the pillow, I closed my eyes.

"Sleep well. See you in your dreams," he whispered.

I kissed his hand and, in my love-spent haze, sighed as his arms tightened around me.

Moments later, sleep pulled me under. Kane appeared almost instantly, radiating with warmth and a honey-toned glow. Overwhelmed, I wrapped him tight in my arms and poured every ounce of emotion from my pounding heart into a long, slow kiss. The honey glow meant one thing.

Love. Deep, soul-filling love.

The kind most people had to spend a lifetime together to achieve. But there he was, just three months after I'd met him, ready to share his soul with me. And I knew I'd share mine, even if my aura hadn't achieved the undeniable color of a person head over heels.

I loved him. More than I'd ever thought possible. My aura would turn one day when it was ready. Though, it would always be tinged with purple, a trait all intuitives shared. Perfect. Gold and purple. I'd be the ultimate LSU fan…if everyone could read auras.

When we parted, he gave me a lazy smile and tucked me close to him. He gently traced his fingers down my arms and over my back. I closed my eyes, concentrated on his soft touch. I'd just about slipped from the dream back into oblivion when a piercing jealousy shot needle-point jabs of pain in all the places Kane's body touched mine.

Still dreaming, I jerked back with a yelp, staring at him wide-eyed. He sat straight up in the bed, reaching for me.

I scooted away, rubbing my stinging shoulder.

"Jade—" Kane's voice went silent as he started to fade away. His lips were still moving, his face pinched with worry lines.

I reached out a hand, but he vanished right there.

A faint trace of triumphant satisfaction entered my awareness. The signature was familiar, but I couldn't quite place it. I scanned the room, wondering if a person had to physically be present in my dream for me to lock into their emotions. I supposed not. But as I flopped back on the pillow, a familiar sheet of pale blond hair caught my eye.

Lailah! Again. She stood in the corner of my apartment, her translucent form rapidly fading into the ether. She raised one hand and wiggled her fingers in a cutesy wave just before she disappeared.

I woke with a start, throwing my arm across the bed. My hand hit something hard and Kane groaned. He didn't move.

"Kane?" I shook his shoulder.

Nothing.

"Wake up. I need to talk to you." The volume of my voice echoed off the walls, making me cringe.

Still, he slept. I got up, padded to the kitchen, and filled a tall glass of water. I wasn't waiting for morning to have this conversation. When I reached the side of the bed, I shook his shoulder in one last attempt to wake him.

Nothing.

Frowning, I lifted the glass and poured the entire contents on his head.

Kane shot straight up, sputtering. "Jade, damn it, what the hell?"

I crossed my arms over my bare chest and glared. "That's what I'd like to know."

He grabbed his shirt from beside the bed and ran it over his face. A moment later he rose, staring at the soaked bed. Anger and confusion flashed in his eyes when he turned back to me.

"Don't give me that look. That's the second time in two days you've left me in a dreamwalk to be with Lailah." I grabbed my terry cloth robe from my closet and wrapped it tightly around myself. With my arms over my chest, I dug my fingernails into my forearms, trying to focus on anything other than the tears threatening to burn my eyes.

Kane didn't bother to cover himself. He just walked over and placed his hands on my shoulders. "I seriously have no idea what you're talking about."

I shook him off, feeling used. "Just now, you were dream-walking me. Then Lailah showed up. First you vanished and she followed. Don't try to deny it. I saw her."

Kane's expression turned concerned. "Just now? The last thing I remember is…" he paused and rubbed his forehead. "Huh. We were lying together, and suddenly you seemed like you were in pain. But when I tried to reach for you, I was locked out of your dream."

I sat on my couch. "What does that mean, locked out of my dream? You left. With Lailah."

He took the seat next to me and grabbed my hands. "I assure you, I was not dreamwalking with her. I was with you one moment, the next you were gone. That usually happens if you wake up or fall into a deeper sleep."

I wasn't convinced. "Last night you said her name."

"What?" He stiffened. "I did not. Nor have I dreamwalked Lailah in the past year. The only time, and I repeat, the *only* time I ever did was when I dated her, long before I met you. If she showed up two nights in a row, the only explanation is she's forcing her way in."

I stood, staring down at him through narrowed eyes. "That explains why you said her name?"

He stood. "It could. If she forced her way in, that means she was in control. But I don't know because I don't remember." His expression turned tender. "Jade, I promise you, I have no interest in that woman. None. You have to know that."

I did know it. Hadn't I just witnessed his love-filled aura not even twenty minutes ago? That wasn't something he could fake. Not to mention he'd never given me any reason to doubt him before. I unclenched my jaw. "I do. But Bea took away her powers. Without them, how did she force her way in?"

He shrugged. "I don't have powers and I dreamwalk. Maybe she has the ability naturally."

The tension in my body eased and I relaxed against him. That was possible. I had empath abilities that had nothing to do with being a witch. At least, I didn't think they did. My gaze flicked to the bed. "Sorry about the water. In my defense, I did try to wake you up the conventional way first."

He chuckled. "I admit it isn't my favorite way to wake up, especially after mind-blowing sex."

Heat burned my face.

He leaned in and brushed his lips across mine. "Don't ever doubt my feelings for you, Jade." He moved closer and untied my robe. His hands came around me, running down my bare back. "I don't know what's going on with Lailah, but trust me when I say, I'll find out. There's only room in my dreams for one woman." Kane lowered his lips to mine, his expert tongue showing me exactly which woman he preferred. "Now," he said in a husky voice. "Let's continue this in the shower."

The next morning, Kane left for work and all I wanted to do was head back to Bea's house. We'd settled on meeting there in the early afternoon to go over the spell we'd perform on the full moon. I glanced at the clock. Five more hours to wait.

I stifled a sigh, contemplating heading to Lailah's to retrieve the portraits she'd run off with. But the thought of seeing her made my blood boil. Besides, if I touched the portraits, I'd likely get sucked back into one of their visions.

Instead, I called Kat again and made plans to meet up at my glass studio. There was no way I could wait around inside my apartment all day. I'd go insane. Besides, I needed to tell her Dan had broken into the club. He was my ex, but after we'd broken up, Kat had dated him too, and we'd all been friends once. She deserved to know.

The walk to the studio was pleasant with the gentle October breeze. Good. The glass studio wouldn't be quite as stifling as usual. I waved to the shop manager and headed back to my workbench. I wasn't teaching today, so that meant I could work on inventory for my online bead store. With everything going on, I hadn't made anything new in over a week.

My hands shook slightly as I lit my torch, and I frowned. I hadn't had any caffeine and I'd eaten breakfast, so it wasn't low blood sugar. Maybe it was the lack of sleep. Guess I wasn't making anything too detailed today.

The anxiety I was carrying started to ease the moment I introduced the first rod of glass into the flame. Nothing calmed me like bead making did. It was the only time I could block out everything and fully concentrate on something else.

I'd just begun winding glass on a metal mandrel, intending to make a long organic tube bead, when the torch flame flared into something resembling a flamethrower.

"Whoa!" Instinctively, I flung myself back in the rolling chair. Keeping a good distance, I carefully reached in to cut the propane, but before I could turn the torch knob, the flame resumed its normal, tight pinpoint.

"Dave!" I cried. "Something's going on with the pressure gauges. My torch just freaked out."

The good-natured shop manager appeared in the doorframe. "Looks okay to me."

"Really?" I gestured to the charred wallboard in front of me. "Does that look normal?"

"It wouldn't be the first time someone let a torch get the best of her." His lips quirked up in a teasing smile.

I scowled and turned my torch off. "Can you check the gauges?"

He shrugged, maneuvering his lanky body gracefully through my shop toward the tanks chained to the wall. After a moment, he switched the oxygen tanks then replaced the pressure gauge. "Okay. Everything looked fine, but I switched them just in case. Call me if you have any more problems."

"Thanks." The torch lit without incident, but the bead I'd been building hadn't survived. I hadn't thought to put it in the kiln to keep it warm, and it had already cracked in multiple places. I was three-quarters of the way through building my second bead when Lailah crept into my mind. What in the world was going on with her? Snatching the portraits, accidentally poisoning Bea, and showing up in Kane's dreams all made me question if she was who she claimed to be: an angel. Don't angels help people? Sure, she'd messed up the spell that had ended with Pyper trapped in another reality, but her heart had been in the right place. At least, I'd thought so.

The misery she'd radiated when Bea had been on death's door had been real. And she'd taken Bea's binding of her powers without complaint. But what I'd felt from her right before she followed Kane in the dreamwalk—

The torch flared larger and more powerful than before. "Holy crap on toast!" I cried and turned it off, this time remembering to throw my bead in the kiln.

"Problem?" a familiar female voice said from my doorway.

"The tank gauges are out of control, and I just about burned the building down."

"I can see that." Kat moved to stand next to my torch station. "Looks like someone needs new wallboard."

The board had done its job, protecting the building, but she was right. It needed to be replaced before my next class. "I'll be right back." I stalked out, vented to Dave, asked him to recheck the system, and strode back toward my studio, vibrating with frustration. Was it a studio issue or was it me? I'd been strumming with power the day before. Could that be the cause? I stopped outside my door and took a moment to search for my inner spark. Nothing. I tried again, and was rewarded with only a slight gnawing in my stomach. Sighing, I went inside, turned off my kiln, and waved Kat toward the door. "Let's go."

"Where to?"

"Lunch."

Five minutes later, we occupied an umbrella-shaded table at Pat O'Brien's. The courtyard dining area was virtually empty.

"Where is everyone?" I asked. Usually the place was filled with hurricane-seeking tourists.

"It's still early. They just opened."

The time didn't stop me from ordering a Guinness.

"Oh good, we're drinking. I'll have a Bloody Mary, go heavy on the Tabasco," Kat told the waiter.

I raised an eyebrow.

"I've been on a spicy kick lately." She went on to order fried gator and shrimp creole.

"I guess so." I passed my menu to the waiter. "I'll have the same." Thinking about what to eat seemed like too much work at the moment.

After our drinks arrived and I downed half my beer, Kat placed her hand over mine. "Are you ready to talk about it?"

That's the beauty of a best friend. She always knows when something's up. I spilled everything about the portraits, being sucked back to Idaho, Bea being sick, Lailah's role in the dreamwalking, and then paused. "Have you seen Dan lately?"

She nodded slowly. "He came by last night after an anger management meeting. Why?"

I was glad they were still friends. Not long after their break-up, Dan had asked Kat for help dealing with his anger issues. She'd been the one to suggest the meetings. We'd all meant a great deal to each other once. But since Dan and I had done our level best to destroy any hope of even a platonic relationship, him coming to me was out of the question. Not to mention, Kane would likely deck him after the way Dan had threatened me that time in the club three months ago. "I'm pretty certain he broke into Wicked." I explained sensing his emotional signature and finding the voodoo dolls.

"Why in the world would he do something like that?"

Shrugging, I stared at the shrimp covered in Creole sauce the waiter had just placed in front of me. I pushed one around with a fork. "It doesn't make sense, but can you feel him out about it? I know it was his emotional signature in the hallway."

She heaved a heavy sigh, sucked down a quarter of her Bloody Mary, and gave me a short nod of acceptance. "I'm not promising anything."

"I wouldn't ask you to."

Two beers and a mild case of heartburn later, I walked with Kat back to her apartment. She had me laughing about a disastrous date she'd been on the previous weekend, when she stopped abruptly and turned to me. "I have to tell you something."

"Okay," I said startled by her seriousness.

"I hope it's okay with you. I mean, it just sort of happened. I didn't plan it."

"What?" Trepidation curled in my chest.

She stopped staring at the brick sidewalk and looked me in the eye. "I have a date with Ian tomorrow night."

"What?" I asked again, stupidly. How could Ian be dating both of my friends?

"I'm not asking permission—it's just that after the Dan debacle, I want to be up-front. I know you guys only had one date and you're with Kane and everything—"

I raised my hand. "Stop. It's fine. I don't care if you date him. Really." I eyed her. "Is Ian the guy you've had your eye on?"

She nodded. "I didn't tell you sooner because I sort of felt weird about it. You know, I don't want to be the friend who takes all your leftovers."

"Kat, please. Ian and I had one date. Nothing happened. I wouldn't exactly call him my leftovers." I raised an inquisitive eyebrow. "Who asked who?"

She smiled. "He did. About two weeks ago. He's taking me to a jazz club he's been wanting to go to."

I nodded, noting how she lit up when she talked about the date. Great. Just what I need: my two best friends dating the same guy. What was Ian up to? Dating them both wasn't cool at all. Should I say something to her about it? No, not yet. Better to talk to Ian first.

Kat chattered on about Ian for a while then laughed. "Sorry. I'm boring you. Tell me what Gwen said when you told her about all this stuff."

Crap! Why hadn't Gwen called me back yet?

"You did tell her, didn't you?" Kat asked.

I shook my head. "Not yet. I left a voicemail."

We walked in silence for the next few blocks. When we turned down her street, I stopped dead in my tracks.

"What?"

"Is that Dan's car?" An older, blue Jeep Cherokee was parked a few spots down from her apartment.

She glanced at it and frowned. "He wasn't supposed to drop by today."

I inched closer to take a peek in the passenger's window. The faded Nirvana sticker on the glove box confirmed it. "It's his. I should go." There was no way I could handle a face-to-face with him.

"But…" Kat trailed off and shrugged.

There wasn't anything to say. She didn't want a confrontation any more than I did. Plus, I was the last thing Dan needed while dealing with his anger management. I gave her a quick hug. "Call me later." I spun, took two steps and froze again. "Kat?"

"Yeah."

"Why does Dan have the portraits in the back of his Jeep?" Right there, poking out from under a blanket, was the edge of Felicia's ornate frame. The other two were there as well.

"No way." Kat nudged me to the side and peered into the vehicle.

"I have to get them." Beyond angry, I frantically tugged at the car's door handles and the hatch in the back.

Locked. Every single one. He had left the driver's side window cracked slightly. If only I had a shim to jimmy the lock. Right. Because I kept one of those in my pocket.

Instead, I slid my hand through the crack, hoping to reach the lock. I got as far as my forearm before I couldn't move it any farther. The tip of my fingers could almost reach, but no matter how hard I tried to jam my arm inside, it wouldn't budge one more inch.

"Damn it!" I yanked my arm out and kicked the wheel. Hard. Hard enough it made my eyes water.

"Hey! How'd you do that?" Kat asked, opening the door.

"What?" I watched as she climbed in and pulled the portraits from the back. "You think I unlocked the car by kicking it?"

"Looks like it. Weird shit just happens around you. I'm used to it now." She had the art pieces wrapped tightly in the blanket and tried to hand them to me.

"No." I shook my head and backed away. "I don't want to touch them after what happened last time." The pain in my foot started to fade, but I had a weird tingling in my gut. Was I going to throw up? I hadn't kicked it that hard. Maybe my frustration had tapped my magic. I'd think about that later.

"What am I supposed to do with them?" Kat climbed out of the car, still trying to hand them off to me.

What, indeed? I couldn't go into a weird trance right there on the street. "Can I borrow your car? I could take them back to Pyper's."

She slammed the car door shut. "That will work. But hurry— Dan could walk up any second."

A minute later, I was in her red Mini Cooper with the portraits strapped into the passenger's seat. "Thanks, Kat. I owe you one."

"Friends don't owe friends." She stepped back. "I'll come by later tonight and pick up the car."

I could have brought it back. Our places were within walking distance, but there was no way I wanted to run into Dan. Especially after he found out they were missing. What the hell was he up to? Did he know they had spirits trapped in them? He had to. Otherwise, why would he take the hideous things?

The heavy traffic in the quarter meant it took twice as long to drive as it would have to walk. I glanced at the portraits and tightened my grip on the wheel, turning my knuckles white.

Unease settled over my already darkening mood. I had an eerie sense the trapped spirits were crying out to me.

Help! Let us out.

Was I imagining it? Were they speaking to me? All I wanted to do was remove the blanket and look into their gruesome faces. A chill ran up my spine and something dark and painful seeped from the passenger seat. The toxic energy started penetrating my senses, making my insides clench and tighten with anxiety. I slammed the accelerator to the floor. The faster I got out of the car and away from the portraits, the better.

A shrill horn sounded. Frantically, I pumped the brakes with both feet. Kat's car came to a screeching stop, missing the taxi in front of me by mere inches. The adrenaline took over, pushing out all foreign energies. Shaking slightly, I eased back into traffic, and a few minutes later pulled into Kane's spot behind Wicked.

I slumped, exhausted by everything, and pulled out my phone. A few texts later, and Pyper was on her way out to help. Leaving the portraits unattended in the car wasn't an option. They'd already been stolen twice.

Sitting there with my head pressed against the steering wheel, my adrenaline started to fade, and something warm and familiar washed over me. An old buried memory of comfort, acceptance, and home touched my soul.

Tears sprung to my eyes as I turned slowly toward the portraits, recognizing the unique energy signature. In a barely audible voice, I whispered, "Mom?"

Chapter 10

I reached out with a tentative hand, but as the signature grew stronger, I lost all sense of caution. Before I could think about what I was doing, I pushed the blanket aside and had Felicia's portrait in both hands.

Her half-burned image slowly faded into a nondescript featureless face then morphed into a beautiful, pale-skinned beauty. Her dark wavy hair was pulled back in her signature low ponytail hairstyle, with a few strands framing her face. The joy radiating from her reached her jade-green eyes, the mirror image of my own.

"Mom?"

She smiled and gave a short nod.

"Oh, God. What happened? How did you get in there? How do we get you out? Did Felicia have anything to do with this?" My questions tumbled out at a frantic pace.

Her energy wrapped around me the way it used to when she wanted to shield me from something.

"No! I can help. I'm a witch!"

A fierce wave of disapproval clouded her energy, and within the frame she shook her head violently. The portrait actually vibrated.

I was so intent on what was going on inside the car I didn't notice Kane's arrival until he had the car door open.

"What are you doing?" He grabbed the portrait from my hands.

All of Mom's energy vanished.

I glared at him. "Give it back." I reached for it, but he shifted it out of my grasp.

"No. I don't know what was going on, but your face was chalk-white and you were yelling at it. Neither sounds like a good idea." He rounded the car and pulled out the other two.

I raced to cut him off before he could stride back into the building. "You don't understand. My mother is trapped in there." I pointed to Felicia's portrait.

"What? Felicia's your mom?"

"No! Just give it back." The dude was standing between me and the mother I'd lost over twelve years ago. Nothing, not even the man I loved, could keep me from investigating now. I lunged.

The impact of my body ramming into his forced the frames from Kane's grip. They tumbled to the ground, but I wasn't fast enough to grab them before Kane caught me around the waist.

"Jade. Stop."

Without thinking, I rammed my elbow into his gut.

His breath came out in a whoosh as he doubled over. Ignoring the sharp stab of guilt in my chest, I reached for Felicia and ran. I'd gotten just inside the building when my world started to fade. A heavy gray mist clouded my vision.

Mom, I tried to scream, but the word rebounded in my head. I took two steps through the blinding fog before I lost all sense of direction and stopped. Foreboding weighed heavily on my conscious. Mom's energy wasn't anywhere within reach. Where had she gone?

I focused all of my concentration on the recent memory of her, and the mist started to fade. A shadowy form materialized, the image growing more defined as it approached.

"Mom?" I eeked out.

A sardonic chuckle sounded from the shadow right before Felicia's face took solid form.

"You!" I said accusingly as I lurched forward. "Where is she, and what do you want?"

"You know what I want, Jade. Help free me from this prison, and I'll lead you to her."

I narrowed my eyes. "But she was just here. Bring her to me first."

Felicia pressed her lips together as her face soured. "No. I cannot risk such a thing. Help me. Then I will help you."

Her ominous tone made the hair on the back of my neck rise. I hesitated, not sure what I should say. Then I decided if we had her cooperation, maybe it would make the spell go smoother. "Tomorrow night during the full moon. Be ready."

A satisfied smile crept over her beautiful features. "I'll be waiting."

The mist reappeared, blinding me, and what seemed like a second later I woke, lying on my bed with Kane hovering over me.

"Jade?" He peered down at me with worried eyes. Something about him didn't seem right, but at that moment, I couldn't put my finger on it.

"How'd I get here?" I pushed myself up on the pillows.

He sat on the edge of the bed. "Are you all right?"

"Fine. What happened?"

He raised his eyebrows at my short tone and straightened, his posture stiff. In a careful, measured voice, he said, "After I recovered from your blow to my gut, I found you passed out, clutching that cursed piece of art. I assumed you'd wake up when I took it from you, but you didn't, so I carried you here. You woke shortly after that." Kane stood and strode to the refrigerator. A moment later, he handed me a bottle of water. His face was blank of all emotion. "Want to tell me what that was all about?"

I rolled it in my hands while I tried to work out what to say. Resentment crept through me as I remembered he'd been the one to interrupt the meeting with my mother. I tried to fight the feeling, knowing he had taken care of me after I'd collapsed in the hall. Though, I wouldn't have been there in the first place if he hadn't interfered. My eyes met his and I had to work hard to keep the glare off my face.

Apparently, I needed lessons on masking my facial features because his face darkened, and a moment later he moved to the door. "I'll be in my office when you're done blaming me for whatever it is you don't want to talk about."

The door snapped shut before I could reply.

"Damn." What was wrong with me? Kane had only been trying to protect me, like he always did. He wasn't even out of line. In his shoes, I would have taken the portrait away from me too. What exactly had he done with Felicia? I glanced around the room. It didn't take long to realize the portrait hadn't made the trip with us. "Double damn."

I picked up the phone, intending to call Aunt Gwen, but before I could hit send, a loud knock sounded on my door, followed by Pyper letting herself in. "Hey. I hear you maybe could use some company."

"Kane sent you?"

She gave a short laugh and shook her head. "No. In fact, he told me to stay the hell out of it. But since I rarely listen to him, and he was vibrating with a case of frustrated male moodiness, I figured you could use an ear for venting."

The refrigerator door squeaked as I reached in for a Diet Coke, wishing it was a chai latte. I held my soda out for Pyper, but she shook her head.

"Don't you have any alcohol in there?" She slid across my wood floors and gently pushed me out of the way. After a quick peek, she pulled out a bottle of Pinot Grigio. "That's more like it."

With my soda can, I curled up at the end of my second-hand couch. When Pyper joined me with a wine glass in hand, I turned to her. "He's angry. That's why he's so moody."

"Kane?" Her eyebrows shot up in surprise. "Really? He didn't seem mad. More like worried and frustrated. You know that look he gets when he can't control everything." She took a long sip of wine. "But I guess you'd know better than anyone."

"Yeah." But her words nagged at me. Had I felt his anger or anything from him? Now that I thought about it, no, I hadn't. I'd been the one consumed with anger, but none of his physical energy had entered my awareness. I'd read his feelings from his facial expression and tone of voice.

A cold emptiness ran through me like I'd lost something special. Ever since Kane and I had gotten together, his emotions had been as real to me as my own. I hadn't even needed to try to read him; they were just always there. Had something happened to me while I'd been trapped in Felicia's energy?

I turned my attention to Pyper, letting her emotional energy wash over me. Her concern warmed my skin. A smile tugged at my lips. After closing myself off from personal relationships for so long, it still took me by surprise to realize I had a network of friends always ready when I needed them. Pyper was one of the best. Kane was even better. My smile vanished. Why hadn't I felt his emotions? Had I been too self-absorbed after what had happened? It was possible, but in the last three months, I couldn't remember a time when I hadn't been intimately connected with him.

I took a deep breath, trying to control the heavy dose of guilt raking my insides. He hadn't deserved my overreaction. "Okay, maybe he isn't angry, per se. But I was. Did he tell you what happened?"

She set her glass down and shook her head. "He just stashed those decrepit, papier-mâché pictures in his office closet and locked it. Then he muttered something about you always getting yourself into trouble."

"Me?" I cried. "What about you? You're the one who ended up with an evil spirit stalking you."

She grimaced. "Don't remind me."

"Sorry. I'm a little stressed out."

Waving a dismissive hand, she turned toward me and lowered her voice. "Ian's been doing some readings with me in my apartment."

All my current problems vanished from my mind. "Why? Did something happen?"

She held up her hands and waved them. "No, no. Nothing like that. He's just being cautious. Or so he says. He says people who have been haunted before are likely to be haunted again. Something about being marked by the other side. I think he's paranoid. Roy targeted me because of our history. Not because I'm some beacon for the dead."

I leaned back against the cushion. "Has he gotten anything from his readings?"

"Nope. I *told* him he wouldn't find anything. But it's okay. I could think of worse ways to spend a few afternoons."

"You like him. A lot." I grinned then sobered, remembering my conversation with Kat. Someone was going to get hurt. I needed to speak to Ian. He had to tell them.

She shrugged and hid a smile. "Maybe. But that's not why I brought it up." She pressed her lips together and sent me a sideways glance. "I think you should let Ian do some baseline measurements on you. I'm not the only one who attracted a spirit."

She was referring to Bobby, the ghost who'd followed me home the first day I'd met Bea. He'd eventually moved on, but his dog had stayed. Eyeing the ghost dog at my feet, I shook my head. "I don't think that's necessary. Duke would alert me if something sinister was going on." When Pyper had been followed by a black shadow, he had barked incessantly every time she was around.

Pyper's eyes followed my gaze. I knew she couldn't see Duke. No one else but Bea could. That meant she was likely studying the nail polish flaking off my toes. I had a sudden desire to tuck my feet under the throw pillow. Before I could muster an excuse for neglecting a pedicure, she spoke. "You have a point, but Bobby had been wreaking havoc in your life and Duke never uttered as much as a whimper about him."

"That's because Duke was Bobby's dog." I stood and crossed the room to my full-length windows. "Look, I don't care if Ian does some readings, but Kane isn't going to be on board. You know how he feels about all this. And about Ian. I've already hurt him enough today."

Kane wouldn't be happy when he found out Pyper was working with Ian, but if I ended up getting involved, it would be a disaster. Even though I had totally and completely chosen Kane, I knew it still bothered him I spent so much time with Ian while working with Bea. Also, he hated when I got involved with anything paranormal. I suspected it was because he had no way to protect me if things went wrong. Hell, who could blame him? I felt the same way.

Except when it came to finding out where my mother was. I already knew one way or another I'd do whatever it took to free Felicia. If it meant embracing my inner witch, I'd do it. Ian conducting a reading wouldn't help. All that accomplished was a bunch of not-so-scientific numbers that meant almost nothing to me. What I needed to do was talk to Bea. She was the one who could help me develop my witch powers.

I grimaced. My witch powers. It was literally the last thing I wanted to explore.

Pyper's face darkened. "He's just going to have to get over himself then, isn't he?"

The massive irritation surrounding her startled me, and I softened my voice. "Really, it's fine. I'm not interested in readings. And if I'm being totally honest, I wouldn't want Kane hanging out with someone he'd dated in the past, either."

"Not that. The part about how he feels about Ian. Ian has been nothing but helpful to all of us. So what if the two of you went on a date? It obviously didn't take. Kane needs to stuff his inner caveman right up his—"

"That sounds uncomfortable," Kane interjected from the doorway.

I jumped, caught totally off guard. When had he gotten there? And where the hell was his emotional signature?

He strode across the room toward us. "And for the record, I don't have a problem with Ian."

Pyper stood. "No. You just have a problem when he and Jade are in the same room together."

He leveled his gaze at her. "No. I have a problem when he's dragging either of you into paranormal activity." Pyper opened her mouth to speak again, but Kane put his hand up and gently laid it on her shoulder. "It's not Ian who's the problem. It's your willingness to throw yourselves into any situation, regardless of the consequences."

His statement silenced her.

He had a point. I was known for doing whatever it took to help my friends and loved ones, no matter the risk to myself. She had shown the same traits. I suspected it was part of the reason he loved us both. It was also why he was so protective.

"So you're going to be nice to Ian the next time I bring him on a date?" Pyper said with a warning in her tone.

He gave a noncommittal shrug.

"Kaaaaaaane," she dragged out.

I sat frozen through the whole exchange. Pyper's irritation and frustration was coming through loud and clear, but I couldn't get a read on Kane at all. The only other time that had ever happened was the first time I'd witnessed him with Lailah. And she was nowhere to be found at the moment.

Kane ignored Pyper and turned to me. "Jade, there's someone downstairs I think you'd like to see."

"Who?" I made no move to get up from the couch. Anyone on my short list of friends would have already come up to my apartment.

He reached his hand out to me. I clasped it, desperate to make a connection. My fingers grasped tightly around his, and when nothing flowed from him, I sent an emotional probe. Nothing. There wasn't a signature. No emotions vibrating under the surface. It was as if I'd never had an empathy gift at all.

Was he shielding his emotions from me? Had I hurt him that much? I wanted to ask him about it, but I didn't want to do it in front of Pyper. This was private.

He tugged me to my feet. "You'll see. Hurry, she's been waiting."

I sent Pyper a look as Kane tugged me out the door. She shook her head and followed.

Chapter 11

When Kane and I got to the bottom of the stairs, I stopped him and waved Pyper on. As she disappeared into the back door of the coffee shop, I wrapped my arms around him and planted a heartfelt kiss on the lips I'd come to know so well.

"I'm sorry," I said. "I didn't mean to snap at you."

He studied me with serious eyes for a long moment. My soul ached to know what was going on inside of him. It wasn't until the lines around his eyes crinkled that I knew he'd forgiven me. "I know. And I shouldn't have stalked off. You have someone waiting. We'll talk later, okay?"

I nodded and let him lead me into the back door of The Grind. My curiosity was only mildly piqued as I wondered who the heck I'd had to come down to the café to meet. "Who is it?" I asked again.

Kane held the swinging door from the back room open and gestured for me to go ahead of him. "See for yourself."

My body blocked the doorway while I scanned the café. I didn't see anyone at first and frowned. But as I turned to question Kane, I caught a glimpse of her curly gray hair and gasped. "Gwen!" I cried and ran to my aunt, sweeping her up in a giant hug. "What are you doing here?"

Her strong, steady love washed over me, filling the void Kane's energy had left. Happy tears sprang to my eyes and she laughed. "My sweet Jade. When did you get so sentimental?"

The old joke made me chuckle. I'd lived with her a full year before I'd allowed her to see me cry. The first time was my sixteenth birthday, and I'd been missing my mother something terrible. Instead of letting her throw me a sweet sixteen party, I'd requested a sleepover with Kat. My only friend really, besides Dan. And no matter how cool Aunt Gwen was, no boy could be invited for a sleepover.

So Kat and I planned an in-home makeover, followed by a bake-off of chocolate cream cheese cupcakes, double chocolate brownies, and chocolate peanut butter cookies, all designed to keep us awake for our all-night movie fest. It wasn't a glamorous sweet sixteen, but it was all I wanted.

But then, Kat caught a case of the chicken pox and had to cancel. There I was, on my sixteenth birthday, with my mother vanished and my best friend sick. When Gwen had suggested she take Kat's place, I'd burst into tears.

She'd grabbed my hand, leveled her gaze at me, and said, "My sweet Jade. When did you get so sentimental?" The curious matter-of-fact tone had startled me into a laugh. I hadn't realized she'd never seen me cry before. In the year I'd lived with her, I'd dealt with the loss of my mother and the horrific foster home experience by blocking it out, not letting myself feel anything.

My laughter had turned to sobs. Gwen had held me while my body shook, purging itself of the bottled-up sorrow. Afterwards, she'd dragged me into the kitchen and, despite my protests, helped me bake every last cupcake, brownie, and cookie. We'd spent the night gorging on sweets and watching *Sixteen Candles* and *Say Anything*. It was still one of my favorite memories. To this day, anytime she sees me cry, she utters the same words.

I looked around. "Where's your luggage? And why didn't you just come up to my apartment?"

"Always so many questions." She picked up a large paper coffee cup and handed it to me. "I got you a chai latte for the road. Something told me you'd need it."

Something. Yeah, that something was her psychic tendencies. Just how much did she know about what had happened? "Gwen," I called after her as she headed toward the door. "I need to talk to you about something. It's important."

"I already know. We'll talk about it later. Right now, you need to grab that young man of yours and hurry up. We have someplace to be." She strode out the door before I could protest.

"You heard the lady," Kane said with a smile, guiding me to the door. "We have someplace to be."

"Do you know where?"

"No idea. But it doesn't seem wise to argue with your aunt Gwen, does it?"

The knot lodged in my chest from earlier started to ease. Everything would be fine now. Gwen would know what to do. She always did.

The shock of Gwen's unexpected visit was nothing compared to when we parked in Bea's driveway, and Gwen ordered Kane to unload her luggage.

"You're staying here? How? Why? Never mind," I sputtered. "Forget it. You're staying with me."

"In your tiny place? Where would I sleep?" she scoffed.

"In my bed. I'll sleep on the couch."

"That's where Duke sleeps," she said flippantly. "At least, that's what you told me, and I don't want to be responsible for displacing an old golden retriever. Besides, you two young people need your privacy."

"Gwen!" I said in a hushed whisper.

"Ms. Calhoun, you are welcome to stay at my house. It's much closer to Jade's and I have a spare guest room. I imagine if you stay there, we can convince Jade to stay over as well." The glint in Kane's eyes made my face grow hot and my ears burn.

"That's a kind offer, Mr. Rouquette. Thank you. But like I said, you two young people need your privacy. Now, could you help me get this suitcase inside?"

"But you don't even know Bea!" I cried.

Gwen stopped at the base of Bea's porch and gazed at me thoughtfully. "Why would you think that?"

"What do you mean? *Do* you know her?" I asked, unable to hide the accusation in my tone.

"As a matter of fact, I do."

Just then, the door swung open and the woman in question glided out onto the porch with a wide, welcoming smile. "Gwen!"

My aunt made her way up the short stairs onto Bea's porch and held her arms open for a hug. The pair embraced as if they were friends reunited after many years. When Gwen pulled away, she had tears shining in her eyes. "Thank you for looking after my girl."

Bea held onto Gwen's hands, shaking them slightly as she spoke. "It's truly my pleasure, my friend. Besides, she's probably done more for me than I have for her."

I stood frozen at the first step of the porch, staring at them. What the heck was going on?

"I'm so glad you took me up on my offer to stay here," Bea told Gwen.

"It'll be like old times."

"Old times?" I snapped out of my trance and took the stairs two at a time. "What the hell is going on here?"

"Jade," Gwen chided.

Bea looked at me quizzically then turned to Gwen. "You didn't tell her?"

"Not yet. I wanted to keep my visit a surprise." Gwen gestured to me. "Come on. Let's go inside."

I opened my mouth to speak, but then closed it. I didn't even know what to say. These two knew each other and had kept it from me? The blatant betrayal made my heart ache. I turned, searching for Kane, and jumped when my shoulder brushed against him. "Sorry. I didn't realize you were right behind me."

He wrapped his arm around my middle and pulled me close. "Really? That's a first. You always seem to know where I am."

It was true. But since he'd been shielding his emotions, he'd been invisible to me. I sighed heavily. Maybe he didn't even know he was doing it.

We followed Bea and Gwen into Bea's sunny yellow living room. Bea ordered us to sit while she busied herself in the kitchen pouring drinks.

Kane led me to an overstuffed loveseat and tugged me down next to him. I leaned into him, grateful for the support.

Gwen mumbled something about helping Bea and followed her into the kitchen.

My eyes stayed glued to her as she awkwardly waited for direction. It soon became clear that if they really did know each other, Gwen had never been to Bea's house. Or if she had, she'd never helped out in the kitchen. Bea told her where to find the lemonade pitcher no less than four times before Gwen uncovered it from the correct cabinet. She also had trouble finding the pantry and ended up battling a mop in the utility closet.

I stifled a giggle. "Aunt Gwen must be feeling really guilty right now. She never offers to help in the kitchen."

"I can see why," Kane said, wincing when Gwen knocked over the full container of lemonade.

It wasn't long before Bea banished her and Gwen returned to the couch, her cheeks the color of her red T-shirt.

"I guess Bea doesn't know you that well," I teased, letting go of some of the betrayal that had been clutching my heart.

Gwen raised her hands in defeat and sat back, waiting for our host.

Just as Bea was heading into the living room, the stairs creaked with light footsteps. Kane and I turned our heads in unison. I tensed.

The so-called low-level angel glided up to the loveseat, waved cheerily at me, and sat next to Kane on the arm rest. When she rested her hand on his shoulder, I snapped.

"Why is she here?" I demanded, turning to Bea. "Didn't she just poison you yesterday?"

"That was an accident!" Lailah cried, burying her face in her hands.

At least she wasn't touching Kane anymore.

Bea leveled a benign gaze in my direction. "She's here at my invitation, dear. Thank you for your loyalty and concern, but Lailah and I are working through what happened. When we've figured it out, I'll be sure to fill you in."

Poisoned? Gwen mouthed in my direction.

I acknowledged her with a tiny nod of my head then leaned back with my arms crossed over my chest.

Kane rested his hand on my thigh. The weight was heavy and foreign, almost as if I were being touched by a stranger. Everything about the scenario grated on me. I jumped up and started pacing. "Can someone tell me what the h—I mean, what's going on?"

"Where would you like us to start?" Gwen asked.

I'd like to know why Lailah was dreamwalking Kane. But I couldn't ask that here in front of Bea or my aunt. God, I was starting to sound like a crazy, jealous girlfriend. Maybe it was because I was so used to reading his emotions. Being cut off wasn't all I'd thought it would be.

Instead, I focused on Gwen. "Start with how you know each other."

Gwen nodded. "Well, you know how you set up that Face-book page for me?"

"Uh-huh." I'd set it up right before I'd moved to New Orleans from Idaho four months ago. I'd thought it would help us keep in touch. But as far as I knew, Gwen hadn't been on the site since the day I'd first logged her on. She never posted anything, not even when I left her messages on her wall. Finally I'd given up, figuring she was a lost cause.

She chuckled. "I found my password about a month ago and decided to check it out. Right when I logged on, there was a friend request from Bea. And the rest is history."

"Wait. You two met on Facebook?"

"Sort of." Bea leaned forward, poured a glass of lemonade, and handed it to me.

I was too polite to refuse it, even though it was the last thing I wanted at the moment. Not unless she'd spiked it with a little vodka.

"Drink," she urged.

The air warmed slightly and a faint trace of ocean tickled my nose. My arm seemed to move on its own, bringing the glass to my lips. After a few sips, all the tension eased from my shoulders, and I sank back down next to Kane.

"Better?" she asked.

"Much." I once again leaned into Kane, forgetting all about Lailah.

"You spelled her," Gwen blurted.

"Just a tiny one to help her relax a bit." She winked in my direction.

Gwen pressed her lips together and shook her head. "She might be fine now, but when it wears off, she's gonna be as angry as a cat on fire. And you said you knew her." She snorted. "Jade hates magic."

"I realize that," Bea said. "But she has to get used to using it. Look at how susceptible she is to it. I barely put anything behind the spell and she's acting as if she's drunk."

I grinned. It was better than being drunk. My senses were sharp enough, and I had no trouble following what they were saying about me. I didn't care. Everything was right with the world.

"Oh, Lord." Gwen rolled her eyes.

"Oh, Gwen. Stop worrying." I waved a hand in her direction. "I'm still waiting to hear all about your Facebook connection."

It turned out, Bea had found Gwen on my Facebook friends list and, on impulse, friended her. Once the two connected, they'd each pumped the other for information about me. If I hadn't been spelled, I'd have probably been more than a little irritated about that, but understood it at least from Gwen's perspective. I was over two thousand miles away and finding plenty of ways to get myself into sticky situations.

Bea wanted more information about my abilities and, given the fact she was the coven leader, I could understand why. Even if it did irritate me.

From there they'd become friends and eventually realized they'd spent a summer together at Summer Solstice, a camp for young witches.

"You went to a witch's camp?" I asked Gwen, confused. "But you aren't a witch."

"Your mother was." Gwen poured herself a glass of lemonade and turned to Bea. "Is this spelled?"

"No. I only altered Jade's."

"Too bad." Gwen laughed and took a sip. "Hope didn't want to go by herself, so I went with her."

The thought of my mother ever needing someone by her side to do anything was totally foreign to me. My entire life, she'd always done everything on her own terms. She'd run her own natural healing shop, bought our house, raised me, and did it all without the help of my father, who'd taken off before I was born. For fifteen years, it had been her and me against the world.

You can do anything you set your mind to, Jade. Don't let anyone convince you otherwise. She'd say that anytime I ever got discouraged about a grade, a project, or any of the small incantations she'd try to teach me.

This time I'd made up my mind I'd bring her home. And I would, with Bea's help.

Bea's face lit with a warm smile. "Turns out, the three of us were cabin mates over forty years ago." Her expression turned gentle. "Your mother was very talented."

"She was, and look at what happened to her." This was my cue to explain all the reasons why exploring my witchy tendencies was a terrible idea. But the possibility of finding her and all the week's events held me back. I got up and moved to

Gwen's side. Gripping her hand, I stared into her eyes. "We have to help her."

"Hope?" Gwen's forehead creased as she frowned. "You know I would do anything for your mother, but after all these years, I don't even know where to start."

"But I thought…" Hadn't she said she'd already known what I had to tell her? "You didn't have a vision of what happened today?"

"Today? No, I thought you were talking about what you did for Bea." Gwen's energy wrapped around me in the way it did when she wanted to protect me. When she spoke again, her voice came out hushed and urgent. "What happened?"

I glanced once at Kane for support then blurted, "I've found her."

Chapter 12

It took a while to explain the portraits and the voodoo dolls. When I got to the part about finding them in Dan's car, I turned to Lailah. "How did he end up with them, anyway? You had them last."

She paled. "I've been working with him."

"Yeah, angel stuff. We know. What does that have to do with the portraits?"

"Nothing. Except…"

Bea, who had remained silent through my explanations, finally spoke, her southern drawl thick with authority. "Except what, Lailah? Under coven law, you are obligated to share your knowledge."

The angel sent Bea a small, grateful smile, and she visibly relaxed. "Thank you. The secrecy bond wouldn't let me say anything."

"Secrecy bond?" I asked.

"It's an angel thing."

"When isn't it?" I muttered.

Lailah sent me a look that could freeze oil. She turned to Bea. "I've been tasked with overseeing Dan Toller's soul."

I froze. Did I hear her right? "Dan's soul?"

She nodded. "I got my orders not long after we brought you back from your coma."

"But his soul? What does that mean?"

Bea cocked her head. "Aren't you aware of what angels do?"

"Make miracles happen? Grant wishes? Spread the word of God?"

Lailah gave me a look of disgust. "I'm not a fairy godmother or a proselytizer."

"I didn't mean it like that." Dang, I didn't know angels were so sensitive. "I mean, do God's work. You know, do good, spread love, that kind of thing."

Bea laughed, breaking the tension. "Yes, angels do that, but their main job is to protect souls. When one is in danger, an angel is assigned to them."

"Really?" Gwen chimed in for the first time. "What happens if you can't save them?"

Lailah's face darkened. "We lose them."

"To Hell?" Suddenly I shivered. It was Dan's soul that was in danger. It shouldn't have been a surprise, considering how terrible he'd been acting lately, but something deep inside me ached.

She nodded. "Something like that."

I didn't want to know what that meant. "And that's why you've been his anger management mentor?"

"Anger is the first sign of corruption. If we can control that, he'll have a chance."

I fell silent, wrapped up in the new information. What had happened after the exorcism that had triggered a soul assignment for Dan? He hadn't been a part of it, so that couldn't have anything to do with his current situation. Could it?

I was about to ask when Lailah pushed a long blond lock of hair out of her eyes and spoke again. "What worries me is we were making progress. Dan took responsibility for the way he'd been treating Jade and even apologized."

"He did?" Kane whispered in my ear.

I held up my hand in a wait motion.

"But then he stole the portraits," Lailah continued. "How did he even know about them? Or where I live? We only meet at the counselor's office once a week."

Everyone turned in my direction.

"How would I know? Before you brought him into the café, I hadn't spoken to him since the night Kane threw him out of the club."

"Did you mention anything to Kat?" Lailah asked.

"No, not until I spotted the portraits in Dan's car."

Bea stood and strode to the center of the room. "Lailah, stick as close to possible to Dan. I know his soul is your highest priority, but we need to find out what his interest is in these portraits." She turned to me. "Where are they now?"

"I have them." Kane spoke for the first time. "I locked them up for safekeeping."

"Good," Bea said. "Keep them away from Jade until we can explore them in the safety of the coven's sanctuary."

"I want to see this portrait of Felicia," Gwen said. "Today." She got up and started moving toward the door, her gray curls bouncing at her shoulders. "Coming, Jade?"

Before anyone could stop me, I jumped up off the couch and met my aunt at the door.

"Gwen," Bea said. "I know you're anxious about your sister, but can you wait one more day? Tomorrow night we'll have the protection of the coven."

"I'm sorry, Bea. But no. I've been waiting for twelve years for a clue to materialize. I will not wait one more minute. Besides, my powers are subtle. I don't need to touch the portraits. Being near them will tell me what I need to know." Gwen linked her sun-tanned arm through mine. "Jade will bring me back when we're done and we can plan from there."

A thin thread of Bea's frustration entered my awareness. It stopped me in my tracks. Had she sent it to me or had it escaped her usually tightly controlled energy? By the pinched look on her face, I decided it had escaped. She wasn't used to anyone telling her no and it showed. At least she still had Lailah to boss around.

By the time we made it out to Kane's new Lexus, he had caught up with us. "You sure you want to do this?" he asked.

"Yes," we said in unison.

Gwen gripped my hand and squeezed it before opening the car door for me.

I paced in my living room, unable to relax. Despite my protests and many arguments, Gwen kept refusing to let me go with her to Pyper's apartment.

"I'm sorry, honey, but I don't want your energy tainting anything I might find," she'd said.

Gwen's a psychic intuitive. She picks up things: impressions, events that have happened or are going to happen. The closer she is emotionally to someone, the better the connection. It's why she almost always knows what's going on in my life before I tell her. She doesn't always know specifics, but she knows when I feel strongly about something. Her gift is different than mine in that she doesn't pick up on random people's emotional energy—she just knows things. It was worth having her inspect the portraits even though I was uneasy about her being alone with them.

"Fine. But be careful. If anything happens…"

Gwen pulled me into a hug. "Don't you worry, little one. Nobody's going to get the jump on this old broad."

I choked out a muffled laugh. "You're not old."

"Whatever you say."

"Come on. I'll take you to Pyper's. Kane said he'd bring the portraits up there for you. She lives next door."

"That's convenient."

I shrugged. "She owns The Grind. It sure makes the commute nice."

By the time we made it down the three flights of stairs in my building and up the two in Pyper's, Gwen's face had turned red and her breathing came out in short, winded breaths. Worry settled in my chest. Gwen owned a farm and spent most of her days either riding her tractor or working with horses. Stairs should not be an issue. "Are you all right? What's wrong?"

A sheepish smile spread across her lips as a faint trace of guilt reached me. She leaned against the wall and flexed one leg. "It's nothing. I twisted my knee a few months ago and have been laid up until recently."

"Why didn't—"

She held up both hands. "You're not the only one who doesn't want people worrying about them."

"Hey, that's not fair. You always know when something's wrong with me."

"And see how restrained I am about not calling every time something is amiss?" She pinned me with a knowing glare.

I had to admit, she was a lot more restrained than I would be. I supposed she had to get used to letting me go at some point. The fact that we talked only once a week was a freakin' miracle. "Point taken. But you still should have told me."

She dismissed me with a wave just as Pyper opened her door. "I thought I heard someone out here. Ms. Calhoun, nice to see you again. Come in, and I'll get you two something to drink."

"Thank you, but Jade has a young man waiting for her." She winked in my direction and, as the door swung shut, I heard her telling Pyper to call her Gwen.

I leaned against Pyper's door, debating. Should I wait there, outside her apartment? I'd told Kane I'd meet him in his office, but if Gwen had a vision, I didn't want to wait to find out about it.

After a couple of moments, my phone beeped, indicating a text. It was from Gwen. *Go away. I know you're still out there.*

Crap. Her message instantly propelled me halfway down the hall. A person can't hide anything from a psychic. The thought made me laugh at myself. No wonder people felt weird around me. With one last glance at Pyper's door, I headed down the stairs.

At the back door of Wicked, I took a second to collect myself before using my key to unlock the door. The music pulsed in rhythm to a strobe light, illuminating a spinning dancer suspended high on one of the poles. She had positioned herself upside down with her back lying against the pole. Only the impressive grip of her thighs kept her from plummeting head-first to the stage.

With skills like that, she should be entertaining a Cirque De Soleil crowd, not the sex-addled patrons of a strip club. Luckily the club was still mostly empty and I didn't get bombarded with the usually thick, frustrated lust that always made my stomach turn. Good thing too, because I'd forgotten to strengthen my defenses before entering.

The music faded and the lighting changed to soft overhead mood lighting. As soon as my eyes adjusted, I spotted Charlie behind the bar. Her face broke out into a genuine smile and she waved me over. "Please tell me you're here to help out? I'd love to spend some time with my favorite girl."

I laughed. "Every female you've ever met is your favorite girl."

"Not true," she said with a pout. "I'd be happy to never see Ariel again. That girl was a mess."

"That's what you get for dating twenty-year-old bi-curious girls. Why can't you find a nice, stable woman to go out with?"

"The young ones are much more impressionable." She smirked.

"You're hopeless." I grinned. "But no, I'm not working. I'm supposed to meet Kane in his office."

Her smile vanished.

"What?"

She glanced toward Kane's office and tugged on a lock of short, red hair at the base of her neck. Her expression suddenly changed, as if she'd just made up her mind about something. "Look, Jade. Normally I wouldn't say anything or get involved in any way, but something is off."

No kidding. Spells, poison, trapped souls. Talk about weird.

"With Kane, I mean."

I stiffened. "How?"

She pursed her lips together and studied me, concern radiating from her chest like a beacon.

"Charlie," I warned.

"Okay, fine. It's that Lailah chick. She keeps showing up here and disappearing with him into his office."

Kane? Lailah? What? The words registered, but the full meaning didn't hit me until she started to speak again.

"I didn't know if I should say anything. I mean, Kane's my boss, and I'm not entirely sure what's going on, but he acts really weird when she's around. I just don't want to see you hurt." Her face softened. "I know you thought I was kidding before, but you really are one of my favorite people. You have a right to know."

I turned to stare at Kane's door.

Charlie moved from behind the bar and stood next to me. The music and lingering emotions in the room seemed to disappear. My Kane and Lailah. It had to be a mistake.

"What exactly did you see?" I asked.

No response.

"Charlie?"

She stepped sideways, just enough to be out of my reach. "I'd rather not say. It's better if you talk to him."

I closed the gap. "You brought this up. What is it I deserve to know?"

She cast a glance once more toward Kane's office and licked her lips. "I…damn it. I walked in on them kissing."

All the air in my lungs vanished. With great effort, I choked out, "When?"

"Ten minutes ago, but—"

I stalked off, not caring what else she had to say. I had my hand on his office door knob when Charlie caught up to me.

"Wait."

I stared at her hand on my arm, wishing I possessed pyro-kenisis. That would be a cool gift. Though, in my state of mind, I'd likely burn down the entire building instead of the traitors presumably on the other side of the door. I shook off the ridiculous thought. It wasn't Charlie's fault my boyfriend was a cheating asshat. She was only trying to help.

"Jade, there's something off about him. I've never seen him behave that way before. And yeah, I'm pissed he was tongue-wrestling with that crazy broad, but it's so far out of character I'd almost think he was spelled or something."

"Oh, God! You too? Not everything bad that happens is caused or fixed by a spell." Without another word, I flung the door open.

Shock rooted me to the floor.

Kane lay shirtless on the desk, Lailah straddling him. All the anger that Charlie's announcement had conjured fled. Pain stabbed my heart. Neither seemed to notice the intrusion. I couldn't breathe as I stood there staring while Lailah clawed and bit at his chest. Her hands moved lower and a strangled cry ripped from my throat.

An electric shock tore through my body at exactly the same moment Lailah flew off the desk, off Kane, and slammed into the wall of the office. She seemed to slide down the wall in slow motion, landing almost gracefully on the balls of her feet. She peered at me in what appeared to be only mild annoyance and moved once again toward Kane, who lay waiting for her.

Pure disgust erupted from deep inside. I spun and ran. I vaguely heard someone call my name. Kane, maybe. But he was the last person I wanted to talk to.

I burst through the back door into the courtyard, gasping for air. No matter how hard I tried, I couldn't seem to fill my lungs. Clutching my chest, I collapsed into a wrought-iron chair and doubled over, staring at the ground. My vision blurred and I didn't notice the stinging until my tears spattered on the faded bricks.

My body shook with silent sobs as the vision of Kane and Lailah played over and over in my mind. Soon, my pain turned to bitter anger. It consumed every part of my being, filling all of my senses.

I heard nothing. Felt no one. Only the betrayal of the one I loved. And that's the only reason I didn't sense Dan sneaking up on me.

Chapter 13

The heavy dose of black licorice on my tongue made my stomach lurch. I curled into a fetal position and moaned. The licorice, combined with the aches in my arms and legs, meant one thing. I'd been knocked out with a very powerful enchantment spell. The same one my mother's coven leader had used on me the night Mom had disappeared.

My eyes didn't seem to want to focus, and I had to blink a few times to clear my vision. After propping myself up on the torn leather couch, I glanced around. A small, thirteen-inch, box-style television sat on a four-person table. A ripped canvas lawn chair was its only seating. The rest of the place, other than the couch I'd been deposited on, was empty.

I stood on wobbly legs, moved toward a window, and fumbled at the latch for some fresh air. The stench of stale beer and fast food burgers in the room turned my unsettled stomach. The latch shifted, but in typical New Orleans fashion, the window had been painted shut. No, not painted shut. Bolted shut.

Shit.

My internal panic finally kicked in, and I ran toward the door. Just as I reached for the handle, it swung open. I dodged, barely avoiding being clocked in the face.

"You're up," Dan said in a conversational tone. He shut the door, but instead of throwing the bolt, he took out a key and locked it from the inside.

"Dan," I breathed. "What's going on here?"

He kept his eyes trained on me, but didn't say another word. Standing there, staring at me, he looked every bit the same man I'd known and dated…until he started to walk. His stiff limbs jerked unnaturally as if he was suffering a full-body spasm. Suddenly he froze, and when he started walking again toward the kitchen, his gait was normal.

"Dan," I said again.

He ignored me and rummaged in the refrigerator.

The last time I'd read Dan's emotions, it had made me physically ill. I'd vowed to never intrude on his personal energy again, but I didn't know what else to do right now. I was locked in a dirty shoebox of an apartment with a crazy ex-boyfriend. I had to know his intentions.

I took a step forward and sent my energy toward him. When nothing registered, I moved closer, sending a stronger probe. A weird thing happened. My energy seemed to swirl around him. No, more like it bounced off him, leaving me nothing to read. It was as if I were trying to read a concrete statue. I gathered my energy together and coaxed it in his direction, pressing when it tried to rebound.

He straightened and turned to face me. "I can feel that. If I were you, I'd stop. Now." His tone had taken on an authoritative edge, making me cringe. His eyes were hard and clear. "When we're done here, you won't be burdened with that particular nuisance of a problem."

"Dan! What has gotten into you?" I cried, balling my hands into fists to keep them from shaking. I was in real danger here. If I couldn't talk my way out of this…"Abduction? Sleep enchantments? This isn't who you are."

"You have no idea who I am." His energy was void, almost as if it had been sucked away.

I shrank back. Everything about him was different. His tone of voice, hard and icy. His empty expression. His awkward stance. He wasn't at all the person I'd once known. I didn't see him for over a year after we'd broken up; not until he'd shown up in New Orleans and started dating Kat. I'd noticed a change then. It would be hard not to, considering he'd morphed into a complete ass. But this was different. His physical being radiated with cold, calculating maliciousness. The kind you don't need empath abilities to know is there.

He stalked forward.

Utter panic took over. A fear I hadn't felt since I'd been fifteen, trapped in my foster parent's house. Only this time Dan wasn't defending me, he was the one hunting me.

"Stop!" With that one word, the spark I'd first found at Bea's house flared through my limbs. The power hummed through my body. It finally dawned on me; it was the same power that had been there all along when I was scared, angry, or frustrated. When my torch had flared out of control while I'd been thinking about Lailah. When I'd unlocked Dan's car. And when I'd thrown Lailah off Kane's body after catching them together at the club.

To my surprise, Dan did stop, but only for a moment. Then he stumbled forward once again in those awkward jerky movements. His mouth gaped open, and his speech came out stilted. "No more…witch…bind power."

For the first time, I noticed a plastic bottle filled with a neon blue liquid in his hand. Something sinister and heavy touched my senses. It took me a moment to register it wasn't Dan; he was still a void. It was what whatever was in that bottle. Everything seemed to move in slow motion as Dan raised his arm and aimed the bottle right at me. The fluid splashed out in large droplets.

Instantly, I jumped back and crossed my arms over my chest in defense. My inner spark expanded, and power exploded from me. I fell backward, landing on my rear with a muffled *oomph*.

A strong honeysuckle stench sweetened the stale air. I wrinkled my nose and glanced around, finding Dan sprawled on the couch covered in blue juice.

"Jade?" He asked in a confused tone.

I scrambled to find my feet.

"What's…wait. Why are you here?" He frowned and glanced around. "How did you know where I live? Kat doesn't even know."

I studied him, taking in his slack, tired expression, the dark circles under his eyes, and general state of disarray. "What was in the bottle, Dan?"

"Huh?" He wiped liquid from his face and glanced around.

I inched toward the window, nodding at the bottle near his feet.

When he rose, I ran. I had my hands stretched out, intending to break the glass with either my power or sheer physical force.

"What are you doing?" He caught up with me and grabbed my wrist. Instantly, the residual power still in my system disappeared.

I yanked my arm from his grasp and stared down at the blue stain on my wrist.

"Sorry." He held both hands up in surrender, his regret brushing my skin.

What was in that bottle? And was it the reason I could suddenly tap into his emotions?

I didn't get a chance to find out, however, because Dan stiffened. His eyes narrowed and panic flared from him, hitting me in the chest. "You have to go. Now." This time he got an iron grip on my elbow and dragged me to the door. "She's coming."

"Who?"

He grabbed the door knob and pulled. Nothing happened. "Fuck." He eyed it as if he couldn't figure out why the door wasn't working.

"It's locked. Dan, who's coming?"

He fished the key out of his pocket and fumbled for a moment before yanking it open. He shoved me out into the dank hallway. Fear, combined with sheer determination, rose to his surface emotions. His eyes bored into mine. "Evil. Now, run!"

His energy faded once again into a void state. Then his body stiffened and his expression turned stony. I bolted.

Two flights of stairs later, I burst through a door onto an unfamiliar dark street. My paranoid-girl intuition kicked in and, without pausing to get my bearings, I ran as fast as I could past abandoned and falling-down homes. It didn't take long for my breathing to turn ragged, but I kept going despite my lungs screaming in protest.

More than a few catcalls came from faceless men sitting in shadows on stoops, but they only propelled me faster. A stitch formed in my side. When I finally made it to a four-way street light, I turned right and almost cried in relief at the sight of a small neighborhood grocery store.

By the time I limped my way to a cashier, my whole body was shaking. I gripped the side of the counter and fumbled for my cell phone. Nothing. I checked the other pocket and came up empty. "Shit."

"Are you all right?" a young man with thick glasses asked. His genuine concern brushed my conscious.

I tried to smile. I'm pretty sure it came out as more of a grimace. "Bad night, but if I could borrow a phone for a minute, I'd appreciate it."

He glanced warily across the aisle at a middle-aged platinum-blond woman.

She eyed him suspiciously. "We're not supposed to let customers use the store phones."

"Okay. I understand. Is there a pay phone?" I could call Bea collect if I had to. Everyone else only had cell phones. I crossed my arms over my body to try to stop the shaking. It didn't work.

"No. Sorry." He pulled an iPhone out of his pocket and handed it to me. "But you look like you could use a break. Borrow mine, unless you plan to call China or something."

His generosity after the awful day I'd had brought tears to my eyes. I blinked them back. "No, just across town. Thank you." At least, I hoped it was just across town.

He sidestepped, presumably to give me privacy, but I stopped him. "Wait, I know this is going to sound crazy, but where am I?"

He didn't miss a beat. "Tulane Avenue."

"Thank you." Thank God. I was still in New Orleans, but not a neighborhood anyone should be wandering around in at night. I automatically started dialing Kane's number, but stopped when the scene in his office flashed through my mind. Betrayal wound its way around my heart.

Instead I called Kat.

Twenty minutes later, she squealed to a stop in front of the market and double-parked. "Jesus, Jade. What the hell happened?"

I hadn't given her any details when I'd called. It was too much to try to do over the phone. I'd only told her where I was and she'd come.

"Get me in the car and I'll tell you everything." The minute my butt hit the seat, all the survival adrenaline I'd been relying on vanished. My hands and feet turned numb, and I barely noticed the tears streaming down my face.

Kat took one look at me, patted my leg, and sped off.

"Go to Bea's," I got out before my throat closed.

Kat didn't speak again until we pulled up in front of the white carriage house. "Want me to call Kane for you?"

"No!" I grabbed her arm. "Don't you dare."

"Jade, whatever happened, don't you think he should know?"

"No. Not since I walked in on him and Lailah making out in his office."

Kat's eyes widened in shock then narrowed as what I'd said fully sunk in. "I'll kill him."

"Not if I do it first." I jumped out of the Mini and slammed the door. I'd gotten on the porch before I realized Kat hadn't followed me. "Aren't you coming in?"

"Yeah, in a minute." She held her phone, tapping in a message.

"Who are you talking to?" I demanded.

She jerked her head up in surprise. "Pyper. She's looking for you."

"You didn't tell her where we are, did you? The first person she'll tell is Kane."

"Um, no, actually. The first person she'll tell is Gwen, who is worried sick, by the way."

Oh, crap. All my anger fled. "Right. Sorry. I'm not thinking clearly. Tell her to tell Gwen I'm fine and to meet me here. But make sure Kane stays away. I can't handle talking to him right now."

"You got it." Kat tapped a few more keys then put her phone away. When she reached my side, she held out her hand. "Use me if you need to."

I bit my lip. "Do I look that bad?" If I got worn down, I could take good energy from people to stabilize. I hardly ever used that particular gift, and when I did, Kat was usually the one to offer. I didn't like doing it. It was too intrusive, but on a few occasions, I'd depleted my energy far enough I'd had little choice.

She nodded. "Sorry, sweetie."

"It's okay. After a day like today, I'm not surprised. But this is only normal exhaustion. And shock. Thanks, though."

"Anytime."

Before I could knock, Bea pulled the door open. "Jade? Where have you been? Gwen's worried sick."

"I know. Can we come in?"

"Of course, dear. Of course." She held the door open.

I waved Kat in and then followed. As I passed Bea, she inhaled sharply. I paused. "What?"

She squinted. "You've been spelled."

"You can tell?"

"I'm a coven witch," she said, as if that explained everything.

"How? Can you smell it?" I brought my blue-stained arm to my nose, but noticed nothing out of the ordinary.

"Magic leaves a signature. I can read it. You would be able to as well, if you worked at it."

"I have no interest in being a coven witch." Exhausted, I moved to the kitchen table and collapsed in a chair.

Bea busied herself in her cheery kitchen while Kat joined me at the table. "Gwen's on her way," she said.

"Pyper's bringing her?"

"Yeah. Is that okay?" Kat plucked at the edge of her black cardigan.

"It's fine." I focused on her, taking in her flat-ironed hair, flawless make-up, and emerald green dress underneath the cotton sweater. "Did you have a date?"

She waved a hand. "It's not important."

"Yes, it is." Elated to have something to talk about other than the horror I'd just experienced I pressed on. "With who?"

She glanced once at Bea and opened her mouth, but Bea cut her off before she could speak.

"With Ian."

"I thought your date was tomorrow."

Kat shrugged with a shy smile. "With the coven stuff tomorrow, he asked if we could reschedule. I figured, why not?"

"Sure. Why not?" If I'd been in a better state of mind, I might have warned her about Pyper. However, dating issues were the last thing I wanted to deal with.

Bea set a mug of tea in front of me. "It's infused with a restorative agent." Before I could protest, she added, "Please, just drink it. Your magic has been compromised and you are more vulnerable than ever to mystical attacks. Drinking this will strengthen you."

It was all I needed to hear. I gave her a short nod and sucked it down in three gulps.

"Good girl." She turned to Kat. "Can I get you anything?"

Kat accepted a regular cup of tea, and once Bea joined us, I filled them in on the whole story. Starting with finding Lailah and Kane in a compromising position.

"I'm sorry your young man disappointed you." Bea grabbed my hand and squeezed hard.

"Disappointed is an understatement," I muttered. "Anyway, that isn't the important part."

"It sounds like it's terribly important."

Kat nodded in agreement, anger streaming off her in waves.

"Okay, yes, to me it is, but there are other things to worry about besides my broken heart."

Bea reached across the table and clasped my hand. "Never underestimate the power your heart holds."

I closed my eyes and chose to ignore her words. I could not focus on that right now. When I resumed talking, my voice came out monotone and detached as I described Dan, his apartment, his crazy behavior. When I finished, I glanced at Kat. "I don't know what to say, other than I think he's turned into a sociopath."

Tears rimmed Kat's beautiful hazel eyes. I knew how she felt. Dan had been our best friend and we'd both loved him. Now he was beyond help from either of us.

Bea excused herself from the table and came back a moment later with a thick leather-bound book. "Your friend is not a sociopath. Or at least, the behavior you described doesn't make him one."

I stared at Bea in disbelief. "How could you know? You've never met him."

She flipped through her book until she found the page she was looking for. "Here." She turned the book around so Kat and I could read it. "Look at this counter spell."

The recipe in front of me contained a lot of herbs and obscure ingredients one could certainly never find in a regular grocery store. I glanced up. "What does this have to do with anything?"

"Look at the last ingredient."

I scanned the list. "Bachelor Buttons? What's that?"

"It's a flower," Kat said. "A vibrant blue one."

"Exactly. It's the main ingredient used in spells designed to neutralize magic." Bea took the book back. "It's obvious your friend was spelled, and once you deflected the neutral-izer on him, he returned to himself. Did he seem normal after that?"

Normal? I didn't know what normal meant for Dan these days. I shrugged. "He seemed more like the Dan I used to know, except for all the fear, panic, and stress."

Bea nodded. "Yes. Being bound to a magical entity will do that to people."

"You mean Jade?" Kat asked. She glanced at me, trepidation pressing down on her aura.

"No, dear. It takes a powerful spell to bind someone to them. Once completed, the witch has the power to control the person. It would appear your Dan is fighting it. The jerky movements are telling. Plus, there's the fact that he let her go as soon as the potion temporarily neutralized the curse." Bea picked up a pen and started scrawling in a notebook.

Confusion radiated off Kat. My head started to spin and I leaned back in the chair, letting her feed Bea the questions. "You mean the potion didn't free Dan from the binding?"

Bea sent her a sympathetic smile. "No. Jade said his energy disappeared. That was a sign the witch had taken over again. Normally that potion doesn't have an effect on bound souls. But if a soul is strong enough, it can help them break away for a short time. He's most definitely not a willing participant in whatever this witch is up to."

"But what would another witch want with Dan—or Jade, for that matter?" Kat asked.

"That's what we need to find out." Bea shifted her gaze toward the front door. "Good, it's Gwen. She'll be useful."

I strained, listening for whatever Bea had heard, but came up with nothing. Minutes ticked by as we waited. When I couldn't stand it anymore, I rose and moved to the window. Outside, the driveway was empty. "You must have heard someone else. No one is here yet."

"They will be."

A minute later, the hum of an engine died and car doors closed, signaling Gwen's arrival. I sent Bea a "you're crazy" look and went to open the door.

Gwen folded me in her arms and hugged me so hard I started to cough. "Sorry. Don't ever do that again. You disappeared, not only physically, but mentally too. I don't like it."

"I'll try not to."

Pyper followed her lead and wrapped me in a fierce hug, but stopped short of cutting off my airflow. When she released me, I turned to close the door, but a tall shadow filled the doorway.

I took one look at his troubled, chocolate brown eyes and slammed the door.

Chapter 14

"Jade." Gwen touched my arm. "Are you sure you don't want to hear what he has to say?"

"No. Not after what happened." I turned to Pyper. "I thought Kat told you not to bring him."

She winced at my accusing tone. "I'm sorry, but he wouldn't take no for an answer. He literally forced his way into my car." Judging by the sympathy radiating off her, someone had filled her in on the details.

"I know you're hurt, hon," Gwen said. "You have every reason to be angry. Goddess knows I would be. But he's been so worried ever since you disappeared."

"He wasn't so worried about me when he was making out with Lailah," I snapped.

"Okay, that's enough." Kat moved to stand next to me. "Jade doesn't want to deal with Kane right now, and she shouldn't have to. She's had a rough night." She turned to me. "I'll go talk to him."

"No, you don't have to do that." Couldn't we just leave him out there to stew? He didn't deserve any explanations. He'd forfeited those rights the minute he decided to let Lailah paw at him.

She shook her head. "I know I don't. But I have a few things I'd like to say."

"Kat," I said with a sigh.

She dismissed me with a wave and disappeared out the front door.

Pyper took Kat's place by my side and led me to the living room.

"I'm fine." I tried to dislodge myself from her grip, but for such a tiny woman, she proved to be a lot stronger than I would have thought. It must have been all the pole-climbing she did at the club when she was filling in.

"You don't look fine. You look like you're one razor blade away from the mental ward. Now, sit." She pointed to the couch. The expression on her face told me it wasn't worth arguing.

I sat, and a moment later, Pyper covered me with the softest knitted blanket I'd ever come in contact with. It took all my willpower to keep from pulling it over my head and pretending the night—hell, the whole day—had never happened.

Gwen took a seat next to me. The worry wrapping around me made my eyes burn with tears. Again. Having Gwen by my side finally made the horror of my abduction sink in.

She put her arm around me and pressed my head to her shoulder. "It's okay now. Aunt Gwen is here."

I sniffled into her sweater, letting her comfort me until my eyes had dried. Then, with Bea's help, I filled her and Pyper in on the night's events.

By the time I'd finished, Gwen's face had turned pale. When she finally spoke, she said, "Poor Dan. He's been through so much."

I jerked back. "Poor Dan? What about me? For God's sake, my mother mysteriously disappeared. I have this terrible gift. My ex is bound to a witch and the pair of them kidnapped me for any number of unknown reasons. My boyfriend was making out with a so-called-angel bitch. And a spirit, trapped in a ridiculous papier-mâché portrait, claims if I set her free, she can lead me to my mother." I threw my hands up and yelled, "This is not a normal life. And you're worried about what Dan has been through?"

Gwen patted my thigh. "There you go. Get it all out."

I gaped.

"No, it isn't a normal life," Bea agreed. "The sooner you realize it, the better off you'll be. White witches attract undue attention. There will always be those who want to tap into your power."

I groaned. "Enough with the witch stuff. I'll do whatever it takes to find Mom, but I'm not going to embrace my witchy side on a regular basis."

"She's always been stubborn," Gwen said, as if I wasn't sitting right next to her.

"I'm sure she comes by it naturally." Bea cradled a cup of tea in her hands.

Gwen laughed. "Hope was as stubborn as they come. I remember this one time at witch's camp—"

"Lord, help me." I curled the blanket around me, and this time I did cover my face.

"I think he has better things to do at the moment," Gwen said, and went on to relay the story of how my mother had first tapped into her magic. "Do you remember Pixie Maythorn?"

"The one from the east coast who never stopped talking about how she was missing out on her Martha's Vineyard vacation?" Bea supplied.

"That's the one. Anyway, Pixie had her eye on Hope's boyfriend. She kept inviting him on midnight strolls, suggesting skinny dipping, and asking him to help her with her love potions."

I pulled the blanket off my head and stared at Gwen. "Love potions? You can't be serious?"

Gwen laughed. "Oh, yes. Pixie could mix powerful ones, too. The problem was, the camp didn't stock most of the ingredients and Pixie wanted someone to help her find plants and herbs in the woods. Since no one was allowed to leave the camp alone, she kept hitting Thomas up to help her. And he was too polite to say no."

"Much to Hope's dismay." Bea chuckled.

"Thomas was Mom's boyfriend?"

"Sort of. I mean, they both liked each other, but we'd only been at camp two weeks. It's hard for fifteen-year-olds to form a solid relationship in that amount of time. Hope had yet to demonstrate any real magical ability other than basic telekinesis, which everyone could do. But Pixie could whip up almost any potion spell if she knew what ingredients it needed. Anyway, Thomas was intrigued."

"And he spent a lot of time with her in the woods, did he?" Pyper quipped.

"Ha!" Gwen laughed. "No, because Hope got so mad, she spent all night envisioning the pair of them with a severe rash. And wouldn't you know it? The very next day they both ended up with poison oak, even though the camp swore the plant didn't exist on their grounds. The head witch had spelled the property herself."

"That's mean," I said.

"I think Pixie might have deserved it," Bea said with a wicked smile. "I remember that girl. She was four kinds of awful."

Gwen shrugged. "Maybe, but since Hope had worked the spell, she had to reverse it. As soon as she put her mind to it, Thomas's rash cleared right up. But Pixie's didn't. Hope couldn't get over her grudge long enough to let the spell go, so poor Pixie spent the rest of the summer hiding away in a private cabin covered in calamine lotion."

"That's the risk you take when you mess with another witch's man," I muttered.

Gwen chuckled. "I don't think Hope did it on purpose— leaving her that way, I mean. She'd been so stubborn holding on to her anger, she hadn't been able to reverse the spell."

"What happened to Pixie?" I asked. Poor thing. Her only crime was liking a boy. I frowned. Liking boys at any age wasn't worth the B.S.

"She made herself a neutralizing potion. It was actually ground-breaking work and landed her a scholarship at Boston U. Their humanities department is actually a secret witch's program, specializing in history and spell development. Last I heard, Pixie was working at Witches Against Curses, the institute for spell reversal research. She's very highly regarded, actually."

"So Mom kind of did her a favor?"

"That's one way of looking at it. I bet Pixie would have found a way into BU's door anyway. She was an academic sort of witch. Unlike you and your mother."

I sat back and crossed my arms, wondering if that was an insult.

Silence filled the room. Then Bea asked, "Gwen, did you find anything about your sister when you checked out Felicia's portrait?"

Gwen sighed. "No. Not a damn thing."

"Nothing?" I asked.

"Not with the portrait." She softened her voice. "But then, shortly after I tried to tune in, a stone settled on my chest and all I could see was red, followed by a gray haze."

"I'm sorry." The stone always represented something painful involving me. Gwen always knew when I was hurt. Emotionally and physically. "Did you have enough time to check before my…situation arose? Or do you think you should try again?"

"Not tonight, sweetie. This old lady needs some rest." Gwen stood. "Bea, if you don't mind, I'd like to retire for the evening."

"Of course." Bea stood and waited for Gwen by the stairs.

"Come by the café in the morning for breakfast," I told Gwen. "We'll talk more then."

She gave me a hug and disappeared to the second floor.

The minute Bea reappeared, I asked, "What are we going to do about Dan and the trapped souls and spirits?"

She took her time getting situated in her chair then gazed at me with intense eyes. "What do you want to do?"

"Obviously we need to help them." Hadn't we already decided that?

"Even Dan?"

"Yes," I said without hesitation.

"Really? Even if he bound himself willingly to his master?" She picked through her knitting basket and pulled out a skein of lavender yarn.

"He didn't."

"How do you know?"

"I just know, okay? Dan hates everything to do with the unexplained. I don't know how he got mixed up in this, but I know he didn't go willingly."

"And you're sure about that?" She didn't even look up as she questioned me.

"Bea?"

When I didn't elaborate, she finally looked up, her knitting needles clicking in a smooth rhythm. "Yes, dear?"

"Do you know something you're not telling me?"

"Well, technically I know a lot of information that you have yet to learn. But nothing pertaining to our current conversation."

"Oh, good Lord!" Pyper jumped up. "You two are more dizzying than a tilt-a-whirl. Bea, Jade wants help with the trapped souls and Dan. Jade, I'm pretty damn sure Bea is going to require you to do the heavy lifting." She turned to Bea. "Am I right?"

Bea laughed. "I like you."

Pyper tilted her head and raised her eyebrows in question.

I chewed on the side of my cheek. I would do what was needed to help, but if I had to do all the work, they were doomed.

"Yes," Bea said. "And not just because she needs to learn so she can protect herself and the ones she loves, but because she has a strong connection to Felicia and Dan."

"I don't—"

Bea silenced me with a pointed stare. "You do. Look at how adamant you are about helping them. You share a connection with Dan, and now through your mother, you have one with Felicia as well. Even if she's lying, the link has been made. I'll help you, but you need to perform the rituals."

I stood. "Fine. When can we start?"

"Tonight, as soon as Lailah arrives. We'll walk you through what you need to know for tomorrow night."

"Lailah?" My voice came out high-pitched and strangled. There was no way I could stomach being around the boyfriend-stealing backstabber. "Why her? She isn't even a witch."

Bea went back to knitting. "She's good with rituals."

Pyper snorted. "Yeah. Look at how good the last one turned out."

Three months ago, Lailah had worked a spell intending to rid Pyper of a black shadow. The result ended with Pyper in a coma and her soul trapped in another dimension.

"The ritual worked perfectly," Bea said, not even missing a beat. "She asked Jade to focus on the spirit haunting her, and when Jade focused on Bobby, he became trapped in the circle. It's a shame no one realized there were two spirits."

I hated to admit it, but the ritual spell Lailah used had been impressive. "True enough," I said. "But I'm not willing to work with her. There must be someone else, or I'll learn it on my own."

A squeak from the front door grabbed my attention. Kat's red curls obscured half of her face as she poked her head in. "Jade? Can you come here for a moment?"

Her trepid tone and energy baffled me. Kat was many things, but meek wasn't one of them. I met her at the door and asked cautiously, "What's going on?"

"I think you need to hear something."

I raised my eyebrows and waited.

"But you need to hear it from Kane."

"No. I have more important things to deal with right now. Send him home. Or call him a cab if he needs one." I gently nudged the door, but she braced it open with one hand.

Her energy changed to one of pure insistence. "Jade, please. He isn't going to leave until he gets to speak to you, and I really think you need to hear what he has to say."

I stared hard at her and delved deeper into her energy. Confusion, determination, and frustration all mixed together and showed in the tension on her face. "Fine. It's a good thing you're the one asking."

"That's what I told him." She pushed the door open and stepped aside.

"I'll be right back," I told Bea and Pyper.

"Take your time," Bea said, reaching to dig into her knitting basket.

Bea's blasé attitude was really starting to irritate me. Lives were hanging in the balance and she was acting like it was just another night. It took all my willpower to keep from scowling.

"I'll be in here if you need me." Kat stepped into the house.

"I'd prefer if you stayed as moderator." With Kat around, I'd be less likely to start crying or, worse, begging for answers. Her presence always made my emotional energy stronger. One of the perks of having a best friend.

"You're not going to need me this time." She closed the door with a soft click.

I stood there facing the door, trying to find the will to turn around. Knowing Kane was nearby, but not being able to sense him, made me shiver in the warm breeze. For three months I'd been connected to him in a way I'd never been with anyone. The loss brought a deep sadness to my soul.

My body twitched, itching to go back inside. How could he have been seeing Lailah, and I'd never sensed it? Not even once. Had I ever even known him at all? The love I'd been so certain of had soured in that awful moment back at the club. There wasn't anything he could say to undo it now.

Finally, wondering if he was still there, I turned. The moonlight highlighting his chiseled features would have made my insides gooey if the vision of him and Lailah hadn't been imprinted on my brain. Instead, I crossed my arms over my chest and glared.

"Are you all right?" He took a step forward.

I glanced down the length of my body then back at him. "It would appear so."

He stepped back and leaned against the rail.

"Kat says you have something to say. So say it. I've got more important things to deal with."

"More important than us?" he asked in a hurt tone.

"Us? There's an us? It sure as hell didn't look like that when you were horizontal on the desk with the *angel*." My anger took over and I strode to him. "When did it start? The first night she showed up in your dream, or earlier? Have you been seeing her this whole time? God! I should have known three months ago when I first saw you two together. I thought it was weird you could turn your emotions on and off. You're getting really good at it."

He ran a frustrated hand through his hair. "Damn it, Jade. I really have no idea what you're talking about."

"Whatever. Play innocent if you want to." I turned to go back in, but he caught my arm.

"Wait!"

I stopped and stared at his hand on my arm. "Let go."

"Not until you hear what I have to say."

This man, the one I'd been so head over heels in love with for the last three months, was now actually making me sick. Though for once, it wasn't an empath side effect. It was all my own conflicting emotions making me nauseated. All I wanted to do was run away, but some morbid curiosity took over. What kind of pathetic excuse had he dreamed up? "Fine. You have five minutes. Then I'm going in."

"Okay, good enough." He let go and stepped back. "Can you tell me what you saw when you walked in my office this afternoon?"

I gaped. "You want me to describe the scene. In detail?" What was wrong with him?

"No, but a brief overview would be helpful."

"So you can work on your cover story? Sorry, Kane, but seeing you lying on your back with Lailah straddling you and savaging your body with her mouth pretty much means you're screwed in the excuses department. Nothing you can say is going to make this go away."

He grabbed the railing behind him, tightening his grip until his knuckles turned white. "What if I told you I don't remember any of that? What if I said I have no knowledge of even seeing her today? What if I told you I lost a whole two hours of my day, and I have no recollection of what happened at all?" The tone of his voice softened, and his deep chocolate brown eyes searched mine. "Would that make a difference?"

"Denial? That's your strategy?"

"No. I don't have a strategy. Do an energy probe if you have to. I'm not trying to weasel my way out of anything. If you say it happened, I believe you. But I don't remember it. And I sure as hell don't have any interest in Lailah," he said angrily. Or was it frustration? I couldn't tell.

"I would," I spat, "but you've been concealing your emotions from me, so I can't."

"I am?" His eyebrows pinched in confusion as he paced the length of the porch. "Why didn't you say anything?"

I shrugged. "You're entitled to privacy if you need it. What would I say anyway? How come you aren't sharing every little feeling with me? I guess I have my answer."

This time when he spoke, there was no denying the anger. "What answer? I haven't been hiding anything from you. I thought our relationship was built on trust." His voice softened and his eyes pleaded with me for understanding. "Here I am, telling you I don't know what happened today. I sure as hell wish I did. Then maybe I could make sense of everything."

The built-up hurt that had been clenching my heart lessened. Unless he'd been taking acting lessons, he wasn't lying. Vulnerability wasn't something he showed often, and at that moment, I no longer believed he would intentionally hurt me in such a way.

I moved forward, intending to lean against the rail beside him, but the sound of a car stopped me. "Who's that?"

A white Ford Mustang came to a stop behind Pyper's Bug. A moment later, Lailah unfolded herself from the driver's side. Kane's eyes narrowed and he took a step in her direction.

That's when I flew past him, down the stairs, and ran full force toward the angel.

Chapter 15

Before I even realized what I was doing, my hands wrapped around Lailah's slender neck and squeezed. Not enough to totally cut off her airway, though I wanted nothing more than to do just that. Instead, I shook her a few times and backed her up until I had her pinned against her car.

"What the hell do you think you're up to?" I demanded.

She coughed and clawed at my fingertips. "Get...off...me."

"Not until you answer my questions. What did you do to Kane today, and why have you been in our dreams?"

The shock of my attack wore off and her face twisted into outraged indignation. Staring hard into my eyes, she dropped her hands from her neck. The next thing I knew, a slow burn started from the middle of my palms, moving outward toward my fingertips. Her eyes narrowed and my fingers suddenly burned as if they were on fire.

I yelped and snatched my hands back. When had she gotten her power back? The red ring around her neck made me retreat as the mortification of what I'd done sank in. "Oh my God," I mumbled.

"He's not likely to help you after you assaulted one of his angels," she said angrily. "Who do you think you are?"

"The girlfriend of the man you bewitched then seduced today in his office!"

Kane appeared by my side and put a hand on my shoulder. "Maybe we could try discussing this in a calm manner."

"I doubt it," I said, returning to the porch. "But we can try, I suppose."

Lailah took two steps and made a show of rubbing her neck. No doubt for effect. "Kane, what is she raving about?"

I still couldn't read his emotions, but his tense stance betrayed his anger. "You tell me. I have about two hours of my life I can't seem to remember and I'm told they were spent with you."

"What?" Lailah moved to stand in front of Kane. It took all my willpower to not attack her again. "I haven't seen you at all today. What would make you think that?"

"You have got to be fucking kidding me," I said. "I saw you, mauling him in his office. And I don't mean I glimpsed someone. I saw your face. You looked right at me before you bent over him and bit his chest."

Lailah, who always kept her emotions close, dropped her guards. Total confusion, mixed with fury, shot straight at me full blast. No, she hadn't just dropped her guard; she'd intended to let me experience exactly what she felt. Fine. If she was sending it, I'd do my best to understand exactly what was going on inside her.

I took it all in, letting Lailah's emotions flow through all my senses until everything she felt was my own. Hurt, indignation, anger. It consumed me down to my soul. There was no need to delve further; she'd sent me everything she had. My arms twitched, trying to release the foreign energy. Slowly I pushed it away, letting it ease into the night. All but the last of her energy was gone when I noticed the shift. It was barely there, but beneath all the angry denial was a hint of doubt. Doubt about what?

"What aren't you telling us?" I asked.

"I don't know what you're talking about." She closed herself off again and brushed past me toward the door.

I wrapped my hand around her arm, applying just enough pressure to stop her. "You're the one who opened yourself to my probe. I got it. You're angry I'm accusing you, and your level of righteous indignation appears to mean you don't believe what I said. But you have doubts. What are you questioning?"

She turned sad blue eyes on me. "I'd rather speak to Bea." She tugged her arm out of my grip.

I stood there watching as she disappeared inside. "There's something off about her."

"You're just now figuring that out?" Kane pulled me down into a wooden swing. He turned me to face him. "You believe me, don't you? I really don't have any memory of what happened today. And the way I feel about you…well, it would take a lot more than some freaky fuck-up of an angel to get me to risk what we have."

A soft wind kicked up, blowing a lock of hair over his eye. I reached out and smoothed it to the side. As my fingers trailed over his skin, his aura suddenly glowed golden, the color of a man deep in love. The same color I'd seen before his emotions had been hidden to me. I shook my head, trying to clear my vision, sure I was seeing things. But when I looked back, his aura only glowed brighter.

I blinked back tears and nodded. "I believe you. I don't know what's going on, but I believe you."

His arms came around me and he pulled me into a hug, crushing me against him. "Make me a promise."

"What kind?" I stared over his shoulder at the lights lining Bea's pathway.

His hand came up to my jaw and he moved my head so I was looking him in the eye. "Promise me the next time something goes haywire, you won't run."

"I can't promise that. Think about what you would do if you found me in the arms of another man. Would you politely ask to speak to me or wait until I was finished?"

A low, sardonic laugh rumbled from his chest. "No, I'd pull him off you and proceed to explain exactly why he should disappear before I lost control of my temper."

I cocked my head to one side. "So the reaction I just had to Lailah was about six hours too late? Should I have stalked into your office and beat the shit out of her?" Never mind my magic had thrown her against the wall. Neither one remembered that, apparently. Besides, I hadn't done it on purpose. It just happened.

"That would have been preferable to you running. Yes, definitely preferable."

I smiled. "I bet."

He laughed then sobered. "This is only going to work if we can communicate. I understand your reaction, but clearly there's something unexplainable going on. I don't want our relationship to be the victim of whatever it is. So for now, at least until we figure this out, please, promise you won't run."

The look on his face, more than any of the words he'd said, made me nod my agreement. "No running. I promise. But don't think I won't lose it if I walk in on another scene like that."

"I wouldn't have it any other way." He leaned in and caught my lips in a slow, meaningful kiss that left me breathless when he pulled back. "Ready?"

"No." The only thing I wanted to do was go home. To his home, and sleep for two days. But I stood anyway. "Let's go."

He joined me, but before we reached the door, it swung open, slamming against the inside wall with a bang.

We glanced at each other. Kane clutched my hand and pulled me forward. Inside, Kat and Pyper stood with horrified expressions as they gaped at Lailah. She hung suspended by nothing in the middle of the living room, white-faced and rigid.

Bea's ball of knitting yarn had rolled beneath Lailah's feet. I followed the single string of yarn back to Bea. She sat sprawled in the chair, unconscious. I gasped. "What happened?"

The stairs squeaked, catching my attention. Gwen inched her way down into the living room to Bea's side.

"Gwen?" I asked.

She knelt down and touched Bea's wrist, searching for her pulse. "She's just knocked out. If you send her some energy, she'll perk right back up."

I moved to her side and picked up Bea's hand. "I can do that, but she told me not to transfer my own energy. Something about weakening my powers."

Kat appeared beside me and held out her hand. "Use me. You've done it before. I know what to expect."

"That's sweet, Kat. But I think it's better if she uses me," Gwen said. "My lighter energy is easier to transfer."

"It is?" I'd never thought of that.

"Of course. Now, hurry." She clutched my hand.

I focused on Gwen's emotional signature. Instead of slipping away like Ian's had, I didn't have to do much but nudge it in Bea's direction.

After a moment, her eyes fluttered open and she sat up. "Well done, Jade. You're finally getting the hang of it." Bea squeezed my hand before letting go.

"What happened?" I demanded again, staring at Lailah's lifeless body.

Bea shifted in her chair and leveled a glare at the angel. "We engaged in a magical duel of sorts."

"It was crazy," Pyper said. "One minute, Bea was questioning how Lailah recovered her powers, and the next, Lailah went into a rage and threw some freaky green light at her. Bea blocked it and it rebounded, turning Lailah into the levitating zombie, but it knocked Bea out."

"She attacked you?" My voice rose in disbelief.

Bea stood, using Kane's arm for support. We walked with her around Lailah's limp body. She peered at her assistant then glanced back. "Jade, have you tapped her energy lately?"

Startled, it took me a moment to respond. "Yes, a few minutes ago when we were outside."

"And was it different than it normally is?"

"I have no idea. I try not to do that if I can help it."

"Do it again," Bea said.

"Why?"

"Jade." Bea's tone implied impatience. "I want to compare what you feel versus what I sense radiating off her. Please, time is limited."

I gave her an odd look, but didn't ask any more questions. It was likely I wouldn't get anything from Lailah anyway, since she appeared to be unconscious. I sat in the overstuffed chair Bea had vacated. "Okay. Give me a minute."

Pyper and Kat stopped whispering to each other and the room fell silent. I closed my eyes and breathed deeply. Focusing usually wasn't an issue, but it had been a long day. With six people in the room, I'd figured sifting through each emotional signature would take at least a little bit of effort, but Bea was masking hers, I still couldn't find Kane's, and Kat's and Gwen's were so familiar to me that I touched on them each and quickly set them aside.

That left Pyper, and she was hardly a stranger. She had a fair amount of curiosity swirling around her, but somewhere buried deep inside, a thread of fear threatened to take over. She did a decent job of holding it at bay, though. I admired her strength. After what she'd been through with Roy, it was amazing she still tolerated any paranormal activity at all. I wouldn't if it was at all possible.

With Pyper's energy out of the way, I sent a slight probe in Lailah's direction. When I found nothing, I pushed harder. My inquiry was met with a void. The eerie familiarity set my nerves on edge. I'd encountered an empty emotional state only once before. It had happened with Pyper right after her soul had been stolen by a ghost.

My eyes flew open. "She's not there," I gasped. "Exactly like before, when the ritual went wrong and we lost Pyper."

"What?" Panic broke through Pyper's calm and her face turned white.

Bea crossed the room and put a reassuring hand on her arm. "You're safe here," she told Pyper then turned and stared me in the eye. "She's there. Search deeper."

Her commanding no-nonsense tone made me stand and move to Lailah's side. Sometimes physical contact helps. Despite my overwhelming desire to cringe away from her, I placed my hand on her arm. This time, when I sent my probe, I didn't hold back. I used every ounce of strength I could muster. My energy burst into her, instantly finding her essence. Her hidden emotions spilled into mine, filling me with hatred and fierce determination.

A rage I'd never known burned within my soul. My hand instinctively tightened around her arm as I pulled her through the air. I couldn't focus on anything except the overwhelming desire to end the existence of those standing in my way. As Lailah's body glided toward me, my other fist clenched and an odd hissing escaped from my lips.

"Jade!" Bea's voice cut through the blinding anger.

I jumped back, recoiling from the venomous energy. Whatever was inside her was pure evil.

Lailah moved, awakening from her enchanted slumber. Still suspended in the air, she raised her arms above her head. A round, green mass, of what I could only assume was a spell, materialized between her hands, and without uttering a word, she threw it directly at me.

My imaginary glass silo, the one I used to block out other people's emotions, snapped in place. The green mass shattered through it, but on contact, the glass took solid form, scattering glass shards around the room. I barely registered the yelps and shocked cries from my friends as a surge of power appeared from the depths of my being. Instinctively, I used it to block the attack. Most of the spell rebounded, but a small, hot bolt struck me just above my heart. I yelped, clutching my chest as it throbbed. A second later, a burning sensation sizzled through my limbs. It reminded me of the anesthesia I'd received when I'd had my appendix out as a kid. I sank to the floor, flexing, trying to regain the feeling in my appendages.

"Jade? What did she do to you?" Kane asked.

I turned toward the sound of his voice, but my vision blurred. I blinked. No, not my vision—his imaged blurred. I could see everything else in the room clearly. He'd moved to kneel beside me, but when I reached out to touch him, my hand glided right through him as if he were a hologram. "What the heck?"

His eyes focused on my hand groping around for solid form. I tried to meet his gaze. Through his flickering image, his face turned confused. His hand came up, trying to grab mine, and horrified panic flashed over his face right before he disappeared altogether.

"Kane!" I cried, groping for his missing body.

Lailah's cold laugh rang through the room. "Draining you would have been faster, but I'll enjoy my time with your lover much more." Her blue eyes flashed yellow right before she evaporated into thin air.

Chapter 16

I scrambled to my feet and nearly fell due to the numbing spell. Clutching the chair, I sought out Bea. She sat on her cheery sunflower-print couch, holding her head in her hands. "Bea?"

She looked up, her face pinched with pain. It took only a moment to notice the blood seeping between her fingers.

"Oh my God." I stumbled to her side and inspected the jagged scrape near her temple.

Gwen touched my shoulder. In her other hand, she held a thick white towel. "Let me." She glanced over her shoulder. "Kat, check the bathroom for a first aid kit."

Kat got halfway up the stairs before Bea spoke. "It's in the hall closet, dear." Her small, wobbly voice made her sound like a feeble old woman.

Kat nodded. "I'll be right back."

I scanned the room for Pyper. A strangled cry escaped my throat when I spotted her feet poking out from behind the loveseat. I sprang up. "Pyper?"

Her foot twitched, but she didn't respond.

"Oh, no." My feet prickled as my limbs started to come back to life, but it wasn't enough. Right before I reached Pyper's side, I fell. Hard. I landed with a thud and curled into a ball, holding my shoulder. All the numbness had fled, and fireworks exploded down my arm.

"That was graceful," she whispered in a shaky voice.

I rolled over and grimaced at the stain of blood on the carpet. "You're hurt," I said.

She grunted in agreement.

My initial inspection found several shallow scrapes. Then I spotted it. She had a sizable shard of glass sticking out of her thigh. Around it, only a small amount of blood stained the dark denim. I frowned and looked at the blood-stained floor. "Where did that come from?"

Pyper turned, revealing a gash on the side of her head. "Scalp wound."

"Son of a…Kat, I need that first aid kit."

Kat hurried over, took one look, and whipped out her phone.

"No ambulances!" Pyper demanded.

"But—"

"No. I'll go to the hospital, but I won't be the one riding the emergency express again." She tried to sit up, but winced and lay back down.

"Pyper," Kat said. "How are we going to get you in the car?"

"Kane can carry me."

Silence filled the room.

"What?"

Kat bit her lip and glanced at me.

I swallowed and my voice cracked when I finally spoke. "Lailah abducted him."

Her face scrunched up in confusion. "What does that mean? There's no way that waif of a girl could overpower a six-foot-two, one-hundred and eighty-pound man."

"With magic," I choked out, fighting the sobs building in my throat. "Just like my mom." My voice cracked on the word mom, and suddenly, Gwen was there with her arms around me. All the terrible emptiness I'd worked so hard to suppress after my mom had disappeared came rushing back.

I vaguely heard Kat talking to someone about fetching Pyper. Relieved to have someone taking over, I buried my head in Gwen's shoulder and silently let the tears fall.

Sometime later, I excused myself to the restroom. I stood there, staring into my vivid green eyes, appearing a deep emerald rather than their usual jade color. It must have been a side effect from the magic. The sadness reflected in them made me straighten my spine. I wasn't a helpless fifteen-year-old anymore. Whatever it took, I'd find Kane and bring him back. Even if it meant taking down an angel. Surely waging magical attacks and abducting people wasn't in her job description.

While splashing my face with cool water, the front door slammed. A moment later, a muffled male voice stood out among the chatter. My heart sped up. Kane? I hastily dried my face and ran back to the living room.

Disappointment stopped me short at the end of the hallway. Ian had knelt beside Pyper and was smoothing her hair back. Tension and worry filled the room, but no one's emotions were stronger than Ian's. And all of it was directed at Pyper. My gaze landed on Kat. She stood apart from the rest of the group, her eyes trained on Ian. A tiny frown tugged at her lips. I couldn't help but feel a little pang of sadness for her. It was obvious that Pyper and Ian would end up together sooner or later. I hoped Kat's heart didn't get battered in the meantime.

A small moan brought my attention back to Pyper. Ian now had her in his arms as Gwen held the door open. I followed them out. "I'll meet you in the ER."

"No," Pyper said over his shoulder. "You work on finding Kane. I'll be fine. If you leave, send me a text letting me know your whereabouts. Otherwise, expect to see me back here in a few hours."

Ian already had the door open and was depositing her in his car.

The fierce determination surrounding her strengthened my own. I found myself nodding. "Fine. Get yourself put back together. I have a feeling I'm going to need you."

"Jade," Ian warned. "She has a two-inch piece of glass in her leg."

"She knows that, Ian," Pyper said. Her pointed gaze met mine. "I'll be back as soon as possible."

Ian sighed and shut her door.

I cocked my hip and sent him a defiant look. "You're always the one dying to do paranormal readings. Here's your chance. Bring your equipment when you come back."

His face shifted into cautious surprise. "Why this time?"

"Because I want every piece of data we can get. Even if it turns out to be useless, it's worth a shot."

His energy shifted and a hint of defensiveness tickled my senses.

"Don't be offended. You study ghosts. I'm asking you to measure anything paranormal. I want to see what you can come up with."

He made a concerted effort to relax. "I've already experimented a little with that. I'm sure we can find something useful."

His car door slammed, and a moment later, the tires squealed when the car darted out of the driveway.

Leaves rustled from a light wind. I shivered in the chilly air. Still, I stood on the porch, staring into the night. How had this happened? Kane's disappearance felt like some surreal dream. People didn't vanish into thin air.

Except people I loved, apparently.

Not too long ago, I would have taken that as a sign to distance myself from those I cared about. Only, to help Kane, I needed them. This time I'd do whatever necessary to bring him back. Even if it meant embracing my inner witch.

I marched through the front door and found Bea in the kitchen. "Are you all right?"

"I'm fine. Are you?" Her tone implied she had her doubts.

"More than ready. Where do we start?"

She reached up, pulled a copper mixing bowl out of the cupboard, and handed it to me. Over the course of five minutes, she filled it with various herbs, spices, and wheat flour, and then finished by adding a can of condensed milk to my haul.

"Baking?"

She snorted. "Locator potion." She pointed to her wooden table. "Sit."

"Are you sure this is a good idea?" Gwen asked cautiously.

"It's fine," I said before Bea could respond.

Gwen rested her hand on my shoulder. "It's been a difficult day. Spells can and often do go wrong when the caster is under emotional stress."

I stared at her. "How would you know?"

She sent me a look intended to put me in my place. "I am your mother's sister. Just because I don't have strong magical skills doesn't mean I didn't pay attention when she was learning."

"Okay, okay. I've never heard you talk about any of this. I had no idea you were so well-versed in witch studies."

"You'd be surprised at what I know," Gwen muttered, taking the seat across from me.

Bea settled into a chair to my right and turned to Gwen. "You know, all of this would have been smoother for her had she learned the basics when she was younger. Witch knowledge ages and becomes refined over the years. Knowing she had the potential to be a witch would have primed her psyche for acceptance. For the talented ones, that's half the battle."

Gwen huffed. "You have no idea what you're suggesting. This child would've preferred breeding snakes to learning magic back then."

I shuddered. The thought of a snake made my skin crawl.

Gwen's voice softened. "After her mother…"

Bea's expression shifted to understanding. "My apologies, my dear friend. It wasn't my place to chastise you."

Gwen nodded her acceptance.

In the meantime, I'd unloaded the mixing bowl and had all the ingredients lined up. "If you two are done discussing my lack of skills and apparent shortcomings, can we get started?"

"Of course," Bea said, returning to the commanding coven leader I'd expected. She paused then called over her shoulder,

"Kat, grab another copper bowl. I have something for you to do as well."

"Me?" Kat straightened her spine. "But I don't have any powers."

"Everyone has something to offer. Your intentions are all we need."

Kat glanced in my direction.

I shrugged.

"All right." A moment later, she sat in the fourth chair with an extra bowl in front of her.

"Good." Bea lined up the supplies in front of us. "Each of you needs to channel all of your energy into the mixture. As I said, intentions are important. Jade, I want you to focus on Kane's essence." She shifted her gaze to Kat. "And Kat, you focus on your friend, Dan. We need to find out what or who is controlling him."

"Why?" I interjected. "What does that have to do with finding Kane?"

Bea leveled an irritated glare in my direction. Clearly she wasn't used to being questioned. "Maybe nothing. But since Lailah was assigned to him, whatever it is may be the same thing that's controlling Lailah."

I narrowed my eyes. "How do you know anything's affecting her? How do we know she hasn't turned into a fallen angel?"

Bea took a deep breath. "I would be able to tell. You're letting your emotions get in the way of your common sense."

"Am I? All I know is that whenever she's involved, something always goes haywire. And Felicia said one of our own was close to falling. Seems obvious to me."

All emotion vanished from Bea's face. Her masked expression made me itch to probe her energy. Bea was a master at closing herself off, so it would have been an exercise in futility. I wouldn't have done it anyway. With her power, she'd have noticed the invasion. It was one thing to read emotions people projected to the world. It was entirely another to go searching for them.

When she spoke, her voice held a hard edge. "You don't know Lailah like I do. Someone is controlling her actions. She would never attack me and vanish. If you want my assistance, you'll need to accept that we'll be helping her as well."

"Jade." When I didn't respond, Kat covered my hand with hers. "It doesn't matter what you think of Lailah. What matters is finding Kane. She has a connection to him and Dan. Figuring out what's going on with Dan could lead us to Kane. Besides, Dan needs help, too. No matter what he's done in the past few months. We owe him that much."

The tight ball that had formed in my chest constricted even more. God, I was selfish. Hadn't I seen first-hand that Dan was, indeed, the victim of some other witch's spell? Hadn't he committed to anger management classes and followed through by apologizing to me? He *was* making an effort. "You're right. I'm sorry. Of course we'll do what we can to help Dan."

"Good," Bea said. "Kat, concentrate on Dan—the Dan he used to be before he started showing signs of aggression. Who he was before Jade moved to New Orleans."

I cocked my head. "Are you implying whatever's happening with Dan has been going on for months?" If so, it would explain a lot.

"I don't know. It's possible, but it's better to focus on who he was before his energy became tainted. No matter what the reason. Believe it or not, if you concentrate on finding the good in people, it's easier than finding the evil."

"Really?" Gwen spoke for the first time. "I wouldn't have thought that to be the case."

Bea nodded. "Goodness has nothing to hide. Evil does."

"If that's so, then why is there so much negativity around?" I asked.

"Unhappy doesn't mean evil. It also doesn't mean unhappy people lack goodness. They just haven't learned the skills to show it."

"Okay," Kat said. "I can do that."

For the next half-hour, Bea instructed the two of us in dicing, measuring, and adding ingredients in the correct order. When we were done, I had a dense mixture of something that looked and smelled like an uncooked pumpkin loaf, while Kat's resembled cuttings from a fresh Italian herb garden.

"Why didn't we use the same ingredients?" I asked. "Isn't it the same spell?"

"Yes, it is." Bea stood and started clearing the table. "But ingredients are tailored for the ones involved in the spell. It yields a higher success rate."

I glanced at my fake pumpkin loaf and wrinkled my nose. What did the ugly blob say about me?

When Bea was finished cleaning up, she strode to the door, her oversized canvas handbag slung over her arm. "It's best to invoke the spells in a location tied to the subject. Kane's house will be perfect for his locator spell, but where should we go for Dan's?"

"Not his place. If he's there, it's too dangerous." I glanced at Kat. "Your apartment? He used to live there."

"That will do," Bea said. "Let's go."

We gathered our stuff and followed Bea out the door. Kat and I settled into her Mini, while Bea and Gwen climbed in her Prius.

Bea rolled down her window. "Kat's place first. I'll follow."

I had to bite my tongue to stop the protest poised on my lips. I'd agreed we needed to help Dan, but the selfish girl inside me screamed to find Kane first. It didn't matter that knowing who or what we were dealing with would be useful once we found him. I just wanted to find him. Now. A small voice in the back of my head chastised me. If only I hadn't been so stubborn about learning the craft, I might have been able to do this on my own.

"Why are you scowling?" Kat asked.

"Huh?"

"Don't you trust Bea?"

I arranged my face into a neutral expression. "Yeah. I'm not dealing with this well."

Kat sent me a small smile. "Considering the day you've had, I'd say you're doing remarkably well. Try not to worry. Bea is one powerful witch, and so are you. You'll find him."

I didn't respond. The lump in the back of my throat wouldn't let me. I spent the rest of the drive staring out the window, trying to think about nothing.

Kat lived in the French Quarter on one of the quieter residential streets, but the fact that it was a few days before Halloween meant the city was full of Voodoo Fest party goers and parking was limited. Kat didn't have designated parking, and we ended up four blocks away. By the time we made it up the stairs to her place, my patience had disappeared.

Kat fumbled around in her purse for her keys. After a full minute of her digging, I let out an exaggerated sigh.

"Sorry. I know they're here somewhere." She looked up with an apologetic expression.

I cut my gaze to her door knob and focused. A tingle in my belly grew, and a second later the dead bolt released with a distinct click.

Kat froze. "Someone's in there."

Bea chuckled. "No. That was Jade. Seems she's finally found her inner spark."

Gwen studied me, while surprise from Kat tingled on my skin. I ignored them and strode through Kat's door.

"So, it was you that unlocked Dan's car that day. I knew it," Kat said, standing just inside her apartment.

I set my pumpkin loaf lookalike on the table. "Yeah, but I didn't realize it at the time."

"Strong emotions make it easier to tap into magic," Bea said.

"That's good, because what I have swirling around in me is likely to explode if we don't get started."

"Jade," Bea chastised, "if this is going to work, you need to calm down."

"I can't help it." How could I be anything other than frantic? My ex was possessed and my boyfriend had disappeared right before my eyes.

"You're an empath. If anyone understands controlling emotions, it's you."

How could I argue with that logic? I crossed from the dining room nook into Kat's cozy living room. Taking a seat in my favorite purple, plush armchair, I tucked my feet under my bottom and sat cross-legged. Nobody followed me, for which I was grateful. I needed a second to compose the turmoil raging inside.

A moment later, my favorite song, "Sunrise" by Norah Jones, filled the room. I glanced over at Kat standing near her iPhone dock. I smiled and my heart eased. With all the crazy crap in my life, I still had a best friend who always knew what I needed.

I let Norah's beautiful vocals wash over me as my emotions settled. The worry and anxiety didn't disappear. Instead, I wrapped them up in my overwhelming love for Kane. I let myself bask in the immediacy of my feelings then set it all aside and welcomed my growing determination.

By the time I sat at Kat's modern, black, fiberglass table, I was ready. "What do you need me to do?"

Bea studied me. I didn't react when her steady energy merged with mine. She sat back and nodded. "Very good. I'm going to walk you through the process of casting the spell to reveal Dan's inner self. If Kat can connect with his goodness, his image and the image of whoever is controlling him should be revealed."

"How do I do that?" Kat asked.

"Just concentrate on Dan like you did when you put together the herbs."

Kat fidgeted.

"You'll be fine." I nudged a tiny bit of my determination in her direction.

Her shoulders straightened and the look on her face told me she was ready.

"Let's do this," I said.

"All right. It appears you've found your magic source, judging by your lock-picking abilities." Bea moved to the middle of the living room.

Gwen chuckled.

"But," she continued, "telekinesis is a basic skill almost all witches pick up easily. Casting targeted spells takes more than pure determination. You'll need to focus to pick up on the delicate nuances."

"I can handle details," I said, hoping that was true. So far, pretty much everything I'd accomplished using magic had happened by force.

"Then we're ready. Jade, I need you and Gwen to join me in a circle. Kat, it's better if you stay there. Go ahead and start concentrating on your friend. No matter what happens here, do not break concentration."

"I'll try," she said.

"Not try, do. Intentions are everything in spell casting. Intend to concentrate. Face away from us if you have to."

"You can do it." I patted her hand and got up to join Bea.

Kat stared at the table for a moment. Then she looked up and tilted her head. "Can I use a photo to focus on?"

"Absolutely," Bea said.

Kat disappeared into her bedroom. It didn't take long before she returned with a framed picture I'd never seen before. It was Dan laughing with the sun highlighting his features.

A dull ache of regret surfaced in my gut. I hadn't seen Dan that happy since before I'd confessed my empath abilities. "When was that taken?"

She frowned. "Not too long after we started dating."

From somewhere deep inside, the buried resentment I'd carried after I'd found out they were dating suddenly shattered. There was a joy in Dan's expression I'd never known existed in their relationship. Every time I'd seen Dan, we'd either ignored each other or had words. He'd done and said some awful things once I'd moved to New Orleans, but now I wondered if any of it had to do with who possessed him now. Was it possible when he'd attacked me in Kane's club that he'd already been affected? There wasn't a way to know. But it would explain a lot. He'd behaved in a way I'd never thought possible.

The sadness on Kat's face made me pull her into a hug. "We'll get him back. I promise." We'd all been friends once. Best friends. And no matter what Dan had done, we owed him our lives.

"Thank you," Kat whispered and let go. She sat at her table, facing the dining room wall. She turned back. "I'm ready."

I rejoined Gwen and Bea in our circle. "Do we need to prep anything else?"

"The herbal mixture is all we need." Bea lowered herself to the floor and sat cross-legged on the cream area rug. "Sit."

When we were situated, Gwen held the bowl up. "What do I do with this?"

"Set it in the center." Bea pointed to the empty space in the middle of us. "Gwen, the only job you have here besides completing the circle is to add your strength to Jade. Focus on supporting her intentions. If your psychic abilities kick in and you see anything, keep it to yourself until we're done. We don't want Jade to get distracted."

"Got it," Gwen said.

"Ready?" Bea asked me.

"As ready as I'm gonna to get."

Bea pulled a pack of matches out of her pocket and tossed them to me. "I'm going to give you an incantation to repeat. After we've spoken the words, you'll need to use your power to light a match. Once it's kindled the herbs, infuse the flames with your spark of magic. Then focus on the Dan who kidnapped you. Do you understand?"

"If I'm infusing the flames with my magic, why can't I strike a match and light it the old-fashioned way?"

"Using your magic to set the herbs on fire gives you control over the spell. Lighting it manually leaves the spell open to any who choose to manipulate it."

"Oh." I had a lot to learn. "Okay, so with any luck, Kat will be able to locate Dan using her intentions, and I'll be able to bring forth the entity controlling him. Am I understanding this right?"

"Exactly. But we'll only see hologram images. They won't physically be here."

From across the room, I heard Kat sigh in relief. I knew how she felt. "Good to know. What happens after they materialize?"

"We might be able to speak to either or both. Or we might just see their images. It depends on the strength of your magic."

I didn't know what to think about that. Did we want to speak to them? Dan maybe, to find out what was going on, but what would we say to a soul-possessing witch? *Get the hell out of our friend's body, or we'll curse you?* Thank goodness we had Bea. She was the New Orleans coven leader. She probably had plenty of badass in her arsenal.

Bea reached her hands out to each of us. Gwen and I followed suit, and once our linked hands completed the circle, Bea started to speak. "Power of the coven, your mistress commands your will. Your strength is called upon. Flow freely and bend to our wishes. By the power bestowed upon me by the southern witches of the ethereal plane, I command you."

I waited, since the incantation wasn't the one I was supposed to repeat. Nobody had bestowed anything on me. Invoking power that hadn't been given freely didn't bode well in the craft. Despite my refusal to engage in anything magical, I had grown up with a witch. I knew some things.

Bea nodded to me. "I, Jade Calhoun, seek to reveal the inner spirits of Dan Toller. Come forth and be seen."

I didn't only say the words. I dug deep and repeated them with conviction.

Bea kept her gaze locked on mine. "The power I wield commands it. Let the ties that bind you to the earth break free. Come forth, be seen."

It was as if something rich and important had taken me over. My words came out strong and forceful. The effect made me sure I could accomplish anything.

"Appear before us," Bea continued. "I, Jade Calhoun, niece of Gwen Calhoun and daughter of Hope Calhoun, force your spirit to our circle. Come now. Be free. Bind yourself to me."

A current flowed through my veins. The words took on a magic of their own, flowing from me without thought. As I finished the last line, "bind yourself to me," my voice rose, echoing through the room.

Without releasing my hand, Bea gestured to the open matchbox in my lap. When had that happened? It didn't matter. It took barely any effort to move one with my mind over the herb bowl. The match hovered exactly where I directed it to go. What was it Bea had said? Right. Kindle the match and herbs with my spark and focus on evil Dan. No problem.

My magical spark jumped at the mere thought of using it, instantly lighting the match. I guided it carefully into the bowl and coaxed the herbs into a burn, using both the flame and my magic. The mixture went up in a whoosh of fire. I stared into it, imagining Dan's features as he'd stumbled toward me with the blue potion.

Nothing changed.

I focused deeper, seeking his image, and let myself experience all the fear and hatred I'd felt in his apartment. I was so absorbed, I almost missed Gwen's tiny shudder. The white, flickering flames started to fade, and I began to lose confidence, convinced I'd failed.

Then, as the herbs turned to ash, a mist rose from the smoke and formed a loose ball. The matter split in half. One took the shape of Dan's smiling face. The other folded in on itself, reshaped into a vague, unrecognizable form, and twisted, only to refold in on itself again. The ball repeated the process a number of times. It wasn't until Bea tightened her grip on my hand that I looked in her direction. The expression frozen on her face was one of outright dismay.

I peered at the fumbling mist, trying to make out what she saw. The shape took on a slightly solid form, and for a minute, I thought I might be able to make out a slender face with long, full locks of hair, but it shifted again. The image that materialized made me gasp in shock. "How is this possible?"

Tears rimmed Bea's eyes. "She's fallen. I can't believe it. Lailah's fallen."

"Lailah?" What was she talking about? "What does Lailah have to do with Meri?"

Bea reached up and wiped the tears cascading down her cheeks. "Meri?"

"Yeah, the evil demon trapped in the third portrait." I nodded to the now-solid form in front of me. "The image is identical. Right down to her skeletal face. You haven't seen it yet, so I guess that explains why you don't recognize her."

Bea's face scrunched up in confusion. "What are you talking about? All I see is an image of your friend Dan, and Lailah hovering beside him."

I turned to Gwen. "What do you see?"

She shook her head. "Just mist."

A cackling, ominous laugh filled the room. I was so caught off-guard that it took me a moment to realize it was coming from Meri. Her eyes locked on mine, and I almost thought I could see right into her soul. A vague image of decayed blackness flashed in my brain. I would have physically recoiled if I could, but my body seemed locked in place. Her cackle faded then cut off abruptly when both images vanished.

Chapter 17

Kane only lived two blocks from Kat's apartment. We remained silent during the brisk walk to his house, and I was grateful for a moment to think. Bea had seen one thing and I'd seen another. It's not that she didn't believe me; she just didn't know what to think. Had Lailah really fallen?

I didn't think so. The evil in my vision of Meri had been decayed. Wouldn't it take a while for Lailah's soul to reach such a state? I'd said as much to Bea, but she'd shaken her head and remained silent, locked in her own thoughts.

When we reached the outside of Kane's shotgun double home, I glanced up at the ornate Victorian scrollwork brackets and flashed back to the first time Kane had brought me there. It had been our first date, and the first time I'd known he loved me. He hadn't said it, of course, but one can't hide something like that from an empath. It had been obvious right up until his emotions had become hidden from me.

I unlocked the door and held it open for my friends. Standing there, I almost expected to hear his familiar greeting from the kitchen. I took a deep breath and swallowed the emotion bubbling up from my chest. Breaking down wouldn't help anyone.

"Have a seat," I said when I joined them in the living room. "I need to text Pyper."

I'd forgotten to update her on our side trip to Kat's. Considering she hadn't called demanding to know where we were, I assumed she was still at the hospital. A minute didn't even go by before Pyper replied. She and Ian were on their way.

"I don't understand why you would see one thing and I would see another," Bea said when I sat across from her in Kane's overstuffed, beige armchair.

"But you both saw Dan, right?" Kat asked.

"Yes," we agreed.

"Could you sense anything from her?" I asked. "Like her soul or any thoughts?"

"No." Bea wrung her hands in her lap.

"I did." I got up and paced. "The being I encountered had a deep-seated evil. An evil that had grown with time. If Lailah has fallen, I don't think her soul has had enough time to wither into such an awful state. Nothing about what I experienced suggested it could be Lailah."

"I hope you're right." Bea stared into her lap and suddenly stilled her wringing hands, clenching them into fists at her side. She stood. "Let's get started."

For a second, I thought about waiting for Pyper and Ian, but quickly dismissed the idea. Finding Kane was a lot more important. I picked up my pumpkin loaf concoction, which had started to separate. Thin cracks widened as I stared at it. "Do we form another circle?"

"Not yet. This one requires heat first." Bea took off toward the back of the house, where the kitchen was located.

I hoped that meant we could use the stove and wouldn't have to wrestle up a caldron or use the fireplace.

Gwen fell in step beside me. She touched my arm lightly. "I need to talk to you," she said with an undercurrent of urgency.

Kat gave me a wary glance.

I tilted my head toward the kitchen, indicating she should go ahead.

"What's wrong?" I asked my aunt.

She pulled me back into the living room. The mixture split entirely down the center and slumped on two sides of the bowl. I grimaced and hoped that wasn't going to be an issue.

"I had a vision, but I don't know what it means," Gwen whispered.

I set the bowl aside and gave her my full attention. "Tell me."

"While you were conjuring Dan and...whoever it was that appeared, I got a flash. I can't say where it was because there wasn't anything to identify the location, other than fog or a light mist. I don't know. It was just gray. But I did see Dan, Kane, Lailah, and a woman I didn't recognize."

"What did she look like?"

"Long, black, straight hair, and lots of body like one of those Cover Girl models. Thin, but not skinny. Angular face. She was striking. But it was her eyes..." She shivered. "They were solid black and empty of all emotions."

"Creepy. What was she doing?"

"Nothing, actually. Just watching." Gwen cupped her hand over the side of her mouth to keep anyone from overhearing. "Someone else was there, too." She pointed toward the kitchen and mouthed, *Bea*.

Breath caught in my lungs, and then my heart almost burst with joy. That meant at some point we'd find Kane. Gwen had seen Bea with Kane and Lailah and Dan. Hope I'd been keeping buried rose in my chest. "This is great news."

Gwen's face transformed from worried to something close to panic. "Shhh. You don't understand. Bea was engaged in a magical battle with the black-eyed woman. And she was winning, but..." She clamped down tight on my hand.

"Jade?" Bea called from the kitchen.

"Coming," I replied. "But what?" I asked Gwen, an ominous warning rising in my gut.

"She had the same empty black eyes as the other woman, and everything about her seemed off. Like she was possessed."

"Black magic," I whispered. "Isn't that what happens when a witch invites evil forces?" I'd never actually seen it happen before. My mother had been an earth witch. Their magic was mostly benign: protection spells, intention spells, blessings of seasons, rebirths, and harvests. That sort of thing. Black magic, I'd been told, eats away at the soul. I'd never met a black-magic user, but in all the stories, they each had the same thing in common—black eyes of evil.

"Maybe," Gwen said with a quiver. "It's not something I know much about. I don't know what to think."

"We have to tell her." I tried to pull my hand out of her grasp, but she tightened her hold on it.

"No! The first rule of a seer is to keep the visions to yourself. Interfering is not permitted."

"That's ridiculous." This time I managed to escape her grasp and picked up my withering, cracked potion-loaf. "Would you not tell me if I was headed into something dangerous?"

Gwen's face hardened. A swift current of her stubbornness almost made me stumble. "No, Jade. I wouldn't. When have I ever told you about my visions before they happened?"

Never. Not once. Except on the rare occasion she went into a trance and spoke aloud. But she never remembered those. "Have any of them ever shown me in true danger?"

Strain flashed over her features briefly. Her expression cleared and she nodded.

"Jade!" Bea called impatiently.

I gave Gwen one last impatient look.

"Please don't say anything. Trust I have my reasons," Gwen pleaded as I walked to the kitchen.

"What happened to your potion?" Bea asked, appalled.

"I think it needed to be refrigerated." I set in on the counter next to her.

"Possibly," Bea agreed. "What took you so long?"

Gwen shot me a warning look from the doorway.

"Gwen was giving me a pep talk." I'd honor her request until I got a chance to talk to her again. The last thing we needed was for Bea to go Wicked Witch of the South on us. I'd do whatever it took to spare her.

Gwen smiled in Bea's direction.

"You poor dear." Bea put an arm around my waist. "I can't imagine how difficult this has to be for you. But don't worry. We'll find him."

I prayed she was right. I glanced at the copper bowl. "What are we doing with that?"

Bea's demeanor quickly shifted from nurturing mother to serious witch practitioner. "Does your friend have any copper sauce pots?"

I shrugged and bent to dig around in his cabinets. After moving a half a dozen stainless steel pots and pans, I came up shaking my head. "Doesn't look like it."

"That's fine. Grab the biggest one you can find. We'll use it like a double boiler." Bea turned on the stove while I filled a stainless steel pot with hot water. "This is probably better for the integrity of the potion, anyway." She took the pot from me and placed it on the stove. "At this point, your potion can use all the help it can get."

"What's the goal here?" I wrinkled my nose at the globby mess.

"It needs to solidify." She handed me a wooden spoon. "When it starts melting, stir it until it's smooth. As you did earlier, keep focused on finding Kane. The intentions will help when you invoke it."

Bea excused herself to the restroom. I was about to question Gwen again when a loud knock sounded at the door, followed by Pyper and Ian clattering in.

"What's going on?" Pyper demanded after hobbling in with one crutch. She'd changed into a black T-shirt, black skirt, and black knee high stockings, matching Ian's signature look.

"How's your leg?" I asked.

"Stitched and ready to go." She pulled up on her skirt, revealing the white gauze bandage. "What are you doing about Kane?"

"We—"

Kat cut me off. "You need to focus. I'll fill them in." She rose from her seat at the kitchen bar and herded everyone back into the living room.

I scolded myself for the slight pang of irritation. Kat was right. I had a job to do. I hated not being part of the conversation. I wanted to assure Pyper we'd find Kane. She was tougher than most. But I knew she considered Kane family. Her only family. Losing him would devastate her just as much as it would me. And Ian always had an interesting perspective to add.

"You're not concentrating," Bea said, startling me. "Stop worrying about your friends. Kane is the important one right now."

I glanced over my shoulder. "Right. Sorry."

She didn't say anything else. I put all my worries aside and focused on Kane. I envisioned embracing his emotions and letting our connection be my guide. In no time, the previously disgusting pumpkin blob turned into a cider-colored liquid.

Bea appeared by my side, making me jump. I'd been so focused I'd forgotten all about her. "Good. It's ready. I'll be right back." She headed back into the living room and, a moment later, reappeared with a hobbling Pyper in tow. "She'll be the third one in our circle this time. She's the closest to Kane, right?"

We both nodded.

"That's what I thought." Once again, Bea lowered herself, taking a seat right on the tiled kitchen floor.

"Here?" I asked.

"Yes. Place the pot on the tile." She gestured in front of her.

I did as she asked and helped Pyper to the floor. She sat next to me, her leg angled awkwardly in my direction.

"This is a locator spell. Unlike the one earlier, we—" Bea indicated her and Pyper, "—won't see anything. If all goes well, you'll find him in a dream state."

Pyper stifled a snort.

"Fitting for a dreamwalker," I said.

"Indeed." Bea reached out her hands and we formed the circle. "After the incantation, infuse the liquid with your magic then take a drink. It will cause you to go into a semi-conscious state and you should be able to find Kane."

I stuck my tongue out in a gagging motion. She wanted me to drink the pumpkin loaf? Gross.

Bea ignored my immature facial expression and started her incantation. It was very similar to the one we'd used at Kat's. Only this time I didn't need to light it on fire. That was good. I didn't want to become a fire-eater on top of everything else.

My power flowed as easily as it had before. With the liquid shimmering gold, I brought the bowl to my lips. It took all my willpower to not spit the bitter, dirt-tasting silt back in the pot, and I forced it down in one gulp.

Just as I expected, my gag reflex kicked in. I clamped my mouth shut and swallowed again, determined to keep it down.

My body went limp against the kitchen cabinets. The surreal sensation of not having control over my limbs sent a thread of panic to my brain. But before I could react, a dreamy bliss clouded my mind. I floated effortlessly, content to think of nothing and relax. I'd never taken drugs before, but I imagined it must be similar. Having nothing to care about sure was appealing.

Wait, that wasn't right. I had something—no, someone— very important to care about. To think about.

Kane, I shouted with my mind.

To my surprise, I instantly locked in on his unique emotional signature.

Pain. Kane was in physical pain. It echoed in my limbs. My wrists burned, and my thigh pulsed with a dull ache. I pressed my awareness toward the source and the closer I got, the more the wounds screamed. I saw nothing but a gray sheet of mist. But it didn't matter. Kane's agony beckoned to me. I welcomed the sensation and pressed harder.

It was no surprise when his anger and frustration burst through. But it was so strong the combination of his wounds and his mental state almost paralyzed me. I pulled my energy back just a touch and conjured up every bit of love I harbored for him. When I sought him again, instead of just seeking him, I pushed that love forcibly in his direction.

A thread of recognition materialized through Kane's frustration. My body warmed with the connection I'd been missing the last few days. Something inside me strengthened. All the crazy doubts and suspicion disappeared. He was here somewhere, and he knew I was searching for him.

Kane.

A faint trace of Kane's voice returned my call. *Jade.*

Where are you?

My question went unanswered. Damn it! I had the odd notion I was circling his pain even though I'd stopped moving in this strange world.

Kane? I tried again.

Nothing. I knew he was here. Why couldn't I find him? We'd communicated like this once before. I'd been in another dimension, and Kane had found me while dreamwalking. Was that it? Had he been dreaming?

I pressed harder, searching for him. The harder I tried, the farther away he became. Soon, all his pain vanished. The only thing left was a weak, almost undetectable, thread of our connection. Was he unconscious?

With a start, I woke back in Kane's kitchen. The light stung my eyes and I blinked.

"Where is he?" Pyper demanded.

My mouth opened, but I shut it. I'd been forming a theory. If only I could remember it.

"You found him, right?" she tried again.

I held my hand up to stop her interrogation. "Give me a minute." I'd been in a pseudo-dream state. Had Kane? Is that why I'd almost been able to talk to him? Had he awakened when he'd felt my probe? Or maybe he'd passed out from all the agony. There was no way to tell. There was one thing I was sure of, though.

"He's in another dimension," I blurted.

No one said anything. I looked up to find each of them staring at me with a puzzled expression. "What?"

"We heard him," Pyper said.

"Huh?"

"We heard Kane say your name."

I turned to her, full of hope. "Did he say anything else?"

She shook her head. "What did you hear?"

I shifted and tried to stand, but my legs wouldn't cooperate. I slid back down on the floor and rested my head against a drawer. "I called to him and he called back. But after that, I lost him."

Footsteps shuffled over the tile. Ian stopped in front of me and offered me a hand.

"I don't think I can walk." I glanced at Bea. "Is this normal?"

She frowned. "The spell uses a lot of energy, but it shouldn't wipe you out that much."

My aunt's harsh voice came from across the room. "She performed two advanced spells. Didn't you think it would drain her? It's not like she has a tolerance for magic."

"Gwen?" I shifted in her direction and caught a glimpse of her angry expression before she turned away.

"I'm worried, is all," she said to the wall. "You haven't been schooled. You don't know what's dangerous and what isn't."

"I'm right here." Bea sounded offended. "Do you really think I'd put her in harm's way?"

Gwen jumped up. "How do I know? I barely know you. And so far, you've used my niece to heal yourself. Twice, I might add. And now you have her working spells that are conjuring evil."

Bea stood and matched Gwen toe to toe. "I haven't forced Jade to do anything. I'm here to help her, just as I was when she got herself trapped by an evil ghost. She's a grown woman. If you hadn't coddled her, she likely wouldn't be in the position she is now."

"Hey," I interjected from the floor. "What's that supposed to mean?"

Bea took a step back and shot me an apologetic glance. "Sorry. I only meant if you'd been better prepared, we could fight this together instead of me just instructing. My frustration got the better of me. Forgive me."

Gwen looked ready to pounce, but she, too, took a step back.

"Gwen," I said. When she finally met my eyes, I sent her a twisted smile. "I'll be fine. I think I just need to rest."

She gave me a short nod before retreating out of the room.

I stifled a sigh and looked up. "Ian, can you help me to the bedroom?"

His lips quirked into a teasing smile. "Now there's a request I can hardly refuse."

Pyper shot him a derisive look.

"What?" Ian asked once he had me supported in his arms. He was surprisingly strong, despite his thin build. Through his touch, I sensed a blossom of something close to love tingling through him, and it wasn't aimed at me.

"You're lucky Kane isn't here and that I can't reach you," Pyper said from the floor.

Ian's expression sobered. Either he felt guilty for flirting with me right in front of Pyper, or he was thinking about what Kane would do if he found me in Ian's arms. Either one was enough to wipe the smile from his face.

"Ian? The bedroom's through there." I pointed to the short hallway off the kitchen.

"Right."

There was something odd and a little bit unsettling about having him carry me to Kane's bedroom. Especially since Kane had carried me there more times than I could count. It was even weirder when Ian laid me on the bed and lost his balance. He slipped and fell right on top of me.

"Cozy," Pyper said from the doorway.

Ian scrambled to his feet and hastily made his way back to the door.

I rolled my eyes. I had zero interest in Ian, and I knew he had zero interest in me. Times change. Pyper was now the object of his affection.

I called her over.

She took a seat on the bed. "What can I do?"

"Stay with me. I have a hunch that once I go to sleep, Kane might find me. The spell state was very much like his dreamwalking. I'd like you to witness if anything unusual happens."

"You got it." She stood, supporting herself with her crutch. "Do you want me to help you get ready for bed?"

I glanced down at my jeans and boots, nodding. "Please."

Ian hovered by the door.

Pyper shot him a look that would have had me scrambling out of the room, but he shifted his feet and said, "Jade, you said you wanted me to measure any paranormal activity. Should I set up some equipment in here, just in case?"

"Fine. Come back in fifteen minutes."

"Sure thing." He disappeared so fast, I wondered if he wasn't the one with supernatural abilities.

Pyper chuckled. "Boys."

"I actually think it's a good idea."

"You're not irritated?" Pyper looked unconvinced.

"No. Any information is good information at this point. I'll take all the help we can get."

She squeezed my hand and pulled me up. My right thigh throbbed. I clutched it and swallowed a groan.

"Are you okay?"

"Yeah. The locator spell left me a gift. I'll be fine."

Twenty minutes later, I was tucked into Kane's bed in a T-shirt and sleeping shorts. Ian returned, toting more gear than I'd ever seen. "What's all that for?"

He sent me a slightly guilty smile. "I want to measure each room tonight, if that's okay with you."

I really couldn't have cared less. "Do whatever you think is necessary."

"Thank you." He spent ten minutes preparing his electrical devices and said good night before he left again.

"I'll be right back," Pyper said from the door.

"Take your time." It wasn't like I was going to fall asleep instantly. With everything that had happened in the last twenty-four hours, I doubted I'd get much sleep at all. Gwen showing up unexpectedly, finding Kane with Lailah, being abducted, Lailah attacking Bea and abducting Kane, Dan being controlled by a demon. It was all too much.

I squeezed my eyes shut, trying to block the day from running like a movie reel in my mind.

Instead, I focused on the thread of love I'd felt from Kane. My body filled with warmth again. Before I knew it, my mind had stilled, and I was floating in that place halfway between consciousness and sleep.

I knew he was there before I saw him. His distinctive emotional signature touched me from behind. I turned in his direction and gasped.

There he was with a stake poking out of his right thigh. His wrists were wrapped in thin metal strips, but he didn't appear to be bound to anything. Beside him, propped up against his other leg, sat Lailah.

Her weak voice broke the silence. "Help us."

Chapter 18

I gaped, and stupidly spoke the first thought that came to mind. "Lailah's in your dreamwalk? Again?"

Kane's pained expression turned wary. "She showed up on her own. I didn't bring her here."

What was wrong with me? I didn't have time to play the jealous girlfriend. I waved a dismissive hand. "Never mind. It's not important. Where are we? Do you know?" I took a moment to glance around what appeared to be a study. Or was it a library? There wasn't any furniture. The pair sat near a blackened stone hearth on a thick, vintage-style oriental rug. Candlelight flickered, illuminating leather-bound books lining the walls. If there'd been enough light, I was sure I'd see a thick layer of dust covering the bookshelves.

"It's a ruin," Lailah said.

"What is?" I moved to Kane's side, inspecting his angry, swollen leg.

"This place." She waved a hand, indicating the room. "But it doesn't exist in our world. It probably did at some point, but doesn't now."

Kane tried to grab my hand, but his slid right through mine. He tried again as I stared in disbelief. "You did pull me into a dreamwalk, right? I didn't manifest some new skill?"

"Yeah, I did."

"It's because we're in some other astral plane. That's what I was trying to tell you about the ruin," Lailah said in a frustrated tone. "Or weren't you listening?"

I glared down at her. "I wasn't talking to you. But now that you have my attention, you can explain how and why you're both here."

"I don't know," she whispered and turned away, burying her face in her hands.

I raised my eyebrows at Kane.

"She says she doesn't remember anything after the fight you two had outside Bea's house. She doesn't remember going in or attacking Bea," he explained.

A muffled sob came from Lailah's prone form.

"You've got to be kidding me?" I asked in disbelief. "Again with the lost memory?"

Kane shook his head and closed his eyes. "You weren't here when I interrogated her. I don't know for sure, but I'm inclined to believe she really doesn't remember."

"Really?" Lailah squeaked through her sniffles.

I crinkled my nose in disgust. "It hardly matters if she remembers or not. The fact is she did attack Bea and then pulled you here. Wherever here is."

"She thinks it's Purgatory." Kane reached out once more, but dropped his hand before it could slide through my shimmery form.

"B...but, you're not dead. It can't be Purgatory." Oh my God. He couldn't be dead, could he? He was dreamwalking me. Crap, ghosts visit people in their dreams. I had firsthand experience.

Lailah straightened. "No, we're not dead. But if I don't get my powers back, we'll never get out of here."

"What happened to your powers?" I asked. She'd gotten them there; she should damn well be able to get them out.

"Bea took them. Remember? You were there."

I stared at her, wanting to beat my translucent head against the wall. "Yes, but you also seemed to get them back. It was your power that brought you two here, and your power that took Kane's memory earlier today. It's there. You just have to find it."

Lailah slumped and stared at the floor.

I stifled a groan, turning back to Kane. "What happened to your leg?"

His frustration rivaled mine as he gritted his teeth. "I have no idea. It was there when I regained consciousness, along with these." He raised his wrists to show me the thin metal wires.

"Someone put them on you." I eyed Lailah, but she looked too helpless and scared.

"Who would that be? No one has been here, and we can't seem to leave the room." His feet twitched, and I knew he wanted to get up and pace.

"I don't know, but—"

Lailah suddenly went rigid. "She's coming."

"Who?" Kane and I asked in unison.

Her body went limp.

Beside her, an image with thick, black hair, tied back in a high ponytail, slowly materialized. The severe style highlighted her thin nose. Her wild black eyes stared right at me. "Come to rescue your loved ones, have you?"

Despite the agony I knew Kane suffered, he managed to stand and move in front of me. "Leave her out of this," he said through gritted teeth.

"Shut up, minion." She jerked her hand through the air and Kane crumbled into a heap at my feet.

I gasped and kneeled, wanting to inspect him for damage, but in the dream state, there wasn't anything I could do. I stood and turned my outrage on the demon. "What do you want, Meri?" I clenched my translucent fists. "What could you possibly get out of this?"

Her black eyes dilated the size of quarters. "You have no idea how long I've been waiting."

"For what?" Panic finally started to filter through my anger. Was she going to take me too? She must have had some control over me, since Kane was knocked out and I was still there.

Her lips turned up in a chilling smile. "The angel. I've been waiting twelve long years to escape my prison. Ingenious, really, what those coven witches did, trapping my spirit in an object. They forgot an angel could free me, though." Meri gazed at Kane. "And she had a connection to a dreamwalker. Such a lowly angel, but combined with your lover, it was enough to rekindle my strength."

"You!" I pointed, outraged. It had been Meri using Lailah to enter his dreams and sexually assault him in his office. "If you hurt him in any way, you'll have me to answer to."

Her high-pitched cold laughter grated on my skin. "I already have, white witch. His pain gives me almost as much strength as the angel does. I look forward to our battle. Imagine what I'll be able to do once I've got you under my control."

I stepped back, trying to put distance between us. If I could only find a way to snap out of the dream state.

Meri turned her gaze to Lailah's prone form. "I was exactly like her once. So weak and eager to do God's work." She shook her head and focused on Kane. "Then I fell in love." Her anger was so strong, I was sure if I'd been in solid form, I'd have been knocked over.

A rotten stench clung to her, something very close to death and decay. "Do you know what happens when angels fall in love?"

I shook my head, trying not to recoil in fear.

"They're forever bound to their mate, even when they fall." She jerked her head in Lailah's direction. "She hasn't suffered such a fate." Her expression softened. She looked almost motherly, in a disturbing, twisted, creature-of-the-night kind of way. "Now she can live her life in Hell in peace."

I shuddered. In Hell? Hadn't Lailah said they were in Purgatory? I shifted toward Kane, fierce protectiveness running through my veins. "If you have a mate, what do you want with mine?"

"Him?" She glanced at him in disgust. "Nothing except his pain. It feeds power. I need to hunt down my cowardly mate who left me here to rot with only a few useless witches." She waved a hand and a mystical window opened. Two women lay prone, unmoving in a stark stone room. I recognized them from the dolls. Priscilla and Felicia.

"What did you do to your sisters?" Loathing shuddered through me.

Fury blasted me. "That damn coven separated their souls from their spirits. Now they're prisoners in time. And utterly useless. It's hard to corrupt a soul that isn't there." She jerked her hand as if to wipe away their images and the scene changed, revealing a woman kneeling in a dirt-floor room. Her emaciated body seemed to sway unsteadily as she chopped a pile of dead leaves. Meri snapped her fingers and the woman's head jerked up.

I stared into jade green eyes. It couldn't be. It just couldn't. But then her face lit with recognition. My heart ached with desperate longing to run to her and wrap her in my arms. To snuggle up against her and smell the sweet wisteria perfume she'd always worn. To somehow grasp a hold of her and drag her back home. But I couldn't do any of that in my useless non-solid form.

"No!" My mother stood and faced the demon, her frail body barely holding her upright as she shook with outrage. "You will not take my daughter. She will never succumb to your soul-eating black magic. She's a white witch. Good. Pure. You can't have her."

"Now, Hope," Meri patronized. "If you'd give in already and work the black spells like an obedient slave, I wouldn't have to drain you so."

My mother ignored the demon and turned to me, but before she could speak, Meri waved her hand again and the window disappeared. "Such a shame she's so reluctant. She'll see it my way soon enough. Especially once I add you to my collection."

"She's been here all this time?" Terror rooted me to the floor. "In Hell?"

"You do have a lot to learn. Don't worry, you'll catch on fast. This is Purgatory." She indicated the room we stood in. "Hope spent the last twelve years here, frozen in time. But I rescued her shortly after the angel freed me. Now she's in Hell. It's only a matter of time before the black magic corrupts her."

Fear squeezed my heart. If she fell to black magic, her soul would eventually be lost. "Open the window," I demanded.

Meri took her time, studying me before she answered. "Give yourself freely, and I'll take you to her."

I glared at her. "What is it you really want?"

"Isn't it obvious? Revenge." Her tone deepened and her eyes turned into black saucers. "I was doing angel work with my mate and ended up getting stuck in Hell. I agonized for weeks, waiting for him to come back for me." A thread of sadness escaped her cold demeanor then quickly shifted to betrayal. "But he never did. You have no idea how hard it is for a powerful angel to resist the call of black magic. It would have freed me in an instant, but we're told so many things. That it will eat our souls. We'll never be the same again. We'll be lost to God."

"What happened?" I whispered.

"He. Never. Came. And I fell. Became a demon." Her eyes returned to their normal size and her tone became conversational. "It wasn't so bad after that. I ceased to care about all the whimpering souls I'd been tasked to look after.

"Everything was going all right," she continued. "I was moving up the demon ranks, gaining power. Then, *bam!* My connection to my mate kicked in, and I knew he was finally coming for me. I embraced his energy, welcoming him here. But then do you know what he did?"

I shook my head, overwhelmed by the demon's confession.

"He helped the coven trap me in limbo. The bastard let them use his connection to me to bind my spirit in some horrific craft project. For *twelve years*," she stressed. "Until your angel found me. You see, only an angel has enough power to awaken a bound demon. Lucky break. Now I'm stronger and coming back full force. Soon enough I'll find that traitorous mate of mine. And you're going to help me."

"Think again, demon," Kane spat. I hadn't noticed him regain consciousness. Now he sat leaning against the hearth. "Jade will never be yours. She'll never give her soul over to you or your black magic. Not as long as I'm around."

Meri whirled in his direction and lashed out.

Kane's eyes locked on mine. *Go*, he mouthed as my world tilted and once again faded into nothing.

Chapter 19

I woke breathing heavily, my heart pounding. Clutching my chest, I squeezed my eyes shut, as if to block out whatever torture Meri was inflicting on Kane.

Don't think about it. Not about Kane and not about Mom. Time to make a plan.

It took a moment for my eyes to adjust to the pale, early morning light. I'd expected Pyper to be lying next to me, but I found her and Ian sleeping in a chair in the corner of the room. Ian was stretched out with his feet on the bed, and Pyper had draped herself over him. If I hadn't been so frantic about my dreamwalk with Kane and Meri, I would have tiptoed out of the room to give them privacy.

Instead, I shouted, "Wake up!"

I was already in the bathroom, pulling on my clothes when I heard a thump on the floor, followed by Ian's voice. "Sorry."

I poked my head back in and found Ian helping a hobbling Pyper to her feet. "What happened?" she asked.

"In the kitchen in five. I'll get Bea and Gwen." I turned to leave.

"They went back to Bea's house last night," Ian said.

"What? Why?"

"They wanted beds." Pyper tugged Ian's hand. "Come on, let's go."

Right before we left, I argued we should grab the portraits on the way to Bea's so I could contact Felicia. My interaction with Meri didn't explain how Dan was involved, but I suspected she'd put a spell on him, too. Lailah had been his angel. She had access. And she'd said every demon needed more minions. Right?

But Pyper and Ian overruled me. They weren't doing anything without Bea's input. Of course, once we woke Kat and filled her in, she'd agreed and I was the odd woman out.

I'd been surprised Gwen had gone home with Bea. She would never have left me after the awful day I'd had, using such a flimsy excuse as needing a bed. Kat would have gladly given her the spare room. She must have been keeping an eye on Bea after what she'd seen in her vision.

A cold chill ran down my spine.

Black magic. Was Bea capable of succumbing to such evil? On some level I knew all witches were, but I'd come to believe, despite Bea's health the last few months and her brush with poison, that she was all-powerful. I'd watched her strip an angel of her power, for God's sake.

Once we arrived at Bea's house, we roused her and Gwen from bed.

"Wake up, sleepyheads," Pyper said from the kitchen. "The kids have some answers."

Gwen wrapped a thin arm around my shoulder. "Did you find him?"

"Sort of."

She gave me a tight hug and whispered in my ear. "I'm glad to see you strong this morning. You scared me yesterday."

I gave her a sad smile. "I scared myself. But this witch needs to deal with being a witch. People are counting on me."

She gave me another tight squeeze. "That's my girl."

I tilted my head toward Bea. "Is she okay?"

"So far, so good."

It didn't take long to fill them in on what had happened. By the time we were done, Bea had turned white. "I did this to her," her voice was barely audible. "I revoked her power. She had no way to fight it."

"You don't know that," Ian soothed. "She'd poisoned you. She probably was already compromised."

"You did what you had to do," I said, not knowing if that was true. What did I know about coven protocol? I'd shunned the Idaho witches.

Bea gave us a half-hearted nod then straightened. "I need to see this portrait."

"I told you—"

Pyper's glare cut me off, and I swallowed the rest of the sentence poised on my tongue.

Bea stood. "Let's go."

Pyper pulled to a stop in front of The Grind. I cringed, remembering I was supposed to work that morning. "Did you find someone to cover for me?"

"Holly. Don't worry. She's got it covered," Pyper said.

"That's good," I said, relieved. Holly was the assistant manager and a college student. She could use the extra money.

Pyper turned to the backseat and handed the keys to Ian. Her face transformed into a sultry pout. "Would you mind parking it for me? I told Bea she could park in my space around back. You wouldn't want all of us to get soaked, would you?" On the way from Bea's, the skies had opened up into a steady rain storm.

Ian didn't even hesitate. "You got it."

He waited for us to find refuge under Wicked's balcony before he quickly moved to the driver's seat and sped off. I noted the fresh rain had already washed away the rotten orange smell that usually lingered on Bourbon Street after a large street party. Being so close to Halloween meant the crowds had been in full swing.

Pyper pulled her keys out and went to work on the numerous locks on the club's front door.

"Why are we going in there?" I stared longingly at The Grind, wishing for a hot chai latte.

"Kane locked them in the storage room, remember?" She disappeared inside. I was about to follow when a grip on my arm made me jump back. The door slammed closed with a thunk. I lashed out with my other arm, but only found air when my attacker ducked.

"Whoa!" Holly cried, holding her hands up in a defensive position. "Sorry. I didn't mean to startle you."

"Jesus. What are you doing scaring me like that?"

"I didn't mean to. I called your name, but I guess you didn't hear me over the rain and the racket." She glared at a group of giggling twenty-somethings stumbling into the café. They obviously hadn't gone to bed yet after a night of partying on Bourbon Street.

I gave her a sympathetic look and hoped none of them lost their pastries on the café floor. It happened at least once a month. "Sorry for bailing this morning," I blurted. "I'd help if I could, but we're having a sort of emergency. So unless it's important, I really need to run."

"I know, sorry, but there's someone who's been waiting for you. He's been ranting kind of crazy about that friend of yours, Lailah. Plus, he's insistent he has information for you about Kane." She pointed over her shoulder. "He's inside."

Someone shifted, unblocking my view, and my whole body tensed at the sight of Dan.

Holly apparently noticed. "Or I can call nine-one-one."

I quickly shook my head when I saw her fingertips poised over the screen of her phone. "I know him. How long has he been in there?"

"Since we opened." She touched my arm. "Are you sure you're okay?"

"Yeah," I breathed. "It's fine. You should go back inside."

She gave me one last questioning look before reluctantly heading back into The Grind.

Shortly after, Dan appeared on the sidewalk. The nausea I always experienced around him came on strong, though I wasn't sure if it was due to my normal physical reaction or the high anxiety the sight of him caused.

He carefully worked his way through the small crowd of girls hovering together to stay dry. His movements were stiff and unnatural. Oh, Lord. He was still being controlled by a witch...or demon.

I backed up to the entrance of Wicked and grabbed the door handle. Locked. Damn it! Where was Pyper? Hadn't she noticed I wasn't with her?

Dan stopped a good five feet from where I stood. I would have breathed a sigh of relief if I didn't think I'd lose the little bit of food gurgling in my stomach. "What do you know about Kane?" I demanded.

He closed his eyes for a moment. When he opened them, his intense focus made me try to take a step back. Unfortunately I was already pressed against the door. Dan's voice matched his unnatural jerky gait. "He's lost. She's taken him to the other-world. You can't get him back."

My eyes narrowed as I held his gaze. "Watch me."

"She's too powerful. Save yourself." He blinked rapidly. Then his posture shifted as muscles relaxed and suddenly tensed again. He glanced around as if to orient himself. His gaze landed once again on me, and recognition lit his face. When he spoke, his voice was tense, though familiar. "Jade, please. I beg you, don't get involved. You can't help him. None of us can."

He seemed so normal I reached out to grab his arm, but pulled back at the last second. Instead, I leaned in. "What's going on? What happened to you?"

"I..." His body started to go rigid again. "No time. It's a trap. Stay away. Save yourself." A tremor ran the length of his body. "Go!" he shouted.

Just then the door pushed open, knocking me into a flooded portion of the street. I fell hard on my knees and scraped my hands on the asphalt. I jumped up, ignoring the pain shooting through my palms, and hobbled with each step.

Dan moved toward me. His face tightened, hatred streaming from his constricted pupils. "You're mine," his disjointed voice croaked out.

"Like hell!" Pyper swung a black baseball bat. She connected with his shoulder, sending him crashing into the middle of the street. She reached over and pulled me into the club. From the doorway, I glimpsed a white SUV barreling toward his unconscious body.

"Stop!" I shouted, but the ominous slamming of the door cut off any hope that my cry would be heard.

The faint squeal of tires skidding, followed by the distinct sound of metal crunching, had me reaching for the door again.

Pyper jumped in front of me, blocking my way. "Stay here. I'll send Ian to check."

"Check what?" Ian appeared from the back of the club with Kat at his side.

"We heard a crash out front. Could you please check to see if everyone is all right?"

Ian quickened his pace. "Of course."

"I'll help," Kat said.

I grabbed her hand. "It's Dan."

Her breath hitched, and suddenly she was running.

"Be careful. He's was fighting it, but he's still under a spell," I called after her.

"Shit," Ian said under his breath and raced outside.

Glaring at Pyper standing guard over the door, I sat in the nearest chair and inspected the damage to my burning hands. They needed to be cleaned. I moved behind the bar to run them under the tap. "If he got hit by that car, there's no way he could have the energy to hurt me," I said, not looking at her.

"If he was hit. What if he wasn't?"

I whirled. "Then we just sent my best friend and the guy you're in love with to battle with a possessed madman."

"I'm not…" Her mouth hung open. She seemed to realize it and clamped her lips together. "I'm not in love with Ian."

"Whatever you say." I turned back around and fished the first aid kit out from under the counter.

"Why would you say that?"

I pinned her with a you've-got-to-be-kidding-me look. "Empath, remember? Every time you even so much as look at him, it radiates from you."

"But…" She sank into one of the blue-velvet chairs near the stage.

When my hands were sufficiently bandaged, I gave her my full attention. Her face had gone white, and the chair she sat in wobbled with each nervous tap of her foot.

"Oh," I breathed. "You didn't know."

She shook her head and in a small voice asked, "Does he feel the same?"

Ah, crap. It was one thing to tell her what I felt from her. It was entirely another to talk about Ian's private emotions. She'd have to wait until he was ready to tell her he was falling for her. "I'm sorry—"

Her hopeful face crumbled.

"No, no, no. I was going to say I'm sorry, it isn't something I think we should be talking about."

"You brought it up," she fired back.

I moved to sit next to her. "I know, and I shouldn't have said anything. I lashed out at you when you were only trying to protect me." I gingerly took her hand. "It's Ian's place to tell you how he feels. It's not right for me to betray what I shouldn't know in the first place."

She bowed her head. "You're right. Sorry I asked. I'd kill you if you told him what you know about me."

"Don't I know it?" Smiling, I squeezed her hand and winced. "I will say he likes you, a lot. And that much is obvious to the casual observer. So don't stress. I'm sure once this crisis has settled and we get Kane—" my throat closed on his name, "—home, you'll have time to figure it out."

"Yeah. Now isn't the time." She sat with her feet spread and knees angled together, elbows propped on her thighs. She reminded me of a pensive five-year-old. It took all my willpower to not wrap her in a comforting hug. She suddenly popped up out of her chair. "Come on."

"Where?" I followed her.

"To help your best friend and the man I love. Good God. I've never said that before." She pulled the heavy door open once again and glanced back at me. "It has a nice ring to it."

I smiled, but felt a tug at my heart for when Kat found out.

A small crowd had formed out front in the steady rain. I craned my neck, barely glimpsing a flash of red curly hair. "Kat," I called.

"Over here, Jade. Hurry."

I stumbled past the spectators and found Kat by Dan's side, clutching his limp hand. A blood-soaked, white towel was wrapped around his left arm and shoulder. Another one lay folded over his chest, held in place by Kat's hand.

"Oh, no." I clutched my throat with one hand and backed up a few feet.

"Where are you going?" Kat cried, peering at me with tear-filled, red eyes. "The ambulance is taking too long. He needs an energy transfer if he's going to make it."

I froze, rain drops splattering on my face. "You want me to give Dan an energy transfer?"

"Yes." Frustration streamed off her in massive waves. "Damn it, Jade. He's going to die. Look at him."

And I did, taking in everything I'd missed during my initial assessment. One leg was twisted, lying out at an angle. Blood had pooled around his limp, pasty body. Kat's hand on his chest barely rose as he sucked in extremely shallow breaths. The white SUV was nowhere to be found.

Her total and utter panic washed over me, making my stomach turn. Worse would happen if I invaded Dan's energy. "I don't know—"

"I. Don't. Care." Her voice went hard and cold. "What part of 'he's going to die' do you not understand? Use my energy or whatever you did with Ian and Bea. But do not sit there and let our friend go."

I was about to say I didn't know if I could, but not trying simply wasn't an option. Dan had saved both of us once and we owed him a life-debt. Not to mention, right before he'd been hit, he'd tried to warn me, maybe even save me again, despite being under some black spell.

"You're right." I grabbed her hand and let her clean energy wash through me. We'd done this before, but then it had been me who'd needed her help. I threaded as much of her energy as I could hold. Her grip weakened in mine, and I shot her a worried glance.

She waved the attention away, clearly stressed I'd lost focus.

My body pulsed with the transfer. If it had been anyone else but Dan, I was certain I could have fed her powerful essence into the person without any problem. Unfortunately, I'd developed a sort of emotional energy allergy when it came to him. As soon as I touched him, heat singed my palm. The pain and instinct to recoil threatened my ability to concentrate.

No. I would do what was right.

Kat's unfaltering energy bubbled up. I reached for my magical spark buried deep inside. It came to life as if it had been waiting for my call. My body tingled; all my pain slipped away. A girl could get used to that kind of power.

I closed my eyes and imagined Kat's energy feeding into him. It moved from my core down my arm, sparking in bursts of micro spasms along my skin. It moved quickly, building momentum as it traveled.

I tilted my head back in wonder, enjoying the rush, basking in it even, all the while coaxing it to Dan. The wave hit my fingertips and, instead of the magic pouring into him, it siphoned off into the ether.

Redoubling my effort, I used every ounce of strength I had to send the magic-infused energy into him. Still, the magic seemed to bounce right off him. The energy didn't, though. Soon, color returned to Dan's slack face and his weakened pulse beat stronger under my grasp.

His eyes started to flutter open. Kat's hand went limp in mine. I glanced at her right as her eyes rolled into the back of her head. She fell, her wet rain jacket brushing against me.

I abandoned my treatment on Dan and grasped her shoulders. "Kat? Are you okay? Are you awake?"

A tiny moan escaped her lips. "Jade? Where are we?"

"In the street. Helping Dan."

"Dan? What happened to him?"

"He had an accident. You don't remember?"

"Nuh-uh. Is he okay?" Her head rolled and she slumped back into my arms.

"Son of a...crud," I grumbled.

"You went too far," Bea said from behind me. "Transferring too much of your own essence is one thing, but stealing it from other people is dangerous and reckless."

Her condescending tone made my ire rise. "Steal? I didn't steal anything. She asked me to send him her energy. In fact, she demanded it. Yes, I went too far, but that was a mistake."

Ian appeared beside Bea. "We know, Jade. We heard everything." He crouched down and gently lifted Kat from my arms. "I'll take her to your apartment." He followed Pyper toward the courtyard and the side door of the building.

"Excuse me, miss. We've got it from here." A stocky, black-haired EMT settled next to Dan and went to work checking his vital signs.

Dan's head turned in my direction. His eyes locked on mine, full of something I didn't recognize. Relief? No. It was wonder. I gazed back, unable to imagine what a near-death experience would be like. No doubt he was just happy to be alive.

Another EMT arrived and nudged me out of the way. I stood on extremely wobbly legs. My knees no longer hurt, but I hardly had the energy to stand.

Bea looped her arm around my waist. "You never learn."

"What now?" Her accusation still rankled. If I hadn't physically needed her help to get back inside, where it was warm and dry, I would have stalked off. Instead, I leaned on her as we inched our way toward my courtyard.

"You drained Kat, and when you couldn't control your magic, you sent him not only Kat's energy, but yours as well."

"No, I..." The physical exhaustion. The irritation. The fact that I'd brought Dan from the brink of death with zero magic. I rubbed my forehead, stifling a frustrated scream. "I thought I'd figured it out. I don't have any trouble accessing my magic. In fact, it's still sparking inside me. Why the hell can't I control it?"

My outburst made me dizzy. I paused and leaned against the brick wall beside the entry to my building.

Her eyebrows rose the way a teacher's does when they have a point to make. "You didn't count on competing with black magic."

Adrenaline spiked through my limbs. I straightened and glanced around.

"Not here." She chuckled. "In Dan. He's still under a black spell."

Anger spiked. "But you keep saying I'm a white witch. What's the big deal if I can't even negate the effects of a black curse?"

She pursed her lips and opened the door for me. "You think on that for a moment while we navigate your building."

I took one look at the three narrow flights of stairs and desperately wished Ian would materialize and carry me as well. Kane would love that.

Kane.

We had to figure out a way to somehow bring him, Lailah, and my mother back. With determination, I put one foot in front of the other and slowly climbed one step at a time. When I got to the first landing, I stopped and gasped for air until I could speak. "Can any witch use black magic?"

"Nooo." She eyed me cautiously.

"It takes a powerful one, right?"

"Yes."

"And the powerful ones turn to black magic because...?"

The light went on above Bea's head. "Now you're asking the right questions."

A few moments of silence ticked by. "But you're not going to answer them?"

"I can't. Only the witch in question can tell you that."

I couldn't imagine a worse time for a classroom-style question-and-answer session. I turned and worked my way up another flight of stairs, then the other. By the time we reached my door, I was trembling. Before going inside, I turned to her and forced out, "Witches only use black magic when they think they need more power."

"That's true for some witches."

"And the others?"

"They're just evil."

"But the fact remains, black magic is more powerful than white magic, right?"

"It can be."

"Bea!"

All her schoolmarm pretense vanished. She turned serious eyes on me. "Yes. Black magic is very powerful. Many witches turn to it when they've exhausted all other options. It's wrong, and they almost never recover from it. Once they tap into it, they can't help it. They lose themselves."

Despite the seriousness of her tone, all I could think about was Darth Vader and wondered if some poor black arts witch had been the inspiration for his character.

Once you go black, you never go back.

"Jade, are you listening?"

"Yes." I nodded, biting my lip to keep the snicker from forming.

"The demon controlling Dan is extremely powerful. I seriously doubt you can best her with your white magic."

"What are you suggesting? That I take up the dark arts?"

She stepped back as if I'd slapped her. "Goddess, no. I only meant you'll need help."

"And where would we find that?"

The door opened just as Bea said, "The coven."

I didn't respond, but only because I had an apartment full of people. People I didn't know, who had light and airy energy, just like mine. Witch's energy.

Chapter 20

Duke bounded up to me, his tongue lolling out the side of his mouth. If he'd been alive, his paws would have tapped out a little dance on the wood floors. Instead, he ran silently around me as I took in the scene.

There were at least eight witches in my tiny one-room apartment and, if I wasn't mistaken, two more on the balcony. I could hear laughter wafting in from the open windows.

"Jade, there you are." Kat's voice rose over the chatter. "Get over here."

I sent Bea a glare. Then I maneuvered my way through the women who could only be her coven members. Duke followed, sniffing my black sneakers as I walked. I turned my glare on him and mouthed, *Stop it.*

Kat gripped my arm when I sat on the side of my bed next to her. "Is he okay? Did it work?"

"Yeah. I think he'll be all right, at least physically."

"But he's alive." She sank back down on my pillow with a relieved sigh. A second later, she smiled. "I knew you could do it."

"What happened to you?" Ten minutes ago she'd been so drained, I'd feared it would take her weeks to recover. I'd once done to myself exactly what I'd done to her, and I'd suffered horribly. But maybe I hadn't done as much damage as I'd thought.

Kat averted her eyes. Her gaze landed on a tall, blond, male witch near the window. He shifted in her direction as he sent her a gentle smile.

"Still doing okay?" he asked.

She nodded. "Lucien, this is my friend Jade. Jade, Lucien."

I leveled a skeptical look at him and waved a hand in Kat's direction. "You're responsible for this?"

"Jade." Kat scolded in a hushed tone.

He chuckled. "If you're referring to restoring her energy, then yes, I'm primarily responsible. With the help of the coven, of course."

"No one asked for your help."

He shrugged. "Your friend doesn't seem to mind."

"Jade," Kat said again. "Stop."

"She's not aware of the dangers involved in your kind of magic. Stay away from her. We don't need your help."

"Jesus!" Kat jumped off the bed. "Lucien, I'm so sorry. Jade's had a really bad couple of days. Never mind her. Thank you, for everything." She turned to me and practically dragged me out my front door. Duke growled and started barking incessantly.

Good dog. You tell her who's boss. Too bad she couldn't hear him. I was the only one with that lovely privilege.

Duke's high-pitched protests were cut off when she slammed the door on him. Once we were in the hall, Kat turned on me. "What the hell are you doing?"

"Watching out for you."

"By insulting the guy who restored the energy you drained?"

Anger burned through my chest, but I clamped it down and in a small voice said, "I didn't do that on purpose, you know."

The tension drained from her face, replaced by weariness. "Of course I know that. Why are you so mad at him? He only did the same thing for me that you did for Dan."

I leaned against the wall and, a moment later, slid down into a sitting position. "It isn't the magic. It's working with a coven and letting someone you don't know have control over you. It scares me, Kat. Dan is possessed. Kane is gone. Lailah is…well, I don't know what's happening with her."

"And coven magic is how you lost your mom."

"Yeah. What's going to happen next?"

She sat down beside me. "I don't know. But you have to learn to trust people. You can't do everything yourself."

"I trust people. You, Kane, Pyper, Ian, and Gwen. But a coven I've never met? No. I can't risk it."

"You're going to have to," Bea said from my doorway, her arms folded over. "If you fight black magic on your own, you'll lose. Do you know what a coven does?"

"Of course I do," I said, offended. "They provide a collective of power for the leader to draw on."

"How is that different from what you did when you used Ian's energy to help me, or Kat's to help Dan?"

"Because I trust all of you." Damn it, weren't they listening?

"You trust me?" Bea asked with a tilt of her head.

I hesitated.

"That's what I thought. It's why we never get anywhere with your lessons and why you only seem to produce magic when you're faced with extreme situations. Figure it out, Jade. Kane is waiting." She disappeared back into my apartment.

I stood. "Let's go."

"What?" Kat's face scrunched up in confusion. "But you have an apartment full of witches waiting to help you. Help you desperately need."

"They're waiting to help Bea. She's their leader. I need to find Pyper. Any idea where she went?"

She sighed. "She's with Ian in the club."

"Thanks." I got to the top of the stairs and looked back. "Coming?"

Kat glanced at my door then seemed to make up her mind. "Yeah."

The back door to the club was locked as usual. When our knock went unanswered, I fished my key ring out of my pocket and smiled at Kat.

"You have a key?" she asked.

"Pyper gave it to me when I was helping out here a while ago. I forgot to give it back."

Wicked was almost always dark with barely enough light to see where you were headed, but today all the lights were out, making it pitch black. That was weird. The hall lights were always on. "What did you say they were doing down here?" I asked Kat.

"I didn't. They were supposed to be setting up."

I flicked the lights on and stared at her. "Setting up what?"

She held her hands up in defense. "Hey, don't look at me like that. I don't know. I was the dazed chick getting an energy infusion from a hot wizard or male witch, or whatever you call them."

My lips twitched. "A witch. Wizards are...well, never mind. That's a lesson for another day."

"Fine, a witch. The point is, I don't know what they're up to."

"Okay. Got it. Let's go find out."

We'd moved about two feet when a loud crash came from the office, followed by a muffled groan. My pulse took on a life of its own, and a second later, I barged through the office door, only to come to an abrupt stop. "Oh. Sorry."

I backpedaled, but stumbled into Kat, who'd frozen in place behind me. I turned and tried to coax her out, but her eyes went wide as she stared at Ian, lying under Pyper. Her skirt was bunched up around her waist, and Ian's hands were under her shirt.

"Shit." Pyper chuckled. "Busted."

The misery escaping from Kat almost crippled my ability to say or do anything. Not to mention, I was still weak from the episode with Dan. I forced the words out and gave her a slight nudge. "Kat. Move."

Finally she stumbled backwards, back into the club.

"We'll be right out," Pyper called.

"Take your…" The tears in Kat's eyes made me pause. "Um, I mean, okay."

I pulled her toward the bar, and deposited her on a stool. "Sit."

She did as I said, but stared in the direction of the office.

Crap. We so didn't have time for this. I turned on one of the bar lights and grabbed a bottle of water. "Drink this."

"Did you know?" she asked.

"Know what?"

"Jade." There it was again. Her no-nonsense look.

I took the stool next to her. "Yes, but it's not my place to get involved." I wanted to tell her Ian liked her, too, but I suspected only as friends. However, that just seemed cruel to mention at the moment.

"You're supposed to be my friend. You could have warned me." The betrayal wound through her.

"Kat. You *are* my friend. My *best* friend," I added for emphasis. "But so is Ian, and that wouldn't have been fair to him to share what I may or may not know due to my ability. You said he asked you out on a date, but—and this is pure speculation on my part—I think it's possible he thought it was just two friends getting together. Besides, I'm pretty sure Pyper asked him out a few days after he invited you to the jazz club. No one here is trying to hurt you. You have to believe that."

Her gaze moved from the office to me. She took a moment to collect herself, and when she spoke, her voice was cool and controlled. "I believe you. Let's drop it. You have Kane to worry about, and I have Dan."

"We both have Dan," I corrected her.

"Yeah. Okay."

Pyper strode out of the office, redressed, though slightly wrinkled. Ian followed more slowly and when he got close, the blush on his cheeks turned darker.

"What are you so embarrassed about? I was the one caught in my underwear," Pyper said.

"That's nothing new," Kat said under her breath.

I elbowed her in the ribs, shocked Kat would say such a thing. She'd never made an issue of the fact that Pyper had been a stripper.

Pyper turned dark eyes on Kat, and though I was positive she'd heard her, Pyper ignored it. "Sorry, Jade. We were waiting for you and Bea and...I'm sure you understand."

I chose to ignore the whole situation. "The portraits are here?"

"Yes. We separated them and Ian has equipment monitoring each one. He said sometimes darkness helps, so that's why we turned the lights off." Pyper glanced at Kat and frowned.

I followed her gaze and found Kat transfixed, staring into the darkness.

"Kat?" I asked.

She didn't respond, only stood and headed in the direction she'd been fixated on.

"Where are you going?"

"She's calling me." Kat's voice took on a soft, dream-like quality.

I jumped down from my stool and grabbed her arm when I caught up with her. "Who?"

"Her." She pointed to a dark corner of the club.

Was it another ghost? What the hell had Pyper and Ian been thinking, setting up in the club? The place was cursed.

"It's Meri. She wants me." Kat ripped her arm from my grasp and bolted.

"Shit," Pyper said. We stared wide-eyed for a second then ran after her.

Kat had her hands stretched out, almost grasping the frame when I tackled her. "No!" I cried.

We tumbled to the ground, knocking a few chairs over as we went.

"Omph." A whoosh of air exploded from my lungs. I stared up into the shocked face of Pyper. Her gaze flickered past me.

"Kat?" I flipped over and struggled to get into a sitting position. A few feet away, I found her already on her feet, moving toward the portrait once more. "Stop her."

Ian moved in front of her. "Hey, Kat. What's going on?" He tried for a conversational tone, but it came out hurried and stressed.

Kat's jaw tensed. "Move, Ian."

He feigned a hurt expression. "But Kat, we're recording paranormal activity. You don't want to do anything to compromise the results, do you?"

She cocked her head to one side. "If I hadn't just found you rolling around on the floor with one of my friends, that school-boy charm might have worked on me. However, I'm not feeling especially charitable at the moment, so get the hell out of my way."

My mind whirled with what I'd just heard come out of her mouth. In a normal frame of mind, Kat would never have said something like that, no matter how much it hurt to see Ian with another woman.

When Ian didn't move, Kat shoved him out of the way with both hands. I lunged after her, but a second later she gripped the portrait and started screaming.

"Holy fuck." Pyper ducked and covered her ears, trying to block out the piercing sound.

But it wasn't the noise that put fear into my heart. Kat's newly restored energy grew into a bright beacon and just as quickly started to fade. Her unique signature stretched and twisted until it started to morph into something unfamiliar and dark.

Black magic.

"Ian! Get Bea and the other coven members. Run!" I didn't have time to check if he followed my order. All I could do was send every last bit of strength I had into my friend before a demon stole her soul.

Chapter 21

Abruptly, Kat let go and stopped screaming. Instead of retreating in horror as I expected her to, she stood transfixed on Meri.

Was her soul lost? Had I been too late? *Dear God, please, please don't let me lose her, too.* Tentatively, I probed her essence. She seemed to be protected by a shield of some sort, but when I touched her, dark, evil-tainted magic crawled over my fingers.

Meri had gotten to her.

My love for Kat swelled in my chest. I grabbed onto it and started pushing back on the demon's tainted energy.

When nothing happened, I studied Kat. Her catatonic expression sent a chill through my heart. If I could force my way through the blackness, I could help her. Focusing, I reached for my magical spark. But no matter how hard I tried, it wouldn't come. I was empty. Frozen. Stuck in a magical void.

"Damn it, Meri, what could you possibly want from Kat? She doesn't have magic."

The portrait hung on the wall, silent and mocking.

If I touched it, would she communicate? Better to wait for the coven. My energy was already compromised, and I couldn't find my magic. I closed my eyes and prayed I wasn't making the wrong choice.

I sensed the coven before I saw them. Their collective power filled me, rekindling my spark. The combined strength of the group overpowered the imprisoned demon. All of the iciness vanished and my heart swelled with warm, clean white magic. I would have basked in the purity of it if I'd had the chance. Why would anyone choose darkness over the headiness of something so pure?

I stood tall and stretched welcoming arms, abandoning all my reservations about the coven. The group parted and Bea came to stand beside me, a pleased smile warming her face.

Suddenly, the hateful vengeance seemed to lock into me. Not into my power source, but my essence. All my joy vanished, and darkness filled my soul. My magic spark actually seemed to grow and take over, feeding off the evil building inside me.

"Argh!" I cried and tried desperately to focus on my mental glass silo. The walls appeared, but blinked away before I could imagine myself protected inside.

I had no control over anything. The black demon played tug of war with the coven's pure magic, holding me suspended in the middle.

In my limbo, I silently pleaded with Bea to take control of whatever was happening. But to my horror, something seemed to break, and all that pure, lovely white magic flowed from the coven, through me, and toward Meri. It wasn't mine, it was the coven's collective power, and I was only the conduit.

"Stop!" I yelled. "Bea, stop. She's only getting more powerful."

With my words, Meri's hold weakened slightly until Bea commanded the coven to keep feeding her power. Was she insane?

"Please," I cried.

Bea seemed to strengthen her efforts to counter Meri, but it made no difference. The more power the coven fed into me, the more she took. "If we let go now, she'll take you."

The realization of what she'd said sank in, and something broke loose in my heart. I would be lost to the dark side. "If you don't—" I gasped for breath, "—she'll take us all."

I met Bea's gaze and knew my words rang true. She mouthed, *sorry*, and a second later the coven's power vanished. My gaze shifted to Kat. I tried to convey in one look all she'd meant to me as the evil blossomed and morphed into sick, perverted vines that slithered over my limbs.

Bea started to chant in what I thought was Latin. The coven joined her, their voices filling the club.

The vines stopped their assault, almost as if they'd been distracted. Slowly, they started reluctantly retreating, one strand at a time. Soon enough, my familiar spark appeared, untainted. My instincts took over, making my magic explode, expelling the evil from my being. It burst from my center in a large, black cloud.

My knees buckled. Relief flooded through me. The black cloud hovered over me, pulsing with the Latin chant. Silver threads of coven magic wrapped around it, tethering it in place. The chanting picked up pace. It took me a moment to realize they were binding Meri's power. But binding it to what?

In perfect unison, the chanting stopped. Silence loomed as we all stared, transfixed, at the ball of evil levitating in front of me.

Then the silver strands burst, and the ball shot straight at Bea. I braced myself for a magical duel, but she didn't even flinch. The mass hit her with such force it knocked her backwards. She would have crashed to the floor had it not been for Lucien, who caught her.

"Bea!" Somehow in my battered and weakened state, I made my way to her side. The light, pure energy I'd come to expect from her had vanished. It now curdled with rot. I flinched, but held by her side. "Why did you do that?"

She raised her hand as if to cup my cheek, but stopped short of touching me. "For you. You're the future, Jade. Find Kane and Lailah. I'm certain she's a victim in this." She paused and squeezed her eyes shut. She blinked rapidly, and when she met my eyes, I stared into deep black pools.

"Oh, no. Bea," I whispered. "We'll get you back. I promise."

Her head moved in a sad shake. "It's too late. The…" She swallowed. "It's already here. The coven is yours now." She paused and fixed me with her empty, black eyes. "Don't let them down. They need you." She took a ragged breath. "Lucien, do it now."

"You heard her," he said.

My body started to tremble as the terrible realization of what she'd said sank in. The darkness had seized her. And she'd saved me. Again. My breath came in short, shocked gasps as the members formed a circle around us, hands clasped. Each one started whispering another chant. No, not a chant, a song. In perfect harmony, the lullaby rose, and the silver threads once again appeared. They gently wrapped around Bea, her spirit and soul.

She'd commanded Lucien to bind her. Not just her power, but everything that gave her life. Essentially, she was being put to sleep. Only, she wouldn't be dead. She'd be in limbo, exactly like Sleeping Beauty.

A tear rolled unchecked down my cheek. With a spell that powerful, it would take a hell of a lot more than a kiss from a prince to save her. Fear burned through my body. How could we save Bea, Kane, or Lailah without losing anyone else? It seemed impossible. The darkness was too strong.

Lucien broke from the song. He caught my attention and whispered, "We need you to seal the spell."

"Me?" I whispered back.

He nodded, fixing me with one of those determined stares each of them seemed to be so good at producing. "You're our leader now."

Bea's words came back to me. *The coven is yours now. Shit!*

"Jade!" Lucien's harsh demand startled me back into the present.

"Okay." I really had no choice. If we didn't bind Bea, we'd be dealing with two evil beings.

Lucien joined the coven in the lullaby once more. I focused on his voice, letting the spell they wove work its way into all the voids left by the attack. It pulsed in a give-and-take until I was certain all the magical elements of the binding were present.

I'd barely touched the spell with my magic when it spiraled from me, whipping and tightening around Bea. In no time at all, Bea's body became limp. Lucian gently laid her on the floor, cradling her head with his jacket.

I stepped back when the coven closed around her. As a group, they bowed their heads in respect and mourning.

Goosebumps ran up my arms and down my spine. What had Bea done? She'd given her life for me. But why? I was a terrible student. Hadn't learned even a fraction of what I needed to know to be a coven leader. But I didn't have any choice. She'd given me the job. When one leader gives her power to another, you simply cannot say "thanks, but no thanks." It's yours until you give it to someone else.

There was no way I'd betray what she'd done for me by backing down. I owed her my life. If she wanted me to lead, I'd lead. Besides, she'd already made it clear none of them were powerful enough for the job.

Except, that might not be true. I focused on Lucien. His power had been plenty strong when I'd honed in on him. Though, I supposed working with the coven could have strengthened his ability.

She meant for you to have the job.

Right. With that thought, I put all the second-guessing aside. We had loved ones to save.

I moved to Kat's side. "Are you all right?" It was a dumb question. Clearly she wasn't. Her anguish over Bea, mixed with my own, almost brought tears to my eyes again. I blinked them back.

Kat shook her head soundlessly, and her lips quivered.

I wrapped her in my arms. "It's going to be okay. I promise. I'm going to fix this."

"You are?" Ian asked from behind me. "You're going to fix my aunt? How exactly are you going to do that? Just reach inside yourself and force it to happen?" His voice had risen with each word and by the time he'd finished, he'd been shouting at me.

I held my ground and, in a steady, sure voice, promised something I had no business promising. "Before this is over,

I'm going to have Kane, Lailah, and Bea back with us. Whole and untainted."

Ian held my gaze, his eyes full of skepticism. But beneath his angry exterior, fear and pain fought to break through his cold demeanor.

Pyper stepped up beside me, full of determination. "Of course you are. And we'll be right here to do whatever you need us to. Right, Ian?"

Silence.

"I'm in," Kat said, stepping up on my other side. "But only if Dan is included in that vow."

"Of course," I said without hesitation.

"Ian?" Pyper coaxed. "It's not Jade's fault any of this happened."

He closed his eyes and softened his voice. "I know that." When he looked at me again, he sent me a weary look. "I'll help however I can. I just don't want anyone else to get hurt."

"Someone's bound to get hurt," Lucien interjected. "They always do when fighting black magic." He studied me with interest. "You really think you can do that? Bring Bea back?"

"Jade can do anything she sets her mind to," Pyper said.

Her confidence gave me strength. "With the help of the coven, yes, I think we can."

"You're taking the job then?" Lucien glanced at his group, still hovering around Bea.

"Was there ever any question?"

"You're joking, right? After the fit you had earlier when all I did was a simple energy transfer? I thought Bea was exaggerating when she said you were anti-coven. I should have known she was being straight."

"She said that? Anti-coven?" The statement irritated me. It shouldn't have because it was one-hundred percent true.

"She was right."

I nodded and realized I wasn't irritated at the statement. It bothered me she'd talked to someone I didn't even know about it. "Why were you two discussing me at all?"

He gave me a startled look. "I'm…or was…the lead member. You know, the one who's in charge if anything happens to her."

Could this day get any worse? I'd insulted him, caused his coven leader to be magically bound, and taken his job. "Damn, Lucian. I'm sorry. I had no idea. Otherwise I'd never have accepted the job."

"What? No. I don't want it. Besides, you're much better suited."

"Why do you say that?"

"Your power, for one. The amount of magic you used to bind Bea is totally unheard of. It should have taken much more than you used."

"I used the power of the coven. Any one of you could have done it."

"No, Jade. We couldn't. I might have been able to with great effort. But that caress of yours? The light spark? That's rare. Extremely rare. You're more powerful than Bea. I'm certain that's why she sacrificed herself and put you in charge. Bea's an extremely smart woman. She wouldn't leave us in a mess like this with just anyone."

Was he crazy? There was no way I was stronger than Bea. Even if that was true, I had no training. Why would anyone appoint an ignorant witch? Still, Bea had named me coven leader. The position always fell to the one with the most ability. "If my power is as great as you say it is, then maybe she took my place because she wasn't sure if she could bind me."

Lucien shrugged. "Maybe. It's entirely possible. But Bea's never run from a fight. The question is, would you?"

"Not when her friends are involved," Pyper supplied. "She'd do what Bea did and more if it meant saving anyone of us. Now, stop interrogating her and tell me what happened. Why was Kat possessed by that…thing?" She waved a hand at the now-covered Meri portrait. "I was under the impression only magical people were affected by her. For instance, I don't have any magic or special ability and nothing happened to me when I carried the thing in here. But Kat seemed drawn to it. Why?"

"I think I have the answer," Ian said, holding up one of his ghost-hunting devices.

I leaned forward, giving him my full attention. I'd forgotten all about his equipment.

"The EMF detector showed spikes when Kat and Jade spoke. But not when either Pyper or I did." Ian sat and shuffled through a folder. He held up a color-coded graph. "If I had time to formulate the readings, it would look very much like this."

Pyper rolled her eyes. "That means nothing to us. Can you just spell it out?"

"Oh, right. Sorry. This is the graph from when I tested Lailah. See all the spikes here?" He pointed to a wavy, red line. "Each peak was when Lailah spoke. The blue, flat line is when Pyper spoke. The readings I just got would look very much like this, only replace Lailah for Kat."

"How can that be? I don't have magic," Kat said from the chair next to me. "At all."

"But I'd just infused you with some of mine," Lucian said. "Right before you came down here."

I had to bite my tongue to keep from lashing out at him. This was why I went bat-shit crazy earlier. Magic causes awful shit to happen.

"Holy crap. That's freaky." Pyper put her hands on her hips. "Now what?"

I stood. "Time to make a plan."

For the time being, we laid Bea out on my bed. Gwen, who'd stayed quiet through the entire battle, insisted she needed to stay by her side.

"Something tells me I need to be here," she said.

"But she's bound, body and soul. Nothing can touch her in that state, even death," Lucian argued.

"So you've said. But like I already told you, I have intuitive abilities and right now I'm being told I should stay here."

"You don't mess with Gwen when her senses tell her to do something. There's no changing her mind." I gave her a kiss on her cheek. "Call if anything changes."

She grasped my hand. "Be extremely careful. Your mother…"

The familiar ache touched me briefly, but I clamped it down. I didn't have time for that now. I leaned back in and whispered, "With any luck, we'll find her too."

Gwen leaned back and looked like she wanted to scold me, but she only said, "Don't get ahead of yourself."

"I'll do my best."

"That's not what I said."

"I know." I gestured to Lucien. "We'll be at Pyper's until further notice."

He stood and offered his hand. "It's been a pleasure to meet you, Ms. Calhoun."

Gwen took his hand in both of hers. "Likewise, Mr. Boulard."

"Take care of her."

"You do the same," Gwen said, indicating me.

"Deal."

When we got into the hallway, Lucien turned to me. "How powerful of an intuitive is she?"

"Extremely."

"Do we have anything to worry about?"

I paused. "Maybe. But there isn't anything we can do about it. Gwen has her own set of rules she lives by when it comes to visions. She had one about Bea and black magic, but she refused to let me say anything. Lots of times if one interferes, the consequences can become much more grave." I frowned. "I don't know what would have been worse than losing Bea."

"Her death."

I blanched. He had a point. But Bea had believed she wouldn't ever be coming back. Or had she? I shook my head. "Yeah, that would be worse. Anyway, if she says she needs to be there, then she has a good reason. And before you ask, no, I don't know what it is."

"Fair enough."

We walked in silence the rest of the way to Pyper's apartment. What else was there to say?

Pyper's door swung open just as I was about to knock. "There you are," Kat said. "I was on my way to fetch you."

"You could have called," I said, digging in my pocket for my phone.

"You lost it, remember?"

Right. I clamped a hand to my forehead. "Remind me when this is over to check if I have insurance on it."

"It'll be the first thing I do," Kat said with a heavy amount of sarcasm.

Good. That meant she was feeling better.

We joined Ian and Pyper at the table. Someone had ordered a few pizzas and brought bottled water. "Where'd those come from?" I asked.

"One of the girls from the coven figured we needed strength," Ian said.

"She's right." When was the last time I'd eaten? I couldn't even remember. "Eat first, plan second. Hey, where are they— the coven members?" I asked when it dawned on me I hadn't seen them since we'd all been in the club.

"They went down to the café. They're on call when or if you need them."

How weird was that? I had a coven on call. My appetite fled, and I dropped the slice of pizza I'd been holding. So much for eating.

Twenty minutes later, Ian had one of his notebooks out, his head down, scribbling the first lines of The Plan.

Chapter 22

"The first thing we need to do is find a way to free Lailah. Without her, we have no hope of battling the demon," Lucian said, his voice grave.

I sat back with my arms folded over my chest. "This all pretty much started with her. What makes you think she can fight Meri, especially since the demon has been controlling her?"

"Because she's an angel and that's what angels do. They fight demons and protect those susceptible to them." Lucien rose and walked to the long windows behind the table. He leaned against the molding and gazed out into the street. "I think if Lailah had known she was being used, she would've asked for help to fight it. But everything I've heard leads me to believe the demon found a way to possess her without her knowledge."

It would explain the poisoning, and maybe the boyfriend-mauling. "Do you know any other angels?"

Lucien leveled his deep blue gaze in my direction. "Another angel? In New Orleans? You're serious?"

"Uh, yes." I glanced at Ian.

He stopped tapping the tip of his pen on his thigh. "Angels are extremely rare, compared to witches. There's probably not another one in the whole state."

"And we need to rescue her tonight. If we waste the full moon, it will be thirty days and likely too late to save any of them." Lucien abandoned the window and moved into the living room.

Tonight worked for me. Where Lailah was, so was Kane. "Okay, but how do we get to her?"

"The voodoo dolls," Pyper said. "Didn't Felicia say she'd help you find your mom if you freed her?"

"Yes. You're suggesting we go ahead with the ritual to rejoin the souls and spirits to the witches...and demon, stuck in the portraits?"

"That's exactly what we should do." Lucian came back to the table. "Meri has already fallen, so she's permanently lost. But if we give her back her soul, it will temporarily weaken her. Her soul will be restored, making her whole for a short time, before the darkness eats it away for good. It's our best shot."

"What if Felicia won't help us, or can't?" I pushed the pizza away. I was too nervous to eat.

"If we truly can weaken the demon, Lailah should be able to come back on her own, hopefully with Kane in tow."

I stood. "How much time do we have?"

Lucian consulted his watch. "About eight hours."

"Good." I turned to Pyper. "I'm going to use the spare room to take a nap—"

Lucien cut me off. "A nap? But we need to find the binding spell Bea was working on and go over it with the coven. Plus, there are cleansing rituals. You don't have time to waste."

"We'll have to make time. Lailah and Kane have to be warned, and the only way I can do that is with a nap." I cut my gaze to Pyper. "Will you stand guard over me?"

"You got it." She pushed her chair back.

"I'll get Bea's journal and notebook," Ian said to Lucien. "You can go over everything with the coven, and when Jade wakes up, you can fill her in."

"But..."

No one paid attention to Lucien's protest. Pyper and I had just shuffled into the spare room when I heard Kat speak. "Don't worry. She's new to most of this, but she won't let you down."

Pyper and I shared a smile.

A moment later, Kat poked her head in the room. "I'm going to the hospital to check on Dan. I'll call Pyper if there's anything to report."

"Okay." Hopefully Dan was knocked out on some serious painkillers. The last thing I needed was for him to take her hostage. "Be careful."

"You, too." She closed the door with a soft click.

"You mind if I shower before I take watch?" Pyper asked. "I didn't get one this morning and after everything that's happened...well, I need it."

"No problem. I'll be here, trying to unwind." I flopped down on the bed Kane had once used after late nights at the club. It still held a faint trace of his fresh rain scent. I took a deep breath and almost felt as if he could be right next to me. "Soon," I whispered.

By the time Pyper reappeared from her shower, hobbling on her freshly bandaged leg, my eyelids were heavy. I yawned. "If you notice anything life-threatening, wake me up, okay?"

"I'm sure if it's life-threatening, I'll be dragging you from the room." She propped herself up on the other side of the bed.

"Whatever works." I closed my eyes and, within minutes, found myself floating in an empty dream state.

Kane? I cried in my mind.

"I'm here." His voice echoed.

I turned and found him sitting on a wrought iron bench. There wasn't anything else, just the bench and Kane, looking as handsome as he ever did. I glanced at his bare wrists, and then his thigh. He appeared to be as good as new. I raised an eyebrow in question.

He grimaced. "It's an illusion I conjured for this dream. The bindings and stake are still firmly in place, I just didn't want you focusing on them."

For his sake, I let it go. Besides, there wasn't anything I could do. "Where are we?"

"A neutral place, where Lailah can't interrupt us."

I sat next to him on the bench, longing to grasp his hand. Seeing him and not being able to feel him under my fingers was torture. "We need her help."

His eyebrows pinched, matching his confusion brushing my psyche. "What can she do?"

"A demon was controlling her and is feeding off your pain." I glanced at his thigh, now covered in clean jeans. "How's your leg? I know you're not showing me what you're really wearing."

He shrugged. "Not great, but I'm hoping once you bring me home, it will only be a bad memory."

I sent him a weak smile. "You're that confident I can do this?"

"Never any doubt." He leaned in, miming a kiss on my lips.

"We're getting you home tonight. Tell Lailah to be ready. We're going to weaken the demon, and when we do, it'll be her cue to bring you both back."

Kane looked unconvinced. "She's a basket case and keeps going on about how she failed. I don't know if she can do it."

I stood. "She has to. Make her understand. None of this was her fault." As I said the words, I realized I spoke the truth. Bea had told me Lailah was a victim. She was right. "The demon got to her through the portrait. She never saw it coming. But now's her chance. Tell her to keep trying to get back to the coven circle. Lucien says she should be able to, once we work our spell."

He stared up at me from the bench, apprehension and fear for me spinning around him.

"We're doing this, Kane. Tonight. I won't lose you. Not now. Not ever."

"No. You won't." He stood, staring me in the eye. "We'll be ready."

If there was ever a time I needed to hug him, it was right then. Instead, I raised my hand, holding it up in front of me. He mirrored my movement and we stood there, translucent palm to translucent palm. "Until tonight," I said.

"Tonight," he whispered.

By the time I woke up, Lucien and Ian had returned to Pyper's, and someone had lined the voodoo dolls up on the couch.

"They really have souls trapped in them? How did this happen?" Lucien eyed us suspiciously.

I shrugged, a little offended he'd suspect we'd be involved in such a horrible thing. "We have no idea. They just showed up one day and I felt the purity of their souls."

"They didn't just show up," Pyper interjected from the doorway of her kitchen.

"That's true. Dan brought them here for safekeeping. He took the portraits and left these. I think he was trying to help," I said.

"How can you be sure?" Ian joined Pyper and took the can of Coke she offered him. "It could be a trap or…I don't know. He *is* possessed by black magic."

"He's been fighting it," I said, remembering the terrible emotional flashback I'd experienced the day we'd found the dolls. I'd mistaken the fear and pain for what I'd felt from him years ago in Idaho. It hadn't been that at all. He'd been fighting whoever was controlling him.

Lucien reclaimed a seat at the dining room table. "Is he magical?"

"Who? Dan?"

He nodded.

"Oh, no. Not at all." I disappeared into the kitchen for a bottle of water, and when I returned, they all stared at me. "What?"

"How do you want to work this?" Lucien asked.

"I thought you were going to tell us."

"You're the coven leader."

Right. "Okay then. I assume you figured out Bea's binding spell."

He nodded.

"Good. Since I'm not trained, I'm counting on you to run the show. Can you do that?"

Lucien rubbed his stubbled jaw. "That's going to take a lot of power. The entire coven will have to be there, and you'll need to provide the spark. We're talking rituals, blessings, and specialized herbs."

"When can you be ready?"

"For something like this, ideally prep would take a few days. The coven members need time to practice. Not to mention someone has to get the herbs and candles. And then there are the blessings to prep. You can't go around messing with this kind of power without being prepared."

Pyper scoffed. "Jade does. Look, Mr. Second-in-Command, I appreciate your desire to be thorough. But my best friend, the closest thing I have to a brother, is trapped somewhere that Lailah seems to think is Purgatory. I will not let you leave him there any second longer than necessary. If it were your sister, what would you do?"

"I don't have a sister."

"Don't fuck with me."

Her response made him chuckle. "Never. Besides, I didn't say I couldn't do it. I just wanted everyone to know it's risky."

"Noted," I said. "But we can't wait another month for the next full moon either."

Lucien's face turned grave. "No, that isn't an option."

The fear escaping his tightly controlled energy made my hands tremble. I clutched them into fists. Failing wasn't an option.

Lucien had given us a list of supplies we'd need. Since none of us actually participated in the craft, Ian found Bea's keys to her store in her handbag and left to stock up.

I wondered if Bea had someone else running her store these days, or if it was just closed. I mentally shook myself. Why did it matter? If we didn't bring her and Lailah back, the store was useless anyhow.

While Ian was gone, I headed off to my apartment to check in with Gwen.

I could hear the barking from the second floor landing. Crap. Not again. Dragging my feet up the final flight of stairs, I wished desperately for a pair of earplugs.

"Duke," I cried when I opened the door. "Stop."

The golden retriever continued his growl-fest from the couch, balancing himself with his front paws on the back cushions.

I came to a stop in front of him, blocking his view of Bea's body. "Off."

The dog immediately jumped off the couch and followed me as I led him toward the bathroom. "In!" I pointed to the open door.

He tilted his head in question. I was constantly telling him to get out. Poor ghost dog.

"Time for a bath," I said.

That did it. He happily trotted in.

I slammed the door and commanded him to stay. I infused a bit of my magical spark into the words, hoping I hadn't trapped him in there forever. I turned to Gwen. "You have no idea how lucky you are you can't hear him."

"Where the hell have you been?" Gwen asked when my gaze finally landed on her. I hadn't seen her angry expression since I'd been seventeen and had been caught sneaking back in after a late night out with Kat. "I've been calling you for hours."

I grimaced. "Sorry. I lost my phone." I hurried to Bea's side. "Is she okay? Any change?"

Gwen took her time easing back into her spot at the end of the couch. "She's fine. Or at least the same. But what about you? A while ago your energy disappeared. I couldn't sense you. I had no idea what was going on. Didn't you think about your old aunt at all?" Gwen was good at the guilt trips when she wanted to be.

"Crap. I'm sorry. I didn't go anywhere. All I did was take a nap at Pyper's and visited Kane in a dreamwalk. Maybe that's why you couldn't find me. Anyway, you could have called her."

"I don't have her phone number." She bit off each word and turned her back on me.

Swallowing a groan, I snagged her phone from the table and went to work adding Pyper's, Kat's, Ian's, and Kane's (because we *were* getting him back) numbers into her phone. "There. Now you should be able to find me no matter what happens."

She barely glanced at the phone as I set it on the table.

"Come on, Gwen. Don't you want to know what happened and be filled in on our latest plan?"

That got her attention. She listened intently as I outlined it for her, not saying a word until I finished.

"You think giving them their souls back will release Lailah and Kane?" she asked.

"I hope so. Lucien says it will weaken Meri."

Gwen looked unconvinced, but agreed it was the best plan. The only plan.

"Do you want to come?"

She eyed Bea. "Something tells me I need to be here, with her."

"Any idea why?"

She pursed her lips together and shook her head. "None. Just an intuition thing."

Psychics don't ignore intuition. I kissed her on the cheek and promised to call when we were done.

"I'll walk you out." She stood, but after two steps went rigid. Her eyes glazed over in an unfocused daze.

I froze, not realizing I'd stopped breathing until my lungs started to burn. Gasping for air, I moved to Gwen's side.

A second later, her eyes drilled into mine. Her voice was low and gravelly. "She's going to die."

"Gwen?" I cried.

She glanced around, disoriented, and then sat. "What happened?"

"You went into a trance." I lowered myself onto the couch and grasped her hand. "You said she's going to die."

Her eyes widened, and her shock slammed into me. "Who?"

I slowly shook my head. "You didn't say."

Chapter 23

There was a terrible truth about Gwen's trances: Whatever she said while in one always came to be. On my eighteenth birthday, she'd predicted I'd be covered in walnuts and chocolate. At the time I'd had a nice fantasy involving a bed and my boyfriend.

Three hours later, a delivery truck full of fudge blew a tire and sideswiped me on the highway. My car spun and ended up slamming into the back of it. The impact had forced the doors open, and fifty pounds of fudge tumbled out of banged up boxes onto my poor Toyota. I'd walked away, but the Toyota hadn't been so lucky.

Over the years, there had been a number of other incidents, always filled with truth, but never anything as ominous as a death.

She's going to die.

Bea? Lailah? Me? One of the coven members? There was one thing I knew for sure. If we did nothing, we'd lose more than one person.

In spite of the guilt tugging at my heart, I decided to keep Gwen's warning to myself. If Gwen had taught me anything about her gift, it was that no matter what I did to try to change things, her visions always came true. She had a theory if one messed with the universe too much, it would come back to you seven times worse. I didn't need seven times more trouble. I was drowning in it already.

Much to my relief, Kat hadn't put up a fight when I'd called and asked her to stay home. She'd sounded relieved, even. But Pyper had been another matter altogether. In fact, when I'd gone to her apartment to ask, she'd told me exactly what I could do with my request and it hadn't sounded comfortable. In the end, I'd given up on my arguments and raised my hands in defeat.

"Fine. If I were in your shoes, I'd probably insist on going, too. But promise me you'll stay far away from the coven circle. Spells can and do go wrong, and if anything happens to you…" I couldn't put words to the thoughts running through my head.

"Of course," Pyper quickly reassured me. "I just can't stay here, waiting and wondering."

I nodded my consent and followed her out to her car.

The directions took us uptown on Saint Charles Avenue. "The coven sanctuary is over here, by the university?" Pyper asked.

"I guess."

We turned left and, in no time, we ended up at a park sandwiched between the river and the Audubon zoo.

"Great." Pyper scowled and raised her good leg, flexing her foot. "So much for my cool new find."

I glanced down at her vintage black and white saddle shoes. "Suck it up. They're washable."

She mumbled something under her breath and followed me through the soggy grass toward a circle of oak trees. The moon shone pale yellow as the stale, decaying mud smell of the Mississippi permeated the air. An eerie sense of doom settled over me. I slowed my pace, trying to shake the ominous feeling.

Pyper and I emerged from the trees to find the coven all there, kneeling in a large circle. A ceramic bowl of dried herbs sat on the ground in front of each of them. I paused, holding my hand out to stop Pyper. The earth blessing Lucien led them in was one I knew well. It was my mother's favorite.

Jade, she'd say. *Hold my hand now. Your love is the secret ingredient.*

She'd said that about every blessing she'd ever conducted when I was around. The memory filled my heart with hope. With any luck, we'd free her, too.

When Lucien stopped speaking, they all reached to the side, joining hands. The herbs erupted into twelve individual flames and died just as fast. On cue, all the members raised their bowls and sprinkled the ashes within the circle.

"Wow," Pyper whispered when a pentagram lit up on the ground. "That's cool."

Lucien glanced up, meeting my eyes. Strain had settled over his features, making me wonder how long the group had been there tonight. He rose, and every head turned to stare in our direction.

"Come on," I told Pyper. "We have a coven to meet."

Lucien met us halfway, holding a black velvet robe. "This is yours."

Pyper arched an eyebrow.

"She's the coven leader now. She needs to dress the part."

I reluctantly accepted the robe and held it up. It matched the ones the other members wore, with its gold trim and embroidered pentagram. Except this one also had intricate symbols stitched down the arms. I traced one, and my fingertips lit with a warm magic. I snatched my hand back. "Whose spell work?"

Surprise sprang from him. "The coven's."

Of course. It had just seemed so familiar, infused with a trace of what I'd always identified with my mother. It was odd I hadn't noticed it before, but then, protection spells such as the one woven into the cloak were subtle. Everything else I'd felt from the coven had been balls-to-the-walls save-your-ass kind of magic.

I took a deep breath, trying to fill the sudden hole in my heart. Tonight I'd get Kane back and, one way or another, an answer about my mother. If not, I fully intended to die trying. *She's going to die* echoed in my brain. Well, if that's what it took.

"Let's get this picnic started." I pulled the heavy robe over my head and strode to where the other members waited. "I know Lucien gave you the details about what we're doing here tonight, but I want to make sure everyone's clear. We're going to rejoin the lost souls of two witches and a demon. Somehow, their spirits are trapped in portraits and their souls are trapped in voodoo dolls. Once we recombine the two, the demon will weaken. That will be Lailah and Kane's best chance to break free and come back to us." I paused and made eye contact with each of them. "I believe this has the potential to be very dangerous, so if anyone is not fully committed, please let us know and opt out now. We cannot afford to break our coven circle once we get going."

A long moment of silence filled the air. Finally, a thin voice spoke up. "Will this help save Bea?"

The group parted, and a tiny, dark-haired beauty with big, round eyes stepped forward. She had a fierce, determined look about her. I liked her instantly.

"This particular spell won't help Bea. We're counting on Lailah for that. The angel thing and all."

A glimmer of understanding registered in her expression. She nodded. "I'm in."

The rest of the coven murmured their agreement and moved to form a circle. Pyper retreated to the sanctuary of the giant oaks. I followed Lucien and then turned to him for instruction.

He indicated I should take the open spot nearest the dark-haired beauty. He took the one directly opposite me. Everyone reached out and clasped hands, completing the circle. A lighted pentagram materialized on the ground in front of us.

The combined pure, clean power of the coven poured from each of them straight into me. I dropped my hands. The pentagram faded as I focused on Lucien. "Why is everyone feeding me power? I thought you were leading the spell."

"Sort of. I'll be reciting the incantation, but you're the one who has to invoke it."

The other members shifted uneasily. Their lack of confidence prickled. Crap. I needed to get it together or this would never work. "Okay. But we need to get the portraits and the voodoo dolls from Pyper's car."

"They're right here." Pyper walked out from under the trees, carrying a box. Ian followed right behind her with a second one.

"Dang it, Pyper, I told you not to touch those." The risk was far too great. I ran over and tried to snatch the box, but she pulled it from my reach.

"Who else is going to do it? The rest of you are too susceptible. Besides, Ian was with me."

I refrained from scoffing. Because Ian could save her if anything happened, using his zero amount of magical talent.

"You can put them in the middle of the circle," Lucien instructed. When they were done, he said, "Thank you. That saved us from casting one hell of a serious protection spell just to get them from the car."

"Sure, no problem," Ian said in his easy tone.

I stared pointedly at Pyper. "You're going to stay by the trees, right? And no rushing to help?"

She shrugged, holding up her crutch. "I can't rush anywhere."

Unconvinced, I turned to Ian. "Can you keep her over there?"

"I'll do my best," he said seriously, but as I turned I caught a glimpse of an amused smile.

Within the safety of the circle, Lucien and I dumped the dolls and portraits on the ground.

"Should we match them up?" I'd assumed we'd place each doll with its respective portrait.

"No. The soul wants to be joined with its spirit. They'll have no trouble connecting." The sureness and matter-of-fact tone left me wondering how he knew that. Soul-merging wasn't exactly something one did every day. Or was it? I peered at the group, suddenly suspicious.

But I didn't have time to second-guess my choices because right then everyone's hands rejoined. Both of mine were taken again by the tiny, dark-haired girl on my left and a woman thinner and taller, but about the same age as Bea, on the right.

That raw, energizing power filled me up again. Everything about it seemed right. It didn't matter that I didn't know anyone's name except Lucien's, or that I'd spent the last twelve years shunning coven magic. This was my place. I belonged there, as their leader.

Lucien started the incantation. Power seemed to flow from him in a steady current, circling through each of the members, sinking into me from both sides.

For the first time, I let myself experience the flow of power. My blood pulsed with it.

There was something hauntingly familiar about the sensation. It took me a moment to realize it reminded me of Kane and the last time we'd made love. My heart and limbs ached to be near him. Somewhere in the recess of my mind, it registered that I'd been hopped up on magic that night. No wonder the sex had been so extraordinary.

Lucien's voice rose and the power tightened its hold on me. My eyes locked on his and all my focus channeled to his incantation. "Body to body, spirit to spirit, soul to soul. Goddess of Life, hear our call. We ask you to restore these beings, save them from a great injustice, and make them whole once more. Body to body, spirit to spirit, soul to soul."

The magic shot to the center of my heart and, with a nod of encouragement from Lucien, I pushed it into the center of the pentagram. It flowed seamlessly, appearing to be sucked up by the objects lying there.

Nothing happened.

Thirty seconds. One minute. Two.

There was still a thread of magic pulsing from the coven, but the bulk of it had been fed into the spell. I'd almost given up hope anything would happen when a white glow formed around the voodoo dolls. A ball of light rose from each one then zoomed to the portraits.

Upon contact, the pentagram vanished, along with the little bit of magic still coursing through the circle. A silver mist rose from each of the portraits. It twisted and molded, becoming more solid with each movement.

My heart raced as I watched the three form solid, human shapes. Their deformities had vanished, replaced by newly formed flawless faces. The three women, in what I guessed were their early thirties, stood facing each other with shock and wonder.

Well, two of them had shock and wonder.

The third, Meri, had tears streaming down her face. "Fe? Priss?" The demon's voice wobbled. "I…" She pressed her hands to the sides of her face, shaking.

Priscilla and Felicia shared a questioning glance.

"Meri?" Felicia inched toward her. "Is it you? I mean, really you?"

Meri sniffed and nodded. "I was stuck in Hell. I don't know what happened. I was waiting for Philip to find me, and then there was only darkness. Is he here?"

"No, Mer. He's not." Felicia took the demon's hand. "You don't remember anything else?"

"Felicia!" Priscilla yanked her sister's hand away from Meri. "It could be a trap."

Meri watched the pair with confusion streaming from her. She glanced around the circle. "Did they bring us back?"

"Yes, Mer. They gave us our souls back. We're free." Felicia shook off Priscilla's hold. "Stop. Can't you see she's in there? She has her soul back."

"But for how long?" Priscilla demanded and then softened her voice. "She's a demon, Fe. At any moment she could turn again."

Tears filled Felicia's big, blue eyes. She turned to me. "Can't you help her?"

Shock kept me silent. I had no idea. It appeared by rejoining Meri's soul, she'd returned to the person she'd been before turning demon. I searched Lucien's face for an answer.

He gave me a sad shake of his head.

My stomach clenched. "I'm so sorry."

A lone tear slid down Felicia's perfect face.

"Where's Philip?" Meri asked again.

"He's not coming," Priscilla said softly. "Meri, you're a demon. Philip's an angel. He can't help you now. You're lost to the other side."

"Demon?" Meri straightened. Something seemed to click in her confused mind. "Oh, no. What have I done?" A cloud of anxiety rose up like smoke and consumed her. "I didn't know what I was doing," she told her sisters. "I couldn't control it. And Philip…he never came for me." Her entire demeanor shifted. It was like watching a complete transformation. Anger pushed all her contrition aside and her rage pounded my skull, almost knocking me on my ass.

Luckily, the two witches on either side of me had a death grip on each of my hands, and I managed to stay upright. More importantly, I didn't break the circle. Because a second later, Felicia and Priscilla turned on Meri.

They started the chant I recognized as the binding spell Lucien had used on Bea.

Black magic sprang from Meri, winding around the pair, who now looked remarkably like they could be twins, except one was blond and the other was brunette. Of course, the black magic user would have black hair.

Felicia and Priscilla turned on Meri, both of them raising their hands high, calling for power. It sprang to their fingertips. On reflex, I pushed my own power into the members of the coven, holding us all steady. "Don't let go!" I shouted.

These witches were in a full-on magical battle. We had to keep them contained.

Please, God, don't let Lailah and Kane show up in the middle of this.

The circle held, keeping all three of them and their magic inside. The ripple of their power pushed at me and the coven, but it couldn't break through. The protections Bea had placed on the circle were too strong. I'd always known she was powerful, but I'd had no idea how much until right then. And she'd given it to me, claiming I was stronger.

It wasn't possible.

The two white witches lashed out with their magic, wrapping it around Meri. Soon the black tendrils of her spell weakened and faded into a whisper.

We all watched, awed, as Priscilla circled Meri, her dark hair whipping in a wind none of us could feel. Felicia stood back, controlling the thread of the power coiled tight around the demon.

Priscilla stopped and cocked her head in Felicia's direction. "What should we do with her?"

"We have to send her back to Hell." The sorrow in Felicia's voice made me ache for her. "There's no other choice."

"Don't feel sorry for her, Fe." Priscilla came within an inch of Meri's face. "She stole our lives for power. If we let her go, she'd only go after everyone here—one soul at a time."

Meri's wide, black eyes narrowed. "Stupid witch. What do you think this white coven will do with you when they find out what you've done?"

Priscilla stepped back. An odd probe pushed at our defensive barrier. She laughed. "What I've done? You're delusional."

"Don't, Priss. She's only trying to bait you." Felicia held tight to the magical bonds, but continued speaking in a gentle voice. "Meri, I understand you have a hold over two souls this coven wants back. If you release them, I'm sure we can work something out."

"You want me to give up my angel? Never!" Meri cried, and then shouted an incantation I didn't recognize.

The wind shifted. All of a sudden, a warm breeze gathered until it formed a wind tunnel within the circle. Everything went gray, and when the mist cleared, another form lay in the circle at Meri's feet.

Someone I knew. With his lower left leg bound in a cast, he lumbered to a standing position and then backed up in my direction.

"She can't save you," Meri hissed.

"I wasn't counting on it. But you'll have to go through me to get to her." Dan turned around. His sorrowful eyes met mine. "I never meant for any of this to happen."

Chapter 24

"Dan?" I asked.

But he'd already turned to Meri. "Our deal was void. Release me."

Deal? Dan had made a deal with a demon? Dread formed a sick ball in my stomach. What had he done? And why?

Meri's maniacal laugh grated on my ears. "You have no idea what you're talking about, mortal. You owe me a debt and I'm here to collect."

"No!" Felicia cried. "I won't let you ruin any more lives."

The sisters spread their arms wide. In unison they spoke, "Banish this woman. Banish her powers. Banish her hold on those she binds. Take her where time stands still."

White bolts of light erupted from them in a wave of power.

The magic coursing to me from the coven wavered. The power being yielded in the circle was too much for them. I redirected my magic back into the circle and cried, "Don't let go. If the circle falls, the demon will be free."

The pentagram on the ground shone brighter, fused with the renewed energy.

Meri seemed to fade into the night, flickering as if she were on a bad film reel. Her thick black magic spiraled out of control, seeming to fade into the night, until it vanished completely.

Priscilla and Felicia stepped back in retreat.

Meri glared at her sisters, fury rising off her, along with a silvery substance, appearing suspiciously like the same matter that had restored her soul. It hovered in front of her and then shot at Dan.

He groaned and fell to his knees, clutching his stomach. The silver substance embraced him. "This wasn't the deal," he spat.

"You sold your soul for my help," Meri seethed. "Now you're going to pay."

"You can't have my soul," Dan cried. "The deal was forfeit."

"You should have paid closer attention." She stalked around his prone body. "You wanted to find the white witch's mother. I agreed to help you in exchange for destroying those voodoo dolls."

My heart stopped at the mention of my mother. After all we'd been through, Dan had sacrificed himself to a demon to help me. All the terrible things we'd said and done to each other vanished. Deep down, Dan was still the same person I'd fallen in love with as a teenager.

"But I didn't do it. I couldn't. It was wrong." Dan's eyes met mine. "I didn't know they contained souls. When I found out, I gave them to you for safekeeping."

"I knew it!" Priscilla cried.

Meri screamed as her sisters twisted their magic, trying once again to bind her. She fell to her knees, her breath coming in short pants. When she looked up, she laughed. "Is that all you've got?" The demon rose, focusing on Dan. "Makes no difference, mortal. You've found her." She waved her hand, revealing a vision of my mother curled up on the floor of a dank stone room. The scene floated in the middle of the circle. "She's in Hell, where she belongs for trying to summon a demon."

"Mom!" I tried to break free, to run toward the vision, but my coven members held me steady in the circle.

"That's not what I meant," Dan said through his teeth.

Meri laughed. "You failed, and now you're mine." The demon's silver substance started to meld into Dan and suddenly

I realized she was fusing her soul with his. No matter how this fight ended, unless Dan died, she'd be tied to him and the earth. And Dan's soul would be irrevocably damaged.

"No!" I cried, channeling my magic and the coven's toward Dan. My only thought was to force her soul from his being. She would not have him. He didn't deserve such a terrible fate.

At the same time, the sisters redoubled their attack on Meri. The combined magic collided, shooting a beacon of light toward the sky, taking all the power we'd built with it. The two witches, unconnected to the coven, fell back, spent and useless.

When the impressive spray of light died down, Meri stood in the middle of the chaos. Anticipation flashed over her face. She turned to me. "Summon my mate, and I'll spare him."

Felicia lifted her head from her hands. "You want to summon Philip? He wants nothing to do with you. If he did, he'd have found you long ago."

The truth of her words rang in my ears just as a soul-shattering pain rippled through Meri. The blow to my gut was strong enough to make my knees weaken. Had the damaged soul we'd restored to her actually shattered? Somehow, I thought it could have.

Meri threw a black bolt at Felicia, knocking her out. Priscilla let out a cry and crawled to her prone sister.

The demon's pain turned into an intense need for revenge. "You can do it. You have enough power. Bring my mate to me and I'll let this one go." She waved an impatient hand toward Dan.

"No!" Dan got to his feet. "She's lying."

I didn't know how he knew, but he was right. I sensed it in her energy. She had no intention of leaving behind anyone she could siphon power from.

I leveled a stare at her. "I don't know how, and even if I did, I wouldn't. Not for a demon intent on corrupting a person's soul she claims to love."

"Love?" Meri scoffed. "Love has nothing to do with it."

"It has everything to do with it. Where do you think the bond comes from?"

My words touched a nerve. Meri's face contorted into a terrible fury. "Not willing to help? How about a trip to Hell? First your mother and now you. What a beautiful way to end this tragic soap opera. An ex determined to save you, and my goodie-two-shoe-sisters imprisoned again." Black ropes sprang from her fingertips, twisted around Felicia and Priscilla's wrists.

All I heard was: *First your mother and now you.*

A rage I hadn't known existed erupted with that magical spark Bea had worked so hard to help me find. Well, here it was, in all its glory.

I pulled my hands free from the two coven members and took a step forward. "Let my mother go," I said, a dangerous edge in my tone.

Dan's eyes went wide in shock as he struggled to his feet. "No, Jade!"

"Move, Dan. I don't want to have to force you, but I will."

"This isn't you. Don't do this."

"I don't have a choice."

I vaguely heard Lucien demand the coven to reform the circle. The pentagram had disappeared, and when the magic circle rebuilt around us, it lit once again in a dim shadow of its former self. I had my doubts the coven could contain us.

When Dan held his ground, I forced him aside using only my mind. It was easier than reading someone's emotional energy. Though, that was coming through strong as well. Dan was horrified and more than a little frightened. For me. The coven had a collective fear, mixed with a sad resignation. They were convinced they were going to lose me, too. The message came through loud and clear. But I knew their highest priority was keeping Meri contained.

I turned my attention to the demon. Smugness, deep and satisfied, radiated from her.

"Show me what you've got, witch. I've wanted to see how you'd stack up against a demon."

"Capturing an angel wasn't enough for you," I said.

"Oh, no. But imagine my delight when I was able to add that one to my collection. And now a white witch. Correction, black witch."

"What?" I glanced around, wondering who she was talking about. It was then I noticed the tinges of black on my fingertips. I should have recoiled in fear. Instead, I squared my shoulders and faced her.

She only laughed and slashed a burning sear across my chest with one swipe of her hand.

From deep inside my gut, something bubbled up, more powerful than anything I'd experienced before. I knew if I willed it, I'd destroy her. She'd be obliterated from my life, the earth, and everyone I cared about.

And why shouldn't I? She'd taken my mother, my lover, and my mentor. And now she had her hooks in Dan. Someone I used to love. She deserved everything she got.

Pressure pushed on my psyche. Something familiar, yet irritating. I brushed it away with just a thought and took two steps closer. Her sisters had been rendered useless, and Meri and I held each other's gaze in a stand-off.

"Do it," she challenged.

"You don't scare me."

Her lips twitched. "I can see that."

"Release my mother," I said again.

Her black eyes glinted. "I don't think so." She turned her gaze on Dan and aimed her hands in his direction.

Magic strained to explode from my chest. Not Dan. She couldn't have him. I didn't know a spell, but I knew my intentions. I raised my arms, said a small prayer to the Goddess of Souls, and then turned my fiery gaze on the demon in front of me. "Hell is too good for you." A simple incantation sprang to my lips. I was seconds from unleashing the worst when the coven started chanting.

The air turned to mist again, only this time it held a purple tint. I blinked, and suddenly in front of me stood Lailah and Kane.

I blinked again, sure I was seeing things.

"Jade?" Kane said, looking confused. "What—"

"Move!" I cried as Meri's anger pressed in on me from all sides. The dark power I'd been ready to unleash fled as my love for Kane took over. I pulled him backward, succeeding in shoving him out of the circle just as Meri's black magic slammed into me. Fire exploded through my limbs.

"Stupid witch." Meri laughed. "You broke the circle again. No one is safe now."

I glanced in alarm at the exhausted members of the coven. Some of them had dropped to their knees. Others were hunched over, trying to regain their strength. Holy God. What had I done when I'd plunged Kane right through their wards?

Meri's black threads of power spiraled around Kane. "He's mine now."

"Not if I can help it." Lailah's voice broke through the pain clouding my mind. "Leave it to a demon to fight dirty," she seethed.

Meri's eyes narrowed with hatred. "You'll be just like me soon enough."

"Think again, demon. I've broken your spell." The pair circled each other, readying themselves for a duel.

"Jade," someone hissed. I glanced up to see Lucien motioning weakly for me to take my space in the circle.

Shit! What was I doing? I scrambled to my feet and reclaimed my spot. I grabbed a hold of the two coven members nearest me and choked back a cry when their despair hit me from both sides.

Shame welled in my chest. I'd almost gone over to the dark side. The only reason I hadn't was because Lailah had managed to bring Kane back to me. Even through the coven's magic, I'd sensed him and the bond that had been missing the last few days.

His love had saved me.

I used every ounce of strength Kane's reappearance had given me and spread it among the coven through my magical spark. Within moments, they were all standing. Lucien's voice rose above the coven's murmurings, leading us in a protection chant once more.

And now it was my turn to help Lailah. She and Meri were locked in a fierce battle, each straining with the effort. Praying I didn't repeat the mistake I'd made earlier when I'd neutralized the sisters' power, I sent the coven's magic to Lailah instead of attacking Meri. With any luck, she'd be able to use it to her advantage.

The effect was immediate. Meri's black magic all but disappeared. With each spell she tried to throw, sparks fizzled, sputtering into nothing. "No!" She turned her attention toward the image of my mother, still trapped in the stone room. "Let me go or I'll destroy her soul. She'll be lost forever."

"You don't have the power," Lailah scoffed.

"Watch me!" The scene shrunk smaller and faded until all that was left was the real-life human form of my mother lying on the grass.

My heart soared.

Her gaze found mine and a tiny, sad smile touched her lips. Despite the despair and hopelessness running through her, relief blossomed in my chest. The emotions held her distinct signature. Something that, as far as I knew, couldn't be duplicated. She was here. Finally.

It took all my restraint to hold the circle and not run to her side. I wouldn't risk anyone else. Not again.

"I brought her here. You know what that means?" Meri's voice had taken on a haughty tone. "She's tied to me."

Lailah's magical hold on Meri loosened. Her eyes flicked to me. "Is that your mother?"

I nodded, fear twisting my insides.

"Whatever I do to the demon now, your mother will suffer the same fate."

"What? No. We have to break the connection." My words came out in a high-pitched panic. "Do something. Anything."

Lailah shook her head and backed up. "I can only send them back to Hell. Anything else will kill her."

Mom stood and walked to me. "Jade, you have to let me go." The deep sadness in her eyes made my heart want to burst. "I can't risk all these people." She lifted her hand to my face and cupped it. "You'll find a way to bring me back, Shortcake. I know you will." She stumbled back with tears in her eyes and nodded at Lailah. "Do it now."

"Mom, no!"

Meri reached for her.

Before anyone else could move, Dan managed to maneuver himself in front of Meri. "Time to deal, demon."

A pit formed in my stomach. Why hadn't he left the circle when he'd had the chance? What was he doing?

Meri moved to sweep past him, but he clamped his hand around her arm.

"We made a deal and I'm ready to pay up."

That caught her attention for just long enough.

"By the deal sanctioned by you, demon Meri, I hereby render my soul for one Hope Calhoun. By the deal sealed in blood, I demand you take me in her place."

Meri's face contorted in rage as black mist swirled up around them. They both disappeared into the cloud.

My knees buckled, but before I fell, someone caught me. Kane. His strong, familiar arms propped me against his chest.

Chatter erupted at once. All I could do was turn in Kane's arms and hold on tight. After a moment, he pulled back and kissed me softly. "There's someone waiting to see you."

The only thing that brought me back to myself was the sound of my mother's voice. "Jade?"

I exchanged Kane's embrace for hers. She'd transformed from the emaciated shell of herself back into the woman I'd last seen twelve years ago. It was as if not a day had passed. She'd spent twelve years in the place where time stood still.

My body shook as she held me. Her arms felt exactly as they had when I'd been fifteen years old.

"It's okay now," she soothed, smoothing my hair back. "Shh, everything's okay now."

I shook my head, but didn't have the energy to list the things that were so very wrong. Bea, Dan, me almost turning to black magic. "What happened?" I finally choked out.

"Your friend sacrificed himself for me."

That part I'd figured out on my own. "I know. But where did they go? Hell?"

The sadness in her eyes answered my question.

"Will we be able to help him?"

Nobody said anything.

I turned to Lailah. "We'll be able to help him, right?"

Her expression turned to one of pity. "I'm sorry, Jade. He willfully bound himself to her. I've never seen a spell strong enough to break it."

"Oh, God," I whispered. What had he done? How was I going to tell Kat? If one's heart could literally break in two, it was happening to me at that moment. I clutched my chest and concentrated on breathing. Kane wrapped a strong arm around my shoulder. I leaned into him, fighting back a fresh wave of tears.

"Hey, where are the other two witches?" Pyper's voice came from the middle of the crowd. "Felicia and Priscilla?"

"They disappeared after Jade broke the circle the first time," Lucien said. "Rosalee saw them make a break for it." He nodded to the dark-haired beauty I'd stood next to in the circle. "Nobody else noticed because that's when, well…Jade started to go to the dark side."

"What?" Lailah whirled, magic pulsing from her core.

I took a step back, holding my hands up. "Whoa. I didn't do it on purpose. I didn't even realize it was happening until you and—" I glanced at the man beside me and met dark chocolate eyes, "—Kane appeared."

He clasped my hand.

"What took you so long?" I asked, noting his wrists were unbound and his leg appeared unharmed.

"The circle was too strong. We were locked out. But once it broke, we were able to make our way back in."

"I would have been able to get us here eventually," Lailah said defensively.

"Looks like we made it just in time." Kane stared down at me, his eyes reflecting all the love bursting inside me.

Pyper appeared, and tugged at our arms. "We have to go."

"Where?" I glanced around, looking for my mom.

"Gwen called. Bea's been taken to the hospital."

Dread crawled up my spine. *She's going to die.* I broke into a run, sprinting toward the coven huddled together. I found my mom standing near Lucien and quickly explained.

"You go ahead. I'll lead the coven in a healing prayer," she said as if it were a normal day and not the first time I'd seen her in twelve years.

"You have to come. Gwen's there."

"I'll be more useful here."

"But—"

"You're the leader of this coven. If you can't be here to lead the healing prayer for your friend, then who will?"

"Lucien can do it," I snapped. "Mom, you have to come with me."

Her eyes went dark and slanted as her face transformed into the mother-knows-best look I'd longed to see many times over the last several years. Now that the moment was here, I wondered what I'd missed about it. "I'm staying. Go."

I didn't have time to argue with her, so I told her to stick with Lucien and I'd call as soon as we had word.

Lailah caught up with me near the giant oak trees. "What happened to Bea?"

I shook my head, too winded to speak, and gestured for her to follow me. I didn't know what had put Bea in the hospital, but assuming she was still bound in black magic, Lailah was our best hope.

Chapter 25

Pyper squealed around a corner and slammed on her brakes, skidding to a stop at a red light. "What in damnation happened back there?" she demanded.

I shot Kane a desperate look from the back seat.

"Which part?" he asked.

"The part when Jade turned scary-evil witch and ended up crossing to the dark side."

"I didn't use any black magic!"

"No, but you were on the verge of it."

Kane twisted in the front seat, shooting me a worried look. "You were?"

Tension built near my temples. "I didn't know it was happening. I was so focused on defeating that demon that it came out of nowhere. I mean, it's not like I planned it." I exhaled and softened my voice, turning grateful eyes on Kane. "But then you showed up, and all the terrible darkness vanished. You saved me."

His face softened. "All I did was come back to you."

"That's what I needed."

We stared at each other until Pyper cleared her throat. "And how exactly did Lailah get her power back? Didn't Bea take it from her?"

I hadn't thought of that. "I don't know. Maybe when we bound Bea, it broke the spell."

Pyper slid into a space in the hospital parking lot. "Only one way to find out." She slammed her door and headed off to the emergency room.

"Kane," I said in a small voice.

He reached back and took my hand. "Yes?"

"Don't ever leave me like that again."

He pulled me forward and leaned in. His lips barely brushed mine. "If you make me a promise."

"Anything."

"I'll do my best to stick by your side, but you need to promise to never compromise your soul to save mine."

I leaned back. "I can't do that. I'd give up everything for you."

"I'd do the same. But black magic? It's worse than…" he shuddered. "I'd rather die than lose you to such a terrible existence."

Silence filled the car.

"Promise me," he said again.

"I promise." I gave him a sad smile and opened my door. "We need to check on Bea."

Gwen let out a small cry when I found her in the waiting room. "Jade!" She jumped up and wrapped me tight in her arms. Then she pulled back and gave me a little shake. "I thought I'd lost you."

I ignored her admonishment. "Mom's back. We found her."

"What?" She dropped her arms and took a step back.

"She's here."

Gwen whipped her head around, searching the hospital.

"I mean, here in New Orleans. She wouldn't come with us." I shook my head. "She was determined to take my place with the coven to cast a healing charm for Bea."

"What was she thinking? For the love of…"

"She's okay, as far as I can tell. I'll fill you in on everything, but first, what happened with Bea?"

Gwen's face went white. "I had a vision that she would have trouble breathing. It's why I stayed with her, just in case. But really what happened is she stopped breathing altogether. She was lying there one minute and the next, I just knew something ominous was in the room. But the minute I touched Bea, it disappeared. I called nine-one-one and administered CPR right away. She's breathing now, but the hospital thinks she suffered a heart attack."

"CPR? Her heart stopped?" I sank into a cold plastic chair.

Gwen nodded. "But only for a minute."

"She died," I whispered.

"Oh, no, honey. She's alive." Gwen waved toward the beeping machines. "See, the hospital says so."

A sardonic chuckled rumbled from the back of my throat. "I can see that. Your prediction was, 'she's going to die.' It was Bea." I stood, gave my aunt another hug, and whispered in her ear, "You saved her."

Gwen pulled back. "Anyone else would have done the same thing."

"Of course," I agreed, dropping it. Gwen didn't care for people making a big deal of her gift. The last thing she wanted was people coming to her for predictions. "Do you think it was a heart attack?"

"No. I think something evil came for her, but I scared it away."

"When did this happen?"

"Not too long ago. The ambulance was on its way when I called Ian. We got here minutes before you did."

Something evil. No doubt Meri had come for Bea's magic and soul. Demon, my ass. That bitch was a soul-stealer. If we didn't bring Bea back soon, she'd be lost and Meri would claim her. I was sure of it.

I asked Pyper for her phone and called Lucien.

Thirty minutes later, Lucien arrived with my mother in tow. Gwen rose slowly then hurled herself in Mom's direction. The sisters hugged, hanging on tight for so long, I finally had to gently pull them apart. Both had tear-stained cheeks. It was enough to make my own eyes well up again. I handed Gwen a twenty and the keys to Kane's house.

"A cab is on its way. Please take Mom back to Kane's and wait for us there."

Gwen protested, but Mom stepped in. "It's okay, Gwennie. Jade has work to do, and worrying about us is the last thing she needs right now."

I hugged and kissed them both goodbye, but a little piece of my heart went with them.

"They left without a fight?" Pyper asked.

"Not much of one."

"I didn't realize the Calhoun clan could be so reasonable."

I glanced at my friend and laughed. "Neither did I. Come on. We have a witch to rescue."

You'd think smuggling a comatose person out of a hospital would be difficult. Not when the smugglers were a bunch of witches. Lucien and Rosalee set a memory spell and suggested to the staff that Bea was just fine. After that, Ian had carried her out in full view of everyone. No one said a word.

Despite the coven's pleas to take her to the circle, Lailah had insisted we move Bea to her house. "She has special wards that will keep her safe there. Better than the circle. You'll have to trust me."

It was odd to watch the coven do as Lailah asked. I'd never seen her as a leader. Only a rival and a screw-up. Still, she had a lot more knowledge than I did, and I had little choice but to follow along.

Lucien and Ian laid Bea out on a blanket in her backyard while Lailah pulled me aside. "You'll need to reinstate my magical privileges now."

"Wait, what? But I thought you had them back. You dueled with the demon."

"I was only able to do that because I was connected with the coven. You didn't notice?"

"Um…no." There were so many people there, what was one more?

"Bea took my magic. Not my ability to *use* magic. To do this, I need you to give it back."

"Why me? I don't know how to do that."

Impatience flickered on her face. "You're the coven leader. You're the only one who *can* do it." Lailah's emotions were still hidden from me, but the disgust in her voice was more than enough to let me know what she thought of me and my new title. "Bea must have been really desperate to hand the coven over to you."

The words were on the tip of my tongue to tell her exactly what I thought of her commentary when my heart hardened. A powerful foreign current ran through my limbs, and an image of striking the angel filled my brain.

Whoa. Where'd that come from? I took a step back and focused on something positive. Like Kane standing next to me. Flesh and blood. Real. Solid.

His hand touched my back and my nerves settled. "You okay?" he whispered.

"Yeah." How was he so strong and steady after what he'd been through? I placed a hand on my hip and asked them both just that. "How come you two don't need rest, or food, or a psychiatrist?"

"There are things that need to happen first," Lailah said.

Kane placed his hand on the small of my back. "I'll rest when you do."

It was then I noticed the dark circles under Lailah's eyes and the slight hunch of Kane's weary shoulders. Okay, so they didn't have as much strength as I'd thought. Time to get the show started. "All right. Lailah, tell me what I need to do."

She led me inside. "It's better to reinstate the magic where it was taken. All you need to do is declare the ban lifted. Put intent behind your words and you should do fine."

I nodded and held my hands out to her.

She stared at them, lifted a skeptical eyebrow. "You want to hold hands?"

I bit back a snarky reply, reminding myself we needed her to help Bea. "Yes. It's easier for me to control where my magic goes if I'm in physical contact."

She wasn't quick enough to hide her annoyance, but reluctantly held her hands out.

I rolled my eyes and grabbed them.

Nothing flowed from her. I wondered if I'd be able to penetrate her walls. I didn't really care about knowing how she felt. I could tell. She didn't like me and, to be honest, I didn't like her. But we were on the same team. "It would probably be easier if you dropped your mental barrier."

"Excuse me?"

"You always shield your emotions from me. I think this would go smoother if you let your guard down."

Her fingernails dug slightly into my palms. "If I wanted you to know how I'm feeling, I'd tell you."

I snorted. "Your actions and body language tell me everything I need to know. Fine. Keep your shield, but I'm not guaranteeing this will work. I'm a newbie, remember?"

She huffed. "Fine."

Annoyance so strong it made my skin itch radiated from her. Its overpowering nature almost made me drop her hands. But then the guilt and suffering trickled in, and I found myself pitying her. It made me regret suggesting she let me in. I didn't want to know how badly she suffered. It was easier to just keep blaming her.

It was that moment that I dropped my grudge against her. Hadn't I been the one who'd been spouting the dangers of magic all these years? The poison and Kane had both been the work of Meri. I knew that in my head. It was time to embrace the truth in my heart. If I'd learned anything in recent months, it was that I needed to depend on others. Lailah, for all I'd gleaned from her, did have goodness streaming through her, and she truly loved Bea. And that was enough.

"By the power given to me by Beatrice Kelton, former coven leader of New Orleans, I hereby lift the ban of magic bestowed on Lailah Faust, angel of God."

A warm spark of power jumped from my center and our hands glowed for a second.

Lailah let go first and stepped back, staring at me in awe. "What was that?"

"What do you mean? I gave you your power back."

"Yes, but you also gave me some of yours."

"What?" No. I'd only sent a little bit of power to evoke hers. Right?

"God above. You *are* powerful. The spark wasn't needed. My power came back the moment you said the words." She frowned as she studied my face. "Great. Good going, Calhoun. Now we're magically linked."

"As in…?"

"As in I'll always know what you're up to, and you'll always know what I'm up to. Perfect. Just what I needed." She turned and stalked outside.

I didn't even want to know what that meant.

Outside, the coven had arrived and already formed a circle around Bea. I hung back with Kane and let Lailah lead. This was her deal, after all. When she was ready, she called me over. I gave Kane a quick kiss.

"Be careful," he whispered in my ear.

"I'll do my best."

A pentagram had been drawn around Bea's body. Lailah had me stand at the northern-most tip. She took the place next to me where Rosalee had stood in the park. The black-haired beauty took a place next to Lucien, who stood with his head bowed. The group was much more somber than they had been earlier. Did they doubt Lailah's ability?

"No," Lailah said. "They realize if this fails, we're likely to lose Bea."

"What? How—"

"It's the circle. I can pick up on certain things. But with your gift a few minutes ago, all your thoughts are coming through loud and clear."

Crap.

She clenched her teeth. "Tell me about it."

"All right. Enough. Get on with it."

"With pleasure." She raised her hands high above her head. "Goddess of evil. Hear me, your father's daughter. This woman before you has become a vessel of Hell. Take her darkness as a gift. We ask nothing of you but for her to return to us unharmed."

The coven members repeated her statement, but I was too dumbfounded to do anything but stare. She was calling a Goddess of evil. Was she crazy?

Who do you think takes the black magic, Jade? Lailah's voice rang clear in my head.

Oh my God, she had full telepathic abilities.

Repeat what I said, or it has no meaning.

I gulped and repeated the words. Without prompting, the coven joined in immediately. When our voices trailed off, the wind picked up, but only in the circle.

Lailah shouted over the howling force, "Come for the black magic. Free her soul from the bonds that corrupt."

To my amazement, black strands of power seeped from Bea's chest. They were scattered upward by the wind, disappearing almost as soon as they appeared. All of us watched and waited as we continued to chant, "Come for the black magic. Free her soul from the bonds that corrupt."

Finally, Bea rose from her lying position. She glanced around, her gaze landing on me. Recognition streamed off her and I broke into a huge smile. Without thinking, I took a step forward.

"No, Jade!" Lailah shouted.

But it was too late. I was already in the circle, and so was Meri.

Chapter 26

"Where's Dan?" I demanded.

Meri's face clouded with shock, and then she laughed. "That's who you care about? Not your mentor, lying on the table about to be trapped forever in my most excellent graces?"

My attention shifted to Bea. She'd fallen backwards, her arms bent at odd angles as if she'd passed out. I stepped forward. "You can't have her."

"She's already mine."

"No!" My spark flared. Hot and cold spikes shot to the surface of my limbs. I vibrated with it.

"That's it," she coaxed. "Show us the power you wield. Go on. Do it."

Her taunting only made me that much more determined. My muscles tensed as I focused in on the demon, ready to end her existence. I could do it. My power brimmed with the promise.

Jade! Lailah warned in my head. *No!*

I shook my head violently, as if that would dislodge her voice. "Someone has to stop her."

"Yes," Meri hissed.

"Not like this." Kane's strong clear voice came from just behind me. "You promised to not sacrifice your soul. Remember?"

I whipped my head in his direction. His eyes bored into mine. "It's black magic you hold now. Use it on her, and you'll lose your soul."

"How do you know?"

"We're connected." He reached out and wrapped his big hand around mine. On my other side, a much smaller, smoother hand slipped into my other one.

"Pyper?"

"We're in this together. Whatever happens to you happens to us," she said.

Love, clear and pure, wrapped around me. Warmth spread to my heart, and a tingle of something I'd only glimpsed a few times blossomed inside me. Strong protective magic grew from my core. It pushed out all the hate and anger I'd built up, and I knew my soul was safe.

I clamped my hands tighter around my friends' and pushed the love-filled magic in Bea's direction. This time a golden cloud circled her, pressing around her body, until it melded into her.

Meri screamed. "Stop! She's mine."

"Not anymore," I said, and when Bea sat up again, looking bewildered but strong, I took all that love-filled magic and threw it at Meri.

I hadn't known what it would do, but when it hit her, patches of her skin seemed to burn off as she writhed with agony. Horrified, I stepped back.

Her façade of a young beauty melted away until she was nothing more than the thin-faced hag she'd once been in the papier-mâché portrait. She sank to the ground, her energy draining from her.

I moved forward, bringing Kane and Pyper with me. "One last time, where's Dan?"

Her empty, lifeless expression turned to one of hate. "He's a demon slave," she choked out. A second later, all signs of life vanished. Her form faded into nothing, leaving only the remnants of her charred skin.

What had I done? I stood trembling, wondering if I'd killed the only person who could lead us to Dan.

"Not a person, a demon," Lailah said coming to a stop beside me. "And I doubt you killed her. Demons are almost impossible to kill. My guess is you stripped her power, though I've never heard of a witch being able to do that. Huh. Learn something new every day."

"You can stop reading my thoughts now," I said.

"It'll go away in a few days. And as for Dan, now that Meri's powerless, there's still hope. There are other ways into Hell."

I shivered in the cool breeze. I most definitely did not want to go to Hell.

"Who does?" she asked, once again responding to my thoughts. She cocked her head and looked me over. "You had us worried there, coven leader. Who knew you could switch from the black to the white so easily?"

I gaped. "You mean I ended Meri with white magic?"

"Of course. It's fueled by love. Didn't you know that?"

With a sad shake of my head, I said, "No. I've got a lot to learn."

"Finally." Bea stood a few yards away, holding onto Ian's arm. "We can start real training."

"Oh, Bea." I rushed to her side. "I'm so sorry. I messed up. I didn't know the spell wasn't complete and that Meri would show up here."

"It's all right, dear. You handled it, though I admit it was a little messy. You'll learn."

I nodded, making a promise to myself to do just that. I wouldn't be caught unprepared again. "Let's get you inside." I reached for her other arm, but she swatted me away.

"Ian's got it from here. Go home. See your mother and your aunt. You call me tomorrow and we'll make a plan."

"You know about my mother?"

"Of course. Gwen told me all about it while I was at the hospital." When she noted the shock on my face, she added, "I was bound, not dead—except for that one unfortunate incident at your apartment."

God, that must have been awful. To know what was going on and not be able to do anything. I shivered.

She stroked my arm and then waved her hand in a shooing motion.

I took two steps and stopped. "Wait. Now that you're whole again, can I transfer the coven leadership back to you?"

"Oh, no," she said. "Why do you think I pressed so hard to get you to train? I needed a replacement if I was going to retire. And who better than a white witch?"

"Retire?"

"Don't worry. I'll still be your mentor." She patted Ian's arm, and they moved toward the house.

Pyper handed Kane her keys. "Take my car. I'll catch a ride with Ian later."

I smiled. "Have fun."

She grinned. "I'll try."

"What was that about?" Kane asked when we got to Pyper's car.

"What, Bea? She wants me to remain coven leader."

"I got that part. I meant, what was going on with Pyper?"

I slid into the passenger's seat and sighed in relief. Kane followed suit and tucked himself into the driver's side. He turned the ignition over, waiting for my answer.

"They're dating now."

"And Kat?"

"She's a mess, but she'll get through it. We'll help her."

He reached over and smoothed the hair away from my eyes, loyalty and protectiveness radiating from him. "Of course we will."

The familiar connection we'd always shared was firmly back in place. My heart burst with all the love I'd been bottling up. And that's when I noticed it. The shimmering golden glow of a person's aura when one's in love. Only this time it wasn't Kane's. It was mine.

Grinning, I leaned in and kissed him.

When we broke apart, we were both breathless. He reached for me, but I swatted him away, much in the same manner Bea had just done with me. "Home. Food. Sleep first. Then we can…"

"What?" His eyes blazed, matching his desire caressing my skin.

"I'm sure you can figure it out."

His cocky grin made me laugh, and this time when he reached for me, I met him with fervor.

Kane and I found Gwen watching over my sleeping mother.

"She crashed about ten minutes after we got here," Gwen said.

"Did you get her to eat anything?" I sat next to my aunt and grabbed her hand.

"No. She got down some water and asked to lie down."

"Okay, I'll make some soup." I stood and headed for the door.

"Jade?"

"Yeah."

"Don't expect too much from her. Twelve years is a long time to be gone." Gwen's sadness mingled with my hope, dimming it just enough to cause a pit of unease in my gut.

"You think she's different?"

"How could she not be?"

I nodded, realizing Gwen was right. But right now, all I cared about was having her back. "I'll be in the kitchen."

After a half-hour of chopping vegetables for the chicken soup, I almost felt normal again. Kane emerged from his room, freshly showered and dressed in jeans and a navy blue T-shirt. He looked as if nothing had ever happened. He'd been gone for almost forty-eight hours, but to look at him, you'd think he'd been off for a short weekend trip.

"How do you do it?" I asked.

"What?" He snuggled up behind me and kissed my neck.

"Appear so normal after what happened."

He stepped back. "For me, being wherever I was wasn't that bad, other than the pain. I mean, nothing happened to us there. I think we were in a holding pattern. So really the only awful thing that happened was I couldn't help you. That, and worrying about you."

"So I nearly killed myself freeing you from Club Med underground?"

He chuckled. "I wouldn't call it that. I just meant what you went through was far worse than what I had to deal with."

"What about your leg? Did the pain go away?" I narrowed in on his stance, noting he kept most of his weight on his left leg.

He shrugged. "It's phantom pain. I'm sure it'll fade soon enough."

"I'll ask Bea about it."

"Fine." He moved in again and wrapped his arms around me from behind. "What about you, love? How are you holding up?"

"Surprisingly, I'm okay. But I do need to go see Kat." I placed the lid on the soup pot and set the stove to simmer.

"I'll take you," Kane murmured into my hair.

I wiggled out of his arms. "She's only two blocks away. I think I'll be okay."

Frustration rippled from him, but he tried to rein it in. "Indulge me. After the last few days we've had, I don't want to let you out of my sight."

When I opened my mouth to protest, he held his hand up.

"I'll stay out of the way. I'd just feel better keeping an eye on you."

He had a point. If he was leaving to go see someone right now, I'd be tagging along, too. I reached up and caressed his cheek. "Give me a minute and I'll be ready to go."

In Kane's room, I changed into clean clothes. He'd given me half his dresser weeks ago. Then I stopped by the guest room to let Gwen know where we'd be. "I don't know when we'll be back, but there's soup on the stove. Can you watch it for me?"

"You got it. Give Kat a hug for me."

"I will." I bent and hugged Gwen, squeezing hard enough to make her cough. "Sorry."

She smiled. "Don't be. I love you, too."

All the lights were out at Kat's apartment, but when we stepped onto her porch, I knew she was in there. Her worry and sadness reached me through the door. I'd called to tell her the news, but when I'd gotten to Dan, she'd said she already heard, choked back a sob, and told me she'd call me later. I didn't know who told her. It could have been anyone. But my guess was Lailah. With her being assigned to Dan, it wasn't unreasonable to think she knew a lot more about our history than I wanted her to.

I hesitated before knocking. What would I say? I'd managed to save everyone except for Dan, the person I'd spent the last two years hating. I owed him my life. And now my mother's life, too.

Before I could work up the courage to knock, the door opened. Kat stood in the doorway, eyes bloodshot and her face splotchy. "What are you doing out here?"

In answer, I moved forward and wrapped her in my arms. She hugged me back, and with one sniffle, her body started to shake with sobs. Tears spilled down my cheeks and ran unchecked as I cried with her.

A soft click of the door sounded behind me. I glanced back and found the door closed. Kane's energy told me he was wait-ing outside. I silently thanked him and led Kat to her couch.

I dabbed her tears with a tissue.

She sniffed and held an envelope out. "I have something for you."

I took it, not saying a word.

"It's from Dan. He explains everything that happened from before he moved here 'til now. Or at least, as much of it as he can remember."

I stared at it. "When did he give this to you?"

"When I visited him in the hospital." Her tears started to flow again.

"Tea?" I asked. When she nodded, I left her on the couch and retreated to the kitchen. After filling the kettle, I leaned against the counter, running the envelope through my fingers. At that moment, I wasn't at all sure I wanted to open it. When the tea was done, I took a mug out to Kane, thanked him, and returned to Kat on the couch.

"Thank you," she said.

"Of course." I took a sip of spiced chai and leaned forward. "He's a hero, you know."

She nodded. "A flawed one."

"Who isn't?"

A tiny smile played on her lips before it disappeared. She glanced at the envelope. "Are you going to open that?"

I shrugged. "Do you know what it says?"

"No. He handed it to me before they wheeled him off for x-rays." Her voice hitched. "It was the last time I saw him."

It was her suffering more than anything else that made me open the letter. I read it out loud.

> *Jade,*
>
> *Let me start by saying I'm sorry. Sorry for every-thing. The way I handled things when you told me about your empath gift, the break-up, and everything that happened after. I was hurt and handled it very badly. I hope you can forgive me.*
>
> *I'm writing this down because every time I try to warn you about what's happened, the demon takes over. I've been fighting it, but she's winning.*
>
> *About a month after we broke up, I'd finally started to calm down and became curious about your ability. I went to see a family friend who claimed to be some sort of psychic. Up until then, I'd always just thought she was a kook. But when I got there and*

asked about you and your gift, she started talking about your mom, how she'd disappeared. It started me on my journey to find her.

    I don't know. I guess I thought if I could help you find her, you'd forgive me someday for going home with that other woman. I don't blame you if you can't. I doubt I'll ever forgive myself.

I looked up at Kat. "Did you know he felt this way?"

She shrugged. "I knew he was sorry about the way he handled things, despite the way he behaved around you."

When I'd first moved to New Orleans, I hadn't known I'd be running into Dan. As far as I knew, he'd been still living in Idaho. It came as a shock to find out not only had he moved, he was also dating Kat. It had made for a volatile situation; Dan and I had never made peace.

Eventually, after Dan attempted to assault me, Kat had broken up with him. Now I had to wonder if the demon had been the cause of his attitude all along.

I turned my attention back to the letter.

    My family friend pointed me in the direction of your mother's old coven. I went to see Izzy Frankel, who I believe was the coven leader when your mom disappeared. She was very knowledgeable and put the portraits and the voodoo dolls in my care. She told me they were the key to finding your mother.

    I had every intention of handing them over to you. In fact, it's the reason I kept encouraging Kat to get you down here. But something strange started to happen. With each day I had the portraits, I started to feel less and less like myself. I was angry half the time and depressed the other half. I was lashing out at people—not just you, but people at work, at the market, on the streets. Pretty much everywhere I went, I got into some sort of verbal confrontation.

Often I'd come home and stare at the portraits. They seemed to draw me in. Especially Meri. Then one night, she came to me in a dream and made me a deal. I was to destroy the voodoo dolls, and she'd tell me where to find your mother. I figured once I knew where your mom was, I could get rid of the portraits for good. It seemed like a good idea at the time. But I couldn't do it. I tried, but every time I came close to harming the dolls, something inside me made me stop. Now I know it was the innocence they carried.

I thought things would get better when I moved in with Kat. I even rented a storage locker and kept the dolls and the portraits locked up. But after that night in the club, with you and Kat, I couldn't stay away. I kept going back to the storage locker. Obviously, by then I knew something was very off about them, but I didn't know what. Eventually I threw out the portraits, praying my life would go back to normal.

Honest, Jade. I have no idea how they ended up in Kane's club. All I knew was I was out of control and/ or being controlled. Fearing I'd be forced to harm the dolls, I left them in your care.

I haven't handled any of this well, but I hope now that you have this information, you do find your mother. You deserve it. Be careful.

All my best,
Dan

P.S. Please pass the included note on to Kat.

I checked the envelope and found a folded-up blue piece of paper with her name on it. "Here."

She took it and stared at the note for a while. She didn't look up when she spoke. "He was trying to help you. Like always."

I blew out a breath and sat back. "It seems so."

"And now he's gone." Her voice was so small and childlike it made my heart ache.

"No. Not gone. Just missing," I said in a commanding tone. "I'm not going to let him suffer in Purgatory, or Hell, or wherever he is. One way or another, we're going to find him and bring him back. I owe him that."

"How?"

"I don't know." I reached out for her hand. "You know, I suspected something was wrong, but I was too hurt to try to help. I gave up on him once and I'm not going to do it again."

Tears shimmered in her eyes, but this time she wiped them away. "Whatever I can do to help, you know I'm here."

"I know."

She stood. "Get up. Kane's waiting."

"I can't leave you here by yourself."

"Yes, you can." She practically dragged me to the door. "It's late. I'm exhausted. You're exhausted. Your mom needs you. Go. Do what you have to. Get strong, and when you're ready, we'll find Dan."

Kat had her fire back, and though I knew she was mostly putting on a brave front, something had shifted in her energy. The helpless despair had vanished, replaced by a tiny blossom of strength.

I hugged her one last time and made her promise to call if she needed anything.

She clutched her blue letter. "I have everything I need right here." She opened the door. "Now, go on."

Kane stood and gave Kat a hug of his own. She blushed when he gave her a peck on her cheek, waving him away. "Goodnight, you two." She closed the door softly, and we headed back to Kane's.

When we got to his front door, he turned to me. "Is she all right?"

"She will be."

"And you? Will you be okay?"

I wrapped my arms around him. "Just as soon as you get me into your bed."

The slow, sexy smile I'd come to love so much spread across his chiseled face. "That, my love, is easily arranged." In one quick movement, he picked me up and strode through the door. He didn't stop until he laid me down on his queen-sized bed. "Has it only been two days?" he murmured.

"Feels more like two weeks." I trailed a finger down his stubbled jawline.

"Looks like we have some catching up to do." His mouth covered mine, and when his hands found the curves of my body, everything else ceased to matter.

Kane was home, and he was all mine.

About the Author

Deanna is a native Californian, transplanted to the slower paced lifestyle of southeastern Louisiana. When she isn't writing, she is often goofing off with her husband in New Orleans, playing with her two shih tzu dogs, making glass beads, or out hocking her wares at various bead shows across the country. Want the next book in the series? Visit www.DeannaChase.com to sign up for the New Releases email list. Book three is due out in late fall of 2012.

Lightning Source UK Ltd.
Milton Keynes UK
UKOW04f1628240114

225201UK00013B/280/P

9 780983 797821